The Absentee Detective

Mark Sohn

Paperback ISBN 978-1-78705-340-3
ePub ISBN 978-1-78705-341-0
PDF ISBN 978-1-78705-342-7

Published in the UK by MX Publishing
335 Princess Park Manor, Royal Drive,
London, N11 3GX
www.mxpublishing.co.uk

Cover design by Brian Belanger

Contents Page

This Book is dedicated to the memory
of Pat Sohn, my Mum.

To her, I owe so much, but included in the list
is my love of reading.

The Detective Who Wasn't

'It seems clear enough to me, Holmes; Lord Stonebrook's valet killed him!'

'No Watson...' Holmes stepped forward dramatically, turning slightly to favour his left profile, '*This* is Lord Stonebrook!' So saying, he took hold of the valet's hair and pulled (he had to do this twice) exposing the man's hair as a wig. Taking hold of the wretched servant's nose, Holmes yanked this off to reveal the artifice... and Lord Stonebrook, the supposedly-murdered man. The audience gasped as one as Watson and Inspector Cross both exclaimed 'Lord Stonebrook!' in unison. Suddenly, the disgraced lord leaped across the stage to the castle wall, itself a hurriedly-painted canvas, to wrench a sword down from its mounting. At once, Holmes threw off his deerstalker, removed his Inverness cape and drew his sword-stick from the malacca sheath. The two adversaries squared off with evident relish, the audience cheering as Sherlock Holmes struck the first blow.

The church hall was shaking to applause as Mortimer Knight took his bow and went backstage to the confines of the changing room, a storage cupboard. Sitting on his travelling case he looked in the shaving mirror he used to apply his make-up. Had it come to this? Evidently, it had. Bustling through from the curtain came, 'Watson,' clapping his fellow actor on the shoulder and bursting into a verse from Gilbert and Sullivan as he began to change from his stage costume. *His foot should stamp, and his throat should growl, His hair should twirl, and his face should scowl; His eyes should flash, and his breast protrude, And this should be his customary attitude...* finally, he stopped, paused to look at his fellow thespian. 'Whatever is the matter, Holmes?'

'The matter - *Belmont*, is this; I'm through. Washed up.

1

Finished.' Rolling his eyes, Baxter Belmont reached into the pocket of his tweed coat as it hung from a hook. Taking a hefty pull at the contents of his battered old silver flask, he thrust it out into the air between them. After a defiant pause, Mortimer took the flask and half its contents. Closing his eyes, his mind summoned forth the past; Jekyll and Hyde at the Adelphi. Hamlet at the Lyceum. Sherlock Holmes at the Lyceum. How they applauded! The King Himself was said to have attended incognito, Charlie Chaplin sent a cable congratulating him. Baxter Belmont was the second Watson, that upstart Carlton thought himself above the role. And where was he now? making another of his dreadful B-pictures in Hollywood no doubt. So now this. Touring the sticks in an asthmatic old Morris charabanc that couldn't get up steep hills without a push... the *Piccadilly Players* had reached the bottom.

The *Players* consisted of five actors', two of them being Bill the driver of the coach and the electrician cum, set builder, a consumptive Welshman who went by the name Jones the Sparks without ever revealing his given name. How far away seemed those halcyon days of 1932 when Mortimer and Baxter had set out on the circuit with a cast of fifty and a complete complement of artisans travelling by special train. Gradually, the offers stopped coming, the craze for the cinema leaving troupes adrift. Most of the old theatres had been torn down or converted to show the latest flicks. One by one, the craftsmen and women departed for more reliable wages in the British film industry, one by one the actors followed or retired to Bognor or Eastbourne or wherever it was old luvvies went to pasture. Consulting his pocket, watch, Mortimer saw it was nearly eleven. *Bugger.* Too late to get to a pub... assuming this place *had* a pub.

The village of Middlemarsh was almost slap-bang in the

middle of nowhere; a dot on the map in Exmoor, it had languished in obscurity for several reasons. First, there was no industry of note there, then there was the fact the railway line to Exeter passed some thirty or so miles to the East; the village never prospered as others did from the expanding network of tracks sprawling across the country. The tin and copper mines had all but shut, and apart from the farmers' market at Minehead there was little reason for anyone to use the single track leading to town. There *was* a pub, the *Sir. Walter Raleigh*, a post office too in the village shop, the Salvation Church Hall and the village school, a one room affair set up in an old cow-shed. The village church was a relatively modern affair for the area, nestling on a small hillock at the end of the one street. At the top of the hill at the edge of the village sat the ruin of a much older small church, said to have been built before the time of the Armada.

Apart from this and a few large houses scattered around the moor, that was all Toby Fairweather had ever known. Now, however, he was taking a chance, a big one. Clambering down from his bedroom, he'd taken his father's pushbike, the one he'd be riding to work at the farm in just over four hours. Andrew Fairweather was a fair, decent man, but it'd mean the belt at least and it was often said the man didn't know his own strength. All Toby knew as he clattered and scraped down the hill to the church hall was this was Bobby's only hope. He only hoped he'd be on time, he'd pray as Reverend Cholmondley was always telling the children to, only this time he'd mean it. *A proper prayer...* Bobby was worth it.

Baxter Belmont had changed into his travelling uniform of tweed suit and cloak, but these days Mortimer rarely bothered; why exchange one set of tweeds for another? Where was the sense? The performance at an end, it would soon be time to give

3

Bill and Jones a hand taking the props to the coach. *This is how it ends...* the limelight to the twilight... the knock at the outside door came so quietly, so deferentially that it was only on the third Mortimer heard it. Curious, he tried the door, finding it locked with the key in the lock. A twist of the key found him face to face with a small boy, no more than ten or twelve at the utmost, with a mop of unruly hair the colour of straw and a fresh graze on his left knee, testament to his lack of practice on a bicycle. He wore a bandage round his right wrist, the result, no doubt of some juvenile mishap. 'Yes?'

'I've come... come for help, sir.' Misunderstanding, the actor waved the boy in, pointing at the curtain leading to the backstage area as he perched back onto his trunk. 'There's not much to do, boy, just some boxes to shift.' Turning back to see the child still standing awkwardly, Mortimer raised his hands in theatrical bemusement. 'Well?' Toby stood, not sure how you were supposed to address the great man. Just then, Baxter came through the curtain for his belongings. 'Hullo? What's this? One of the Irregulars?' Seizing on the mention of the famous gang from the old copies of *The Strand* his Grandfather had given him, Toby nodded vigorously. 'Yes Sir, I mean, well, *no* Sir... that is, not *really*, Sir.'

'Well what, then, boy?' Mortimer was in no mood to humour an idiot child. 'If you won't help with the lumber, what are you here for?' Clearing his throat discretely, Baxter reached into the ragged old folio he insisted on keeping his scripts in and produced a playbill and a pen with a flourish. *Ahh, of course!* The penny dropped, Mortimer reached for the pen and signed the bill, it was, of course for *Sherlock Holmes,* handing it to the boy. 'Now run along, there's a good chap - why it's past eleven! Surely you had best be in bed, child?' To the actor's horror and confusion the

4

boy had burst into tears. 'Not if you won't help me, Mister Holmes, I'll run away, I will!'

It came out as a jumble of heartbreak and juvenile misery; the boy's constant companion, a Collie dog named Bobby, had bit him, quite out of character, and then bitten his mother when she tried to help the boy. The next day, on his return from the farm, the boy's father intended to bring a shotgun home and Bobby was under penalty of death. The boy, Toby by name, had heard of the play and, although the family was too poor to pay 3'6 for tickets, had decided to enlist the aid of none other than Sherlock Holmes, the famous consulting detective of 221b Baker Street. Had Mortimer Knight not been so pre-occupied with his faded career, so egotistical – and so tipsy, he might have thought better of it. Instead, he reached for his pipe, (a prop, naturally, as he detested smoking) and his deerstalker. As Baxter rolled his eyes and shook his head, Knight dropped easily into character and asked the boy to describe the details of the mysterious incident.

Dawn broke the next day as it had for generations, the first rays of light throwing the spire of the ruined church into silhouette against the crepuscular sky. Only the baker's lad and the farmworkers were about, men like Andrew Fairweather who was cycling to work, the fresh scrapes to the bicycle's frame and handlebar not un-noticed. *That boy!* Always trying to learn to ride when he wasn't about. He'd have to speak to him though; if he damaged the old Hercules, he'd be for it. *That bike was my Dad's...* still, he could hardly deny the boy if he wanted to ride. If only old Crowley paid more! The farmer was a notorious skinflint, otherwise Toby could have the bike he was always asking about. *Maybe next year...* trouble was, he'd been saying that to the boy for the two years past already. He just hoped Toby would understand what he had to do this evening. Across the valley from the Fairweather's cottage stood the old blacksmith's forge, above which Mortimer Knight stirred uneasily after his night in the old brass bed he'd had to share with Jones the Sparks; accommodations were hardly plentiful round these parts, as the old woman who owned the building had told him. Still, she'd agreed to provide a cooked breakfast and it was the smell from the bacon that drew the tired old trouper from his bed now. He washed in the old-fashioned bowl on its stand in the corner and felt a little better, more alive. Yet something was nagging at him, a vague sense of disquiet; what was it he had said to that kid last night? Something about a dog, wasn't it?

'Lovely grub, that, missus, I will say. Proper food, is that.' Jones wiped the grease from his chin with his sleeve and Mortimer shuddered silently at the Welshman's manners. The old lady seemed delighted, however and took their plates to return with more tea. Letting out a satisfied belch, the Welshman leaned back and reached into the pocket of his waistcoat to produce a bag of the evil-smelling tobacco he swore by. Others, the tired joke ran, swore *at* it. Leaving Jones to produce his roll-up, Mortimer excused himself and went up to pack his things. This was *definitely* his last tour.

Bright and early, Toby panted his way into the village, heading for the blacksmith's yard. If he ran all the way, he reckoned he could make it in twenty-five minutes or even less. With any luck he could still make it to school by eight-fifty; Miss Cardew was known to be strict on time. All he had to do was find Mr. Holmes and the rest would be simple; he'd save Bobby, he was sure of it.

The *Players* had arranged to meet up at the coach at nine-thirty sharp. They had another five engagements booked and had to be across the border into Devon by the afternoon. The tour finished at Truro some two weeks' hence. It was just before half-eight when Baxter Belmont turned up, lugging his case. 'No sign of his Lordship?' Bill the driver shook his head. That in itself was strange; Mortimer Knight was always first at the coach, fussing and checking everything and everyone like a stressed mother hen. A loud burst of cursing heralded the arrival of the final player, Alan Neville; 'Lord Stonebrook' and, thanks to a bit of quick-changery, the suspicious gamekeeper both. It had got to just before nine when Mortimer Knight appeared in a fluster of words explaining what was going on, dumping his trunk by the coach and unbuckling the leather straps securing it, he took out his *Holmes* costume and props; Inverness, deerstalker, walking cane, pipe and glass. 'No time to explain, but Baxter and I will follow on, meet you in Eastwater. Baxter, the game is afoot old friend, costume dear friend, costume! We have a modest, but important performance to attend to.' Arms folded, Baxter regarded this flurry of activity calmly. 'This is that boy. Last night. Isn't it?'

'A promise is a promise, old friend.'
'But he thinks you're Sherlock Holmes! Sherlock *bloody* Holmes... what'll he think when he finds out the truth?' Regarding his long-term colleague with an amused eye, Knight seized on the chance for some fun. 'The truth? What's the truth, when it's at home?' Wearily, Baxter closed his eyes. *Not this again.* 'You know very well, what truth', *Mor-tee-mer,* that you are an actor, not a fictitious detective. Let's just get out of here, shall we? It's never a good idea to get mixed up...' he was interrupted by a jubilant shout from Knight; 'Ah! The lad himself.'

Toby Fairweather had indeed appeared from the direction of the schoolhouse, his expression one of grim determination.

Miss Cardew had not been best pleased by his lateness and when he had cheeked her, had given him six of the best and a promise to take this up with his mother. Now the boy was steadfastly refusing to show any sign of a tear, his faithful dog's peril far outweighing his natural fear of his father finding out he'd been insolent to the teacher. Knight met him in character, issuing a cheery greeting and venomously dragging Belmont into the charade by introducing him as 'My estimable colleague and erstwhile companion, Doctor John Watson.' Hissing under his breath, the old professional slipped into character as easily as a pair of favoured old slippers. Turning melodramatically to 'Holmes' 'Watson' exclaimed; 'Well, Holmes, what can be made of the matter? Have you any thoughts?'

'Naturally, Watson.' Throwing back his Inverness to showcase the famous old calabash – originally selected as its large size and appearance made it more visible for audiences in dim Victorian lighting – 'Holmes' gestured towards the horizon. It had suddenly occurred to him that he usually did this with a script, ad-libs not being a *forté* of his. Looking askew at Belmont from the corner of his eye, any hope of inspiration was dashed by his friend firmly and pointedly folding his arms and cocking his head, as if to say *'You're in this on your own, mate.'* Luckily, the boy proved quicker off the mark than his choice of champion. 'I'll expect he wants to see him, don't you Mister Holmes? Bobby, that is.'

'AHA! Of course! The chief suspect. Very well, boy, take us to this Bobby of yours.'

Waving the rest of the troupe off, Mortimer set off after Toby to his cottage, Baxter trudging along mutinously in his wake. The walk was pleasant enough, the day cloudy, but mild as they climbed a stile and walked across a field leading to a brook. A stone bridge led across to a path that meandered and twisted to bring them out opposite a dolmen, one of those ancient and mysterious stone constructs whose purpose was perhaps to inter the remains of nameless heroes, ones who died before time was time. Glad of the cane, Mortimer was beginning to feel his fifty-one years, while Baxter seemed annoyingly fresh, the result doubtless of his mania for tennis. He carried a racket and whites everywhere he went in the hopes of getting a game. Mortimer Knight detested all forms of exercise, regarding sport as something quite unbefitting someone of his status. Breathing heavily now, he let his mind slip to thoughts of retirement. *Perhaps Hastings...* but then they came to the gate.

The Fairweather cottage was always a hive of activity; as well as raising her sister's baby, Nancy Fairweather took in washing to help make ends meet. The baby, a noisy bundle of joy, had been evacuated along with his mother from London during the Blitz of the previous year. It was on a visit home that Minnie Fairweather had been killed in a surprise bombing raid. Her husband was serving on minesweepers somewhere in the North Sea when the news came; after a hurried compassionate leave, he had agreed to the Fairweathers raising the boy as their own. Andrew had said nothing at the time, but simply asked for extra work at the farm to help pay for the new arrival he now saw as one of his own. The two-bedroom building was easily a hundred or two old, with a large garden mainly given over to the 'Dig for Victory.' The potatoes and carrots grew well enough, but so far, any attempts to cultivate an edible swede had eluded Nancy. She was sat on the back doorstep by the old butler's sink she used to scrub the laundry in, taking a rest and singing gently to little Robin as he gurgled happily in his pram. Hearing the gate squeaking, she made to stand up as the curious delegation made it's entrance known.

Mrs. Fairweather folded her arms at the sight of a middle-aged man in an Inverness cape raising his deerstalker in greeting. 'Good day to you madam, I take it I have the honour of addressing Toby's mother?.'

'I wouldn't know about that. My husband's out at his work if it was him you were wanting.'

'Far from it, far from it; we are here with a serious purpose.' Spotting her son shyly standing next to a man dressed in tweed, it struck her that altogether there was something oddly familiar about these two strangers, but she could not satisfy her curiosity without asking what she felt might be impertinent questions. All the same, that boy had better have a good reason for not being in school! Spotting Nancy's disapproving gaze, Baxter stepped forward briskly and raised his hat. 'Toby has brought us here so that my colleague can examine the dog.'

'Bobby? But he's dangerous! That is, he bit Toby and me.'

'Just so, Mrs, ah, Fairweather, but I assure you our interest in the dog is strictly professional.' This came from the man in the deerstalker and now Toby joined in the pleas to allow 'Holmes' to see the dog. 'This is Sherlock Holmes, mum; he's come to help Bobby!' Awkwardly, Mortimer exchanged a look of unease with Baxter, who had been against this fool's errand from the outset. 'If we could just have a word in private, I am sure I can explain...' Nancy Fairweather's expression made it clear this was exceedingly unlikely.

'So you two gentlemen are actors? From the play at the hall?'

'Quite.' Mortimer Knight paced the small kitchen, stooping his head to avoid a low beam. 'Your boy Toby came to the hall late last night...'

'He did *what*?' Going to the open door, Nancy called out angrily to her boy; 'Toby Fairweather, come over here right this instant!' Mortimer's attempts at placating the outraged mother were foundering fast, but Baxter, used to his friend's knack of getting quickly out of his depth tapped on the window, which was ajar. 'He really is a brave little chap, Mrs. Fairweather. Why not let my friend see the dog, and we can be on our way; it's probably gone mad from heatstroke or the like anyway. What harm can it possibly do?'

'Try telling my husband that, Mister... Watson, I suppose?'

'Yes Mum, he's Doctor Watson and that's Mr. Sherlock Holmes what's going to solve the case of why Bobby bit me and you.' Toby was defiantly insistent as he stood in the doorway. 'Then Dad won't have to shoot Bobby, will he?' Sighing in vexation, Nancy turned back to her washing. 'Oh... bother the lot of you!' Toby let out a shout of elation and ran out to the garden, followed by an apologetic Knight. 'But just you wait 'til your father gets home!'

The shed was at the end of a path at the side of the property, secured by a plank of wood through two rusted iron hasps. Eagerly pulling the wood back, Toby went to pull the door open, but Baxter's hand on his shoulder restrained him. 'Not until Holmes has a chance to assess the temperament of the animal, Toby.' The boy shrugged free of his grip, however and grabbed at the door. 'I know he won't harm me, he never meant to bite me...' A medium-sized collie erupted from the darkened shed and leapt at the boy. 'See?' To the actors' relief, the dog was playfully licking Toby's face, neck and hands in an excited, but decidedly friendly, frenzy of joy. Even Baxter Belmont had to wonder aloud; '*This* is the dog that savaged two people?'

Accepting the offer of a cup of tea, the two actors sat at the kitchen table mulling it over. Clearly the dog had attacked both boy and mother; the bandage Toby was sporting on his wrist was testament to that. Nancy Fairweather had been bitten to the leg, but her coarse woollen stockings had prevented the collie getting a proper grip and further damage. The question had to be,

11

'Why?' Why did the dog, normally a faithful and devoted pet, turn so feral so quickly? What was the cause of it? It was Baxter who finally put his thoughts into speech. 'So, what happened to set the dog against the boy?' Nancy turned to regard her son, now happily playing in the back garden with his pet. 'You'd have to ask Toby that; he was walking him when it happened.'

'Where?' Mortimer quickly added 'Forgive me, Mrs. Fairweather, but where was Toby walking Bobby?'

It was a little over an hour later and Baxter Belmont was despairing of ever rejoining the troupe in Eastwater. The boy and his dog in the lead, they had traipsed over two largish hills and along a valley and now stood on the coastal path. The view was tremendous; from here one could see across the Bristol Channel to the southerly coast of Wales. Several small fishing boats plied their trade in these waters and a larger boat, a freighter of some type was visible cutting through the waters inland towards Bristol or Cardiff, maybe even Newport. A porpoise, perhaps or a dolphin broke the surface some half a mile from shore. What looked to be a falcon of some kind hovered overhead, riding the air currents that soared above the cliff. It was along the path here that Toby had walked and run with Bobby, until, that is they got to the fence. Easily six feet tall, the wire fence stretched as far as the cliff-top, where it disappeared into some brambles. A sign warned trespassers that the cliff area was unsteady and could collapse at any moment. The only way onward was to follow the metal fencing inland to where a temporary pathway angled its way around to the far headland, to meet the coastal path there. Mortimer turned to face Toby, who was throwing a stick for Bobby. 'Toby, where was it that the dog bit you?,

'My wrist, Mister Holmes.'

'No, I mean where were you when this happened?'

'Oh, through there.' To the men's surprise, the boy was pointing at the bramble patch near the cliff edge.

There was, on closer inspection, a small gap in the greenery. Pushing through the barbs that tore at his tweed, Mortimer cursed beneath his breath. *This was the last time he was getting involved with the bloody fans...* finally reaching the fence, he could see a length of the bottom had become exposed, possibly by small animals and children digging it out. By reaching down, it was possible to pull the bottom up and crawl through. Behind his colleague, Baxter was ducking brambles as they came lashing back at him. 'You're not going in there, are you, Mor... I mean, um, Holmes?' The reply came back in a stage bellow. 'That's where Toby was when the dog turned, Watson, that's where our answers lie!'

'But the sign... the cliff could be dangerous!.'

'Not really Doctor Watson, that sign's been up three year now.' This came from Toby, who was bringing up the rear with Bobby, on hands and knees to avoid the worst of the brambles. That decided it; Mortimer Knight bent down, hauled the wire up and stepped back for Baxter to go first. 'Shall I – shall I go first then, old boy?' The smile on Knight's face was a picture. 'Oh, I insist on it dear chap.'

They all stood in a huddle against the prevailing wind, a southwesterly that blew stiffly across from the Atlantic, the smell of salt and the sea strong in everyone's nostrils. From where they were standing, the ground rose and then fell towards a bay, a cluster of huts in the dip before the ground rose on the far side to a scrubby clump of weather-beaten trees. Toby was pointing at a hillock of tufted grass some thirty feet distant. 'That's it, that's where Bobby bit me.' As if to underline the point, the dog lay down with his head on his paw, a sorrowful expression in his eyes and manner. A sharp elbow from Baxter Belmont had 'Holmes' scrabbling for his props, Mortimer Knight producing his pipe to place it in his mouth in a dramatic stage gesture, only to immediately remove it again to speak. 'I think I shall look for clues, Watson.' At which the pipe disappeared to be replaced by the magnifying glass. Stooping over, he began an apparent examination of the blades of grass between his shoes and the mound ahead. 'Ahh, yes... very interesting... well I can say this... there are some interesting details about the, ah, grass here. Yes, indeed Watson. Wouldn't you say?' 'Watson' was about ready to admit the truth to the poor boy, that they were nothing, but actors... when a peculiar thrumming sound came to his ears. *It was as if the earth itself was humming!*

'Holmes' had just put his ear to the ground over the mound when it started, that odd whine from below. What transpired next came as both shock and end to the expedition; first there was a shout and then Bobby, quite literally, went mad. It took both men to subdue the beast, for he had indeed become as such. No more the loveable collie, this was now a deadly dangerous animal, ripping out left and right with his fangs and claws, saliva pouring from his mouth and his eyes quite red. Poor Toby! Seeing his pet turn like this for a second time quite upset the boy, who tried to call his Bobby with a whistle. Indeed, this seemed to still the savage beast, if only for a moment, perhaps recognition dimly dawning in the animal's subconscious brain. Then it was as before; Baxter and Mortimer surrounding the frothing, roaring creature. A terrible transformation!. Finally, Baxter acted decisively, snatching at his friend's Inverness. Seeing his plan, Mortimer quickly divested himself of the garment and Baxter was able to throw it over the convulsing animal, drawing it around him like a tweed bag. Just as he succeeded, the voice called out again, a voice of authority telling them in no uncertain terms to stand where they were.

The man was perhaps thirty, slim if muscular with a poacher's jacket and a shotgun. He walked towards the group with the easy movements of a sailor on a heaving deck, eyes of flint on them the whole time. Mortimer decided to speak first, spurred on by the barrel of the shotgun that somehow never *quite* dropped from his stomach the whole time the man was approaching. 'We are not trespassers, the boy here was showing us where his dog became wild.'

'This land is off-limits. The cliffs here are a danger; you would have seen the signs, Sir.'

'Ah, yes, but you see we are not in any danger, so we shall be leaving.' Baxter's intervention merely made the man's eyes narrow for a second as they refocused onto him. He had the acutely uncomfortable sensation of being marked up for a target. The man spoke again; 'How'd you get in? Through the gap by the cliff face was it?.'

'That's right, mister; not our fault if it had a gap, is it?' Toby's impertinence sparked something like recognition in the man, the craggy features relaxed a little. 'Right you are son, better bugger off the way you came, sharpish like.' *'Bugger off?... bugger – OFF!'* Mortimer Knight was certainly not used to being spoken to this way! Luckily, Baxter knew his friend well enough to head off any protest the fool was likely to make, and clearing his throat loudly dropped back into character. 'Good heavens, look at the time; we'd best be on our way, *Holmes*.' The inflection was warning enough and, with a subdued nod, Mortimer turned to the writhing mass in the Inverness. It took both men to carry Bobby, as the bundle was kicking out desperately. As the singular little party departed, they could not have known the terror running through the sergeant's mind. *'Dear God - it's out of control now...'*

By the time they had dragged the snarling, growling, struggling bundle through the fence, it had gone limp. Concerned, the two men pushed through the brambles to lay the cape down, opening it cautiously to find the dog quite unconscious, breathing shallowly and irregularly. Alarmed, Baxter knelt by the wretched creature and checked its neck; there was, indeed a pulse, however faint. Dropping to his knees by his pet, the boy was beside himself, in tears despite his efforts to contain them. 'Can't you help him, Doctor?' Shaking his head, the actor was cursing himself for a fool.

'I'm not a doctor, Toby, I'm an actor.'

'But you're Doctor Watson, the famous doctor!'

'I wish I was.' Ashamed of the deceit, Baxter rose to stand, wishing the ground would swallow him up.

'You said you'd help!' Producing his calabash, 'Holmes' sparked up again; 'And we shall, Toby!, we shall!' Snatching the pipe from Mortimer, Baxter hurled it over the cliff. 'It's over, Mortimer. Face it, this was a stupid, stupid mistake.' Standing back, his little fists curled tightly, the boy shook his head, realisation dawned.

'You're not even Sherlock Holmes! Liars, both a'you!' Baxter tried to calm the boy, but he ran away down the path, shouting over his shoulder as he went. 'The gyptians! They'll help!'

It was nearly half an hour later. Unwilling to leave the stricken animal, the actors sat with it keeping vigil. Bobby seemed to be sleeping, his breath coming somewhat easier now, his pulse stronger. Any attempt to rouse the dog, however, was met with failure. He simply could not be woken. The creaking and clattering of a cart that chirred into view around the bend made the dejected Mortimer raise his head first. 'Look at this, Monty!' It was quite a sight, a massive dray pulling a flat wagon piled with straw for the horse and a woman who must have been a hundred. The driver pulled up as Toby jumped down from the seat and ran round to help the old woman down. Again Baxter made to speak to Toby, but the lad merely ignored him, showing the wizened

Gypsy woman to where Bobby lay, still comatose. Mortimer raised his deerstalker in deference to the old woman, who gave him a curious look in return. The driver came round, a tanned youth with a chequered shirt and red neckerchief. 'Afternoon, gents. This is Mother Patience, come to see the dog.' The weathered, withered face seemed to radiate wisdom and something more, a wonderful calmness. Seating herself by Bobby's still form, she laid a be-ringed hand on his chest and left it there a full minute.

As Toby and, rather subdued, the actors watched, the woman drew a leather pouch from around her neck and pulled out some herbs. Laying these aside, she took a twist of paper from a pocket in her skirt and opened it out. Inside was a foul-looking paste, to which she added the herbs. She spoke the word 'water' at which the young lad produced a glass bottle, handing it to her with surprising gentleness and deferential manner. Pouring a little of the liquid over the mixture, the watchers, though not the youth, were astonished to see it suddenly fume and belch, producing a cloud of noxious purple smoke. This concoction simmered and hissed until the paper beneath caught fire, at which she poured more water onto the burning mess, this time extinguishing it. Taking up a small stick, the old crone mixed up a paste from the remains of her bonfire, scraping this off into the neck of the bottle. Finally, she reached into another pouch about her neck for what seemed to be common table salt, sprinkling some into the cocktail. The water, which had clouded and darkened, at once became clear again. Reaching over to the stricken Bobby, she opened his mouth and poured a little of the bottle's contents over his teeth and gums. As she repeated this, she uttered a strange and wonderful chant, rising in a low bass from deep within her sparrow-like chest to become a keening wail. *Drabsap Drab, Pattriensis Adrey, Drabsap Drab, Pattriensis Adrey, Bister Zukel, Bister Zukel...* this was all that the audience could discern, the rest being incomprehensible to the Western ear.

Slowly at first, Bobby began to twitch, then shudder until he was shaking as if in the grip of a violent seizure. Alarmed, Toby threw himself on his beloved dog, arms around him in a helpless gesture of devotion. As suddenly as it had started, the fit subsided and Bobby was awake. 'Good God!' Baxter's thought was echoed by Mortimer, neither man able to believe it. Whatever the old woman had done, it had wrought a wondrous transformation in the collie, who now sat up as if nothing had happened. Stepping forward, Mortimer produced his wallet and offered the old lady some silver coins, which she accepted with a graceful bow of her head. Gesturing to her young driver to help her back to the cart, she paused and said something to him. Curious as to this, Baxter raised an eyebrow and shrugged in the universal gesture of wonderment. In answer, the young Gypsy pointed up at the sky. 'Mum says there's no good to come of this place, no birds will fly here.' With that, he turned and clambered onto the seat of the cart, waved goodbye to Toby, gee'd his horse and was gone.

Nancy Fairweather was changing baby Robin when the group trudged wearily back, Bobby slipping past her legs to curl up in his bed in the kitchen corner. Toby came in, took off his boots and ran up to his room. After perhaps a minute, he returned downstairs with a dog-eared copy of a magazine. Handing it to Mortimer, he stood there, a sad look on his young features. The magazine was *The Strand,* open at a page showing an illustration of Holmes and Watson pursuing one of their cases. 'I'm not stupid, I knew you weren't really them, not *really.* I just wanted to show Dad that Bobby wasn't a bad dog. I thought you could help.' Lowering the tattered, faded publication, Mortimer turned to meet the gaze of his friend. Shaking his head, he smiled ruefully. 'And I thought we *could* help, Toby. That's why we came, to help save

Bobby. I must apologise for the pretence; I was carried away I suppose.'

'There is one good thing to come of this, you know.' Baxter squatted down, to look the boy better in the eye. 'We discovered something, I'm not sure what, that made Bobby become savage. He's really a very gentle dog, but you mustn't ever take him back to that place.'

'What place would that be, then?' Turning to the open door, Baxter saw a man standing there with a shotgun under his arm.

Andrew Fairweather listened as the two actors explained everything that had transpired since they had met young Toby the night previous. Not entirely unsympathetic, he was still grimly set on shooting the dog with the gun he had brought back from the farm, finishing early that day so as to be done with it before Toby returned from school. On finding the boy had played truant, his strong features clouded; there would have to be an apology to Miss Cardew and he was still undecided on a belting for the boy, only Nancy's intervention was likely to dissuade him from such drastic punishment. It seemed the boy had been proved right about the dog, but could he afford to take the risk? What if it turned against the baby next? And what of this place where Bobby had gone wild? Baxter broke into his thoughts by asking about the strange compound.

Everyone in the village knew about the odd comings and goings at The Dip – the local name for the spot. Over a bottle of the local ale, Fairweather told his visitors what he knew in the snug of the parlour. It must have been the autumn of '38 when the fence was run up; the workmen were a queer lot and no mistake. Billeted in the village, they kept odd hours, coming and going around the clock. Old Baylett, the retired postmaster had been in the Boer war as a lad and insisted they were military men.

Certainly, they carried themselves with an alert, upright bearing, but said little to the villagers, aside from the odd trip to the pub or shop, they kept to themselves. Local children, however always make the best spies, and not just around Baker Street. The village kids had soon reconnoitred the place and found a way in, but all there was to see was some huts, old, dilapidated Nissen huts. This in itself had seemed odd, as they had been quite new when actually constructed, the children swearing that they had been made to *look* old and rusted. That was all the farm-hand could tell his guests.

There seemed little, if any point to remaining any longer. The two had done what they could, made fools of themselves, but hopefully proved the dog had only been set awry by the mysterious hillock. Baxter was keen to get the next bus to Eastwater, but Nancy had bad news; the Eastwater bus ran only Saturdays now that there was a war on. They had a full three days before the next bus and no-one had any petrol to spare with the rationing. They would either have to walk a distance of some twenty-three miles, or remain until the weekend. Graciously, Nancy had offered to put the men up, but it meant taking Toby's room and neither man was keen to discomfit the boy any more than they already had. Walking back to town, the two decided to put up at the old blacksmith's forge for the remainder. Luckily, Mortimer carried a cheque-book and the old lady was delighted with the sum proffered. It was still light, however and her cooked breakfast many hours distant. Why not, she suggested, take supper at the pub?

The Sir. Walter Raleigh was one of those treasures you so often find in English villages. Built in the 17th century on the site of an earlier inn, the pub was the heart of Middlemarsh. Mortimer and Baxter found the place thriving as they entered, leaving their hats (A homburg in Mortimer's case and a flat tweed in the other) on pegs by the door. They managed to find a quiet bench near the fireplace and were soon enjoying the landlady's speciality, a game pie with potatoes and carrots. Leaving Baxter to indulge with a rare cigarette, as he only smoked when in a pub these days. Mortimer found a space at the bar and propped next to a fisherman. The landlord, a ruddy-faced man named Farley greeted the newcomer with a gruff   'Yes?'

'Two pints I think, what can you recommend?'

'Using your eyes.' To the amused laughter of the locals, Farley nodded his round head towards the pumps. 'Mild, Bitter, Stout.' Unabashed, Knight put on his best and most winning of smiles, one that had softened the flint hearts of many a landlady and creditor.

'And which of these would you suggest?' With a look of exasperation, the landlord placed a flabby hand on the nearest pump handle.

'Mild'll blow your socks off...' the hand moved to the next pumps in turn.

'Bitter's a tad milder and the Stout will set you up for a good night.'

'Two pints of Stout it is, landlord.'

As Mortimer took the mugs back to the bench, a serving-girl was clearing up their plates. Taking his glass, Baxter took an experimental pull at his Stout, savouring the strong, hoppy taste of the beer. This was good stuff and he was quite relaxed for the first time that day. Looking around, he took in the place – the people with their rustic humour, the smoke curling from the pipes and the old pictures hung on the ancient walls. No doubt about it, this was the life!

The evening passed in a convivial haze of good beer and

tobacco smoke. Sometime after nine, a new arrival came in, quite soaked with rain. Neither of the two actors had noticed the weather turn, but a sudden flash of lightning gave the change of atmosphere distinction. Going for another pint – it was Baxter's turn, he found himself alongside the new arrival. This man was perhaps forty-five or so, distinguished, dark-haired and dressed more like a country squire. Sensing he was being scrutinised, the man turned, his bearded face splitting into a puzzled grin.

'Hullo, you'll be one of those actor chappies I suppose?'

'Baxter Belmont and Mortimer Knight, at your service.' The hand that took Baxter's was dry and firm.

'Henry DeLacey, but you might as well call me Sir. Shovel-Alot, as that's my nickname in town.'

'Oh, how so?' Taking his glass of whisky, still not on the ration despite the rumours, DeLacey raised it in toast.

'Your good health.' Feeling he ought to return the man's hospitality, Baxter invited him to join them and soon the three were in conversation.

DeLacey was an affable, easygoing sort of chap and answered the others' questions with a breezy informality. The descendant of Edmund DeLacey, who had fought at Agincourt, he had returned from his mining concerns in South America to establish his claim to the Baronetcy of Dyfant, dormant some three hundred years now. His unusual sobriquet was due to his excavations at Cragston Hall, which, he said were to find the original 10th century walls of the old Abbey. The house itself was mainly a ruin, with a single wing surviving the storm of 1703 and a fire shortly after. It was in this wing that DeLacey had set himself up and very comfortably, for his requirements were modest. Mortimer commented that he had done well to come back before the U-Boats made the Atlantic too hot to consider crossing, but the noble applicant replied he had only returned late last year, he had business affairs in London which called him and he had only spent a total of six months at the Hall. He had a housekeeper who cooked, her husband did duty as a butler of sorts and there were, he said a few Barnstaple men who helped with the digging in between fishing trips. This seemed distinctly odd to Baxter, but he kept his thoughts to himself. Why would a man risk the treacherous crossing from South America when the waters were infested with U-Boats? Surely it would be more prudent to wait until the threat has passed? After all, it was common knowledge the Royal Navy would be gaining the upper hand soon, hadn't the Secretary of State made that stirring speech in the Commons just the other week?. Without knowing quite why, Baxter had decided not to trust this aristocratic claimant.

It was approaching closing time. The storm outside was buffeting the pub, the old building creaking and groaning at the force of the wind. Lightning streaked the sky and the rain lashed the panes with fury. Having consumed several pints of the excellent stout, Mortimer decided on a visit to the lavatory, which was out the back, reached through a short passageway. He bumped into one of the fishermen coming the other way, an uncouth fellow who just pushed past. As he returned, DeLacey invited both men back to Cragston Hall. He had arranged for his butler to pick him up in his car, though petrol was rationed. It was three miles to the Hall and he had seen the weather change during the late afternoon. Neither man was over-keen to take to their shared bed, so they accepted gratefully, though Baxter retained his private misgivings.

The Alvis Speed Twenty had been a beautiful car, but this one had seen better days. The weather in this part of the country was not kind to paintwork nor chrome and several dents and a bent bumper testified to Harris' poor driving. Indeed, DeLacey's butler had never driven a car before this one and, as Henry

DeLacey pointed out cheerfully, his driving was no better after five whiskies. Perhaps to illustrate the point, he banged the brakes on when a tractor pulled out suddenly from the right ahead. Harris himself seemed an odd choice for butler, gruff and severe with little, if any respect for his master. You would be forgiven for thinking the man an unpleasant uncle rather than servant from the way he spoke to his employer, his Cockney accent seeming to underline the contempt in his voice. Bouncing over the rough track leading to the house, the man swore constantly beneath his breath.

Seated in the back of the forlorn automobile, Mortimer and Baxter were thrown around from side to side, a half-rotten leather safety handle coming loose in the former's hand as he clung on for dear life. Finally, thankfully, Cragston Hall hove into view. It was a sad sight, this once-magnificent pile reduced to a single east wing and entrance hall, with little, but rubble to show where the remainder of the house had once stood. Several new-looking outbuildings and a small lodge at the gate, occupied by Mr and Mrs. Harris, made the remainder of the property, which stood some quarter of a mile back from two crumbled gate-posts. The original gate lay rusted in the grass alongside.

Cragston Hall flashed out of the darkness as a bolt of lightning struck the stump of a tree on the hill behind it. It was like something from one of those horror films Mortimer was always dragging Baxter along to see, the remnants of a stone fountain out front, with what seemed to be a griffin or dragon spreading a solitary broken wing over the cracked and broken basin. Harris stopped outside the oaken and barred main door to allow his passengers to hastily alight and sprint through the rain for the sparse shelter of the portico. The Alvis rumbled off around the back, presumably to a garage of some kind. Once inside,

Mortimer and Baxter found themselves inside a surprisingly well-appointed hall dominated by a double stair that led nowhere to the left and to the remaining upper floor to the right. Paintings of ancestors lined the stone walls and there was some oak panelling, along with various chairs and tables. There was even a suit of armour in a niche, while various ancient armaments hung from the original iron fitments. Although there was a heavy chandelier, it was not lit, the sole light a warm, flickering glow coming through from the room to the right. As if reading his guests' thoughts, Henry mentioned he had yet to have the house wired for electricity.

Following their host through to a huge sitting room, the actors could not help but be impressed by what they saw; more portraiture along the oak-panelled walls and an array of antique furniture. Nothing in the room seemed to have been made after 1820, but it was the fireplace that dominated and drew the eye. Fully fifteen feet across, the Portland stone fireplace was massive, the fire within enough to warm the entire chamber. What made Baxter stop in his tracks, however were the two Irish wolfhounds that had risen to their feet at their master's approach. Not unused to the reaction, Henry turned and smiled. Mortimer stepped forward unperturbed by the huge animals.

'Oh don't worry Baxter, a dog won't touch you if you're with its master or mistress.'

'Yes, but do the dogs know that?'

'Otto, Fritz... *Zurück!*'. At this oddly Germanic command, the two hounds immediately retreated to their place by the fire, laying down on a much-abused old rug there.

'Rather fond of these two, but I should warn you they roam the grounds here at night and they only answer to mc, well, Mrs. H. has a way with them, but that's her home-made pork pie; sends, em into a merry funk.' Going over to a sideboard laden with bottles, Henry asked his guests to name their poison.

Sitting in front of the roaring fire with glass in hand, the trio made a convivial group. Henry talked eloquently of his hopes for the old place and of gaining his title, while Mortimer regaled him with tales of the stage. DeLacey told them of the history of the family, the original DeLaceys who were given the land and most of the surrounding area by a grateful King Henry, of the tin mines that brought them wealth and power, then of the terrible reckoning after the Civil War, when the family was driven from their home and lands. The clock in the corner had just chimed twelve, when DeLacey asked what they thought of the village. Reservedly Baxter replied that it was a charming place, Mortimer nodding his agreement. Leaning forward, his glass between his hands, Henry probed further.

'And what did you make of the walk, along the cliffs, I mean?' Baxter gave a start at this; how had he known?. His colleague, however, was well into his cups and seemed happy to describe their meanderings along the coastal path, mentioning Toby and Bobby's extraordinary transformation. Henry was listening to this account intently, as if it had some personal meaning to him. As Mortimer finished his odd tale, Henry went to refill his guest's glasses, giving Baxter the opportunity to whisper across that he felt the man was hiding something and not to trust him.

'You're taking the part a bit seriously old love, the chap's perfectly decent... ah, thank you, sir.' Knight took his glass and smiled pointedly at Baxter as if to emphasise his opinion. Belmont managed a brief smile as he took his own drink. He decided there and then to investigate this unique place, to see if he could discern anything about their host; after all, the country was at war, any man using German commands to control his dogs might well have something to hide...

The wind howled through the eaves and the rain was relentless in its assault on the old house. It was past two when the door to Baxter's room creaked open and out stepped the man himself. Pausing at the landing, he listened carefully and was rewarded with the sound of heavy snoring, Mortimer Knight in drink was always the heaviest of sleepers. Wishing he had a torch, he crept along the hallway, socks around his shoes as he had read the American 'private eyes' sometimes did. He made his way along the hall, stopping to listen every now and then. From what he could gather, the upper floor ran in an 'L', the shorter branch to the rear. DeLacey's bed-chamber was, naturally, at the front and side, commanding ninety-degree views of unrivalled majesty across the land and the sea which was some half mile distant. His and Mortimer's room being at the back of the 'L', he thus would have had to sneak past the master bed-chamber to reach the gallery leading to the stairs. His nerves weren't up to it, so he headed instead for the rear of the house, where he was rewarded by the sight of a narrow passage leading to the servant's stairs. The whole house seemed in darkness, with just the occasional, and heart-stopping flash of lightning to show him the way. Baxter only hoped DeLacey was right about the dogs roaming the grounds at night; he didn't fancy his chances against them. He had made some progress when a phenomenally loud blast rendered the air, causing him to jump and stagger against the wall. It was a lightning strike, extremely close by, the flash and bang being simultaneous. Almost at once, the sound of a door banging open and shoes on stone stairs ahead of him sent him flying back along towards his room.

Whomever it was, almost certainly a servant, Baxter had no time to open his door and slip inside, so he kept going, past the master bed-chamber. It was then that the door to Mr.DeLacey's quarters opened and Baxter was certain he'd been discovered. Fortune, they say, favours the brave; perhaps also the petrified.

The door was opened from the *outside,* the man standing there lit from within. A fisherman by his garb, he was soaked from head to foot, despite the oilskins and Sou'wester he wore. By some miracle, he hadn't seen the trespasser, but Baxter froze, unsure what to do or where indeed to hide. The man made to speak, but was pulled inside by a hand, the door closed behind him. Despite his rising panic and fear of discovery, Baxter tip-toed back to listen at the door. From the chamber came the sounds of an argument; the visitor's voice easy to discern by the local accent. Although he couldn't hear much of the detail – the door must have been fully three inches in thickness, the actor heard snatches. *I bloody told you... more care... Commander...* whilst from DeLacey came *can't go back to Berlin... battle isn't lost... a lightning strike... must remain a secret...* This confirmed it! Not only was DeLacey hiding something, it had something to do with Germany!. Suddenly, Baxter was seized with an awful feeling of absolute horror, that his life and his friend's would mean nothing to such people. Were they Nazi agents? Spies? Perhaps even the vanguard of some terrible invasion? He had to warn the authorities!

Gradually, as he listened, the tone of the conversation turned to joviality, with both men laughing at one point. Baxter knew he had to report this, but felt he'd be laughed at without concrete proof. Perhaps, he thought he should continue his surreptitious search of Cragston Hall before rousing Mortimer and making a dash for it to the village. As he crept along towards the main stairs, however, a chilling thought hit him. This man, this fisherman-visitor was a local. *What if they were all in on the scheme?* He had seen a film like it once, with that American chappie... what *was* his name? There was this hotel and there was a murder and it turned out they'd *all* done it. This might well be that sort of thing, he decided not to trust anyone, but a policeman. There wasn't a station in the village; he doubted they saw a constable more than once a year if that. Perhaps he could get to Barnstaple? But he was at the top of the staircase and the point, in his mind, of no return.

Hoping to find DeLacey's study, Baxter went down the stairs, careful to keep to the edge as he had learned as a schoolboy; his preparatory school was an old pile of similar vintage and midnight feasts in the sports hall were the custom. More than once he had successfully eluded the house master as he prowled his domain by lamp-light. Now, he was pleased to find, his skill had not deserted him as he negotiated the stair with quiet ease. He knew the first door from the entrance was, of course, the sitting room, so tried the second door, finding it unlocked. It was pitch black in there, so closing the door behind gently, he reached in his waistcoat pocket for his matches, striking one and then... dear God!, dropping it. Recoiling in terror, he backed away from the gigantic creature he had seen in the sulphurous flare. Another match, this one lit with a trembling hand, revealed the truth to be a stuffed bear on hind paws, frozen forever in a savage posture, a salmon in its massive paws. Further, he saw a candelabra on a table and hastened across to light it.

By the light of the candles (he had lit all three to avoid one seeming shorter than its companions to any watchful servant) Baxter saw he was in some sort of trophy and gun room, lined with the slightly moth-eaten remains of what appeared to be a good portion of Africa's wildlife. It was a taxidermist's dream, but it was the gun-cases that drew his attention; there were three of them, all filled with shotguns, rifles, elephant guns and pistols ranging from the antique to the more recent in the form of a Webley service revolver chambered for the .455 cartridge. Baxter's father was a subaltern in a highland regiment and had kept his in his own study for many years; he knew the pistol of old. If things turned nasty, he would make for this cabinet, assuming the ammunition would be in the locked drawer below. It was time to move on, however; the door at the end of the room enticing him deeper into his nocturnal survey. Opening the door, he found himself in a dusty ante-room of doubtful purpose, old tea-chests packed high either side of the tiny space. A look in one revealed some old crockery, so he abandoned the room, careful to extinguish the candles before approaching the door back to the entrance hall. As he stepped out, the sound of voices came to him from upstairs, clearly the fisherman was leaving. He groped his way along the gloomy wall until he was at the next door, the sudden sound of an engine starting causing him to pause. The Alvis? Yes, there could be no doubt. Had DeLacey left the house? His mysterious visitor? Or both? Dismissing the thought for the moment, he tried the door, finding it too unlocked. He opened the door.

It was the dining room, with some sort of scullery or pantry adjacent, more of the tea-chests in the latter. With nothing to be gained by loitering, he went back out to the hall. The staircase protruded from the rear wall of the great space, so that the space beneath formed a corridor. Along this and directly beneath the stair, a massive double door opened into another inky-black space, musty with the unmistakable smell of old books. Clearly a library. Stepping inside, the door closed behind, he again lit his candles from the dwindling stock of matches. The chamber was as expected, walls lined with shelf upon shelf of ancient volumes, most bound in faded leather. The library was vast, fully fifty feet wide, with several reading tables and chairs at its centre. A gallery running the entire perimeter was accessible from two sets of steps in iron spirals. Of a study there was no sign. It seemed if DeLacey kept any incriminating papers or even a wireless set, it was in his bed chamber and therefore, inaccessible. *Unless he left in the car...* but the sound of footsteps falling quickly down the main stairs above the library door told Baxter he wouldn't have time to find out.

Henry DeLacey was a worried man. The agent he had placed to watch the base was certain the two actors had penetrated the surface fence. Now Walton shows up and announces he reckons a U-Boat couldn't make the approach after all and they'd need an E-Boat, one of the so-called *Schnellboots* to make a successful breach. Walton was on his way to secure a *fast boat*; better safe than sorry! He turned into the library, pausing at the doorway a second. What was that smell? Something burning? Perhaps; this old house played all kinds of tricks on the senses. Going through the large room, he pushed the book in and leant against the shelf to open the secret panel. He couldn't afford to wait for Walton to reach headquarters, he needed to be sure. He would use the transmitter.

From his position above on the gallery, Baxter lay as flat as he could. He just prayed the traitor wouldn't spot the candelabra he'd left on the table. He needed to hear or even see what was happening, yet he dare not move a muscle for fear of making a noise on the iron work; it would ring like a bell and he was lucky to get up there without being detected, the amount of vibration it caused through the ironwork. To his horror, he heard the unmistakable sound of a wireless set being warmed up, with a sudden burst of clicking. It was clearly Morse Code of some kind and Baxter cursed himself for not learning it. The clicking might as well have been Dutch to him. Or German...

The day dawned as days must and the Alvis was back from its mystifying errand. Harris had woken both men bright and early and, as DeLacey had not yet awoken, both the actors trooped down to the entrance hall to await the car's arrival outside. Hurriedly, Baxter whispered to his friend to keep quiet about what he had shared with him in the small hours, when he had stolen into his friend's room to inform him their host – along with unknown other locals, was a Nazi traitor. Surly as ever, Harris drove them to the old forge in a belligerent silence, and Mortimer's cheery wave of thanks was answered with a face of stone. The two went into their lodgings, the old lady pleased to see her errant lodgers had at least turned up for her breakfast.

This being only Thursday, the two found themselves adrift in a village filled with God-knew how many Nazi sympathisers. Enquiring as casually as he could, Mortimer asked the old lady if there was ever any trouble in Middlemarsh. 'Oh, nothing to speak of, sir; there was that business with the Randall girl the year before last and old Bob Sykes got drunk and crashed his tractor into the church on Jubilee Day in '35. Why ever would you ask, sir?'

'Oh, no particular reason. I just wondered if the local constabulary had much to do, that was all.' The kindly face wrinkled with the smile across it.

'Why, there's no need for such a thing, unless you mean Bernard Lean, the Bobby and he's been retired ten year or more. No, if you want the police, you'd need to go to Barnstaple; you could always ring them from the post office, or I suppose the vicarage. Reverend Cholmondley has a telephone at the vicarage.'

There was, both men agreed, little point in telephoning from the post office; hadn't they both heard about saboteurs and spies taking over whole areas? Gossip was rife in modern Britain, but that didn't mean it was *all* rubbish! No, the vicarage seemed the place. Asking directions from their landlady, they set out after finishing their meal. The walk to the place seemed to take an age, but the house itself was set back from St. Winifred's itself. A middle-aged man was stooped over a rose-bush with secateurs in his calloused hand, rising at the sound of the gate. 'Good Morning, it is a lovely day.' The vicar stood, smiling, evidently waiting for his visitors to speak their business.

'Reverend Cholmondley? The landlady at the old forge recommended us to you.' Baxter stepped from behind his friend to add; 'We understand there's a telephone here. We wish to ring for the police.'

The two men sat, despondent in the *Sir. Walter Raleigh.* Their attempt to call the authorities had been thwarted by, of all things, the vicarage phone line coming down in the previous night's storm. *Of all the luck!* The Reverend Cholmondley had proved most charming, however, insisting on them coming in for tea and biscuits – well, carrot cookies at any rate. Rationing was hitting home everywhere these days. Their new friend had proved most charming, even Baxter had to admit the fellow was first-rate... and certainly no Nazi. He had established that in conversation, although he was cautious enough not to reveal everything, he warned the Reverend about DeLacey.
Cholmondley was shocked, especially at a local landowner; if the man were some city type he might have believed ill of him!. He had waved them off with the assurance the line would soon be fixed; he had sent off to town for a GPO man. Mortimer had wanted to call from the post office, but Baxter was nervous as to how far the spy ring's tentacles reached. No; safer to wait for the Reverend's telephone line to be mended.

The night passed slowly, uneventfully. Apart from the arrival of the Reverend Cholmondley, there was little to occupy the two hapless companions. All they could think about was warning the authorities about the Nazi spy in the ruined stately house. Playfully, the Reverend reminded a few of his more wayward flock of the Church Drive for Victory, everyone was expected to donate money, goods or labour to help buy a Spitfire and already the fund stood at thirty pounds. Think of it! Their little village able to raise perhaps a hundred pounds towards victory! So far, he reminded the landlord, only old Jones had failed to turn out, oh – and Mr. DeLacey, of course, but the man was busy and couldn't be expected to find the time...

'You hear that?.' Mortimer leaned closer to his friend. 'DeLacey wouldn't contribute!' Baxter had heard all right. Then again, why would a Nazi contribute to the British war effort! It just confirmed it; the swine! He had a good mind to... but then the door to the pub opened and Harris stood there, squinting into the murk and fug. Clearly he was looking for... them! Shuffling over to the pair, DeLacey's servant was his usual cheerless self. 'The Master wants me to tell you how you're invited to dinner tonight. He apologises for not seeing you off this mornin', but he had urgent business to attend to.' Coming from this man, this was quite the discourse. Sensing reluctance in his counterpart, Mortimer quickly spoke across him.

'Why yes, that would be lovely.' Looking across at the Reverend, who had accepted a pint from a local, he added loudly; 'Yes, we would love to have dinner at Cragston Hall. *TONIGHT...*' Harris looked as if the man had gone mad, but merely added; 'Car's waiting.'

Cragston Hall was perhaps even starker by moonlight. The sharp light threw the tiniest feature into a sharp relief and made dark, unwelcoming shadows where there would normally be nothing sinister. The lights, at least, were burning brightly and their host met them in the parlour with the drinks ready. DeLacey seemed slightly tense in his manner, but both his guests assumed this part of his guilt and did not remark on it. He proposed a toast, to the King.

'So you are a Monarchist, then, Mr. DeLacey?'
Mortimer's comment raised an eyebrow from Baxter, but Henry DeLacey merely nodded.

'Not exactly fashionable, perhaps, with half the World overthrowing their Royal Houses. But yes, yes, I am something of a traditionalist.' Waving them over to the now-familiar seats, he set down his glass on a table and picked up a cabinet box of cigars, bringing it over.

'Pre-War. Cuban.'

'Not for me, thanks.' said Baxter, but Mortimer leaned forward to take one, managing to discretely elbow his friend. They weren't, after all, meant to be aware of the man's duplicities.

'Nonsense old boy, when will you get the chance again? Not 'til we've given Jerry the thrashing he deserves, eh?'
Proffering the cutter, then a lighter, DeLacey paused.

'A noble sentiment, but I think you'll find the Nazis are far from beaten. I'm afraid it will take more than England alone; we need the Americans and the Russians to dig us out of this one I'm sorry to have to say.'

Enraged at the man's dismissal of Great Britain's fighting forces, Baxter contrived to hide it – it took all his acting skill, by making a show of coughing at the first puff.

'Erm, sorry, the smoke, not used to such luxuries you know.' Mortimer took a sip of his drink and then lit his own cigar. Although not a tobacco addict, he was partial to a good cigar in the right company. This wasn't it. Something about the lighter caught his eye; a modern, almost new model made of silver with a leather covering, it was embossed with the words *'Pour Jean Avec Gratitude'.* Handing the lighter back, Knight asked smoothly who Jean was. His expression clouding, DeLacey pocketed the lighter before replying.

'Just a friend.' *He's been in France recently...* Mortimer put the thought to the back of his mind as he savoured the fine cigar.

Thinking over Baxter's evidence from the previous night, he stood as if to stretch his legs after a long day. 'Well, this is very good of you, Henry, but I wonder, is it possible to see round the house?' DeLacey answered with a wolfish grin. 'Thought you'd never ask.'

With an hour until dinner was to be served, the presumptive baron showed his guests the features of the ancient house; the elegant carved staircase they had seen, but not noticed the armorial panelling to its foundation, nor had they known the identities of the worthies depicted in the paintings. By the time they'd reached the tenth ancestor, both men were reeling from all the information they'd been gifted. Realising the Nazi would never reveal his secret hideaway, Mortimer rapped experimentally at a panel.

'Sounds solid. Don't these old places have priest-holes and the like? You know, secret passages and dungeons, that sort of thing.' Eyeing Knight with what seemed like open suspicion, DeLacey nonetheless nodded.

'The family fortune was built on tin mining; there was a secret passage between the west wing and the entrance to one of the mines, but that's of course long since vanished. None of the painting's has eye-holes, though, if that's what you mean!' All three men laughed at this, but then a bell chiming drew everyone's attention. 'That's odd, wasn't expecting anyone else. Please excuse me, gentlemen and I'll answer it; Harris is ringing from the gate-house.' Striding over to a mahogany box by the front door, DeLacey opened it to reveal a field telephone. 'Yes?' The voice at the other end did not carry to where the two actors stood. Their hosts' expression one of irritation, he answered. 'Well, yes, if it's alright with Mrs.H. Well, all right then, send them up.' Turning to his guests, DeLacey shrugged. 'It seems we are to have company for dinner.'

36

The Reverend Cholmondley stood beaming inside the hall, a young lad of no more than eighteen or so standing next to him in the uniform of a submarine rating.

'I really must apologise for my frightful intrusion, Mr. DeLacey, but you see I had no idea Charles was on leave... may I introduce my nephew, Charles Jones, currently serving in His Majesty's Navy.'

'Submarines, I see.' DeLacey stepped forward to shake the youngster by the hand. 'Delighted to have you, both of you, naturally!' Waving the group through to the sitting room, Henry DeLacey followed them in before going to make the drinks. No-one saw the look forming on his face. It was a look of pure hatred.

The conversation was lively that night, DeLacey drinking rather faster than his guests and becoming quite the *bon vivant* with his tales of Paris before the war and South America. He was particularly companionable towards young Jones, taking a keen interest in his movements, even asking him what flotilla he was based with. Determined to foil his scheme, Baxter cut across briskly, telling his host the submariner would not be able to reveal such secrets. The Reverend was quick to agree;

'Yes, Henry, I'm surprised at you.' The sound of a throat being cleared heralded the arrival of Mrs. Harris. A short, tweedy woman, Mrs. Harris was a little more friendly than her husband. She announced dinner more in the tone of an aunt calling her nephews than a servant and gratefully, everyone made their way to the dining room.

The meal hardly suited the baronial surroundings, but as DeLacey explained to his guests, there was a war on. Mrs. Harris had worked wonders with the ration card, and, Mortimer suspected, some under-the-counter cash. The starter was pancakes, with some unheard-of syrup. After this unexpected luxury came more basic fare in the form of cauliflower cheese and bacon with an apple crumble for dessert. Throughout the meal, the wine kept flowing, a pre-war Vouvray followed by a Latour that had eyebrows raised around the table. Sipping his, Mortimer hummed his appreciation, whilst Baxter went for the throat.

'Delightful. How *do* you get wine like this, Henry? Do you have a U-Boat bring them in at night?' The eyes scrutinising him over the glass didn't mirror the smile beneath.

'Why, no. I had the foresight to stock the cellar before the war. Care to see it?' Baxter Belmont could hardly believe his luck; keen to see as much of the house as possible. Perhaps he would learn something from the excursion.

The doorway to the cellar was concealed behind a tattered tapestry depicting a joust. As with the rest of the house, electricity hadn't been laid on, DeLacey handing Jones and Mortimer a lantern each, adjusting the flame on his own.

'It's dark as pitch down here, so watch your step.' This said, he started down the steps into the gloom, the glow from his lantern lighting the massive stone blocks of the stairway beneath and the wall to their right. The cellar had originally been a storage area, but it had the air of a dungeon; chilly, slightly damp and morose. Baxter silently noted the tarpaulin-covered shapes here and made his mind up to explore further later. Divided into three huge chambers that ran beneath both the extant and destroyed wings of the house, the cellar was the oldest part of the house.

Pausing at a curious circular stone pit, DeLacey heaved the wooden cover from it to reveal a well. Extracting a coin from a pocket, he held it up in the lamp-light with a dramatic gesture.

'Listen to this.' Dropped, the coin made no sound for a full three or four seconds, when a distinct *plok* echoed up. 'This well is at least eight hundred years old. The cellar was once part of a priory, but we've had little luck finding out more.' Sliding the cover back in place, DeLacey added local legend had it that King Charles II had taken refuge here overnight on his flight to France from Shoreham, his convoluted route across country one of desperation and necessity. Apparently, he had been forced to hide down in the cellar as Cromwell's troops ransacked the house, escaping from a secret tunnel that had never been found since, its location long-forgotten. 'Who knows? Perhaps the King drank water brought up from this very well.' The Reverend Cholmondley, no doubt thinking of testing the Nazi spy, spoke;

'Perhaps King George will have to drink from it. If the Germans invade, that is.' Apparently puzzled by this, DeLacey shook his head.

'The English aren't easily invaded.' Walking onwards, he missed the exchange of glances between the actors and the vicar. *This would be the perfect chance...*

Reaching the wine cellar, even Baxter was taken aback by the stocks of wine there; DeLacey had arrived with the entire stock of the Maison D'Lorient, the famed hotel just outside Biarritz. When Mortimer asked how it was he'd managed such a feat under the noses of the Nazi hordes invading France, the man simply smiled.

'One has one's methods.' Turning to the racks of dusty bottles, dust from the cellar in France, DeLacey stated it would be an insult to make such a pilgrimage without reward, selected a bottle of 1924 Pape Clement and turned to find Baxter toying with a piece of rope. 'Practising knots?' His resolution to overpower the spy fell away as DeLacey pushed rudely past. Mortimer rolled his eyes; this was the ideal opportunity to jump the bounder, tie him up and get help, but it seems some things are easier thought than done. He resolved to have a quiet word with Jones the sailor later on; surely he would have more nerve!

After the miserable failure in the cellar, the night took a subdued turn, with Mortimer claiming to have developed a headache. As the night was a clear one, the Reverend and his nephew declined the offer of a lift home and elected to walk instead, buoyed by the excellent wines they had consumed. The Clement sat empty, testament to the night and DeLacey was left alone with his thoughts by the fire, the two actors taking a ride with the brusque Harris back to the old forge. Out to sea, a sleek black shape rounded the coast off Milford Haven, and in the wheelhouse Walton consulted with his navigator, a lean, hawk-nosed man with narrow eyes and a face lined by long years at sea.

'How long until we hit the target?'

'No more than an hour and twenty minutes, *Mein Kapitän*.' Eyeing the grin on the man's features suspiciously, Walton's own, craggy face broke into a grim smile.

'Piss off and get me the approach chart.'

Friday announced itself with rays of brilliant sunshine, Mortimer and Baxter taking their breakfast in silence. Finally, Mortimer could contain himself no longer.

'We should have done it last night. There were four of us for God's sake!' Setting his fork down, Baxter wiped the grease from his mouth before replying.

'We leave tomorrow. We'll have to go back today or this night.'

'Well, what will we do with our last day here?'

'I'm for taking another look at that place Toby took us to.' Knight sipped at his tea thoughtfully.

'What about Cragston Hall?' Through a mouthful of egg, Baxter made an impatient humming noise.

'I doubt we'll find out anything; we already know the man's a spy, that he has a radio there to contact his Naz... Ah! Our landlady.' The elderly lady came and asked if they wanted more tea, taking the plates away when they politely declined. The old dear fussed over her guests like a mother hen, but the wonderful breakfasts made it worthwhile. The two men went upstairs to prepare for their excursion, Mortimer digging out his opera glasses. When he saw them, Belmont let out a laugh;,

'Whatever did you bring those for?'

'Well, you never know when such things might prove handy.' The two set off for the coastal path, unaware they were being watched as they did so by hostile eyes.

The compound seemed eerily deserted, with no sign of shotgun-wielding guards. The two found they were able to stride past the notorious hummock and stand at the edge of the cliff – at least they *would* have stood had not Baxter suddenly grabbed his friend, pulling him down to the grass behind a convenient tussock.

'Look! There!' Following the outstretched finger, Mortimer Knight was astounded at the sight that met his eyes. There was a small cove, the inlet providing natural cover for a small boat. Such as the German E-Boat that lay tied up to the little jetty. Covered with a camouflage netting, the unmistakable lines of the fast attack boat lay in perhaps twenty feet of water, waves gently lapping against the hull. The two watched as Walton emerged from a doorway set into the rocky cliff. Although they couldn't hear what he was saying, he seemed agitated, waving his arms and shouting at the crew of the *Schnellboot*. The crew was dressed in Aran sweaters and blue trousers or boiler-suits and seemed to be loading the boat with what looked like heavy crates. This was it! They were clearly stealing whatever had been hidden underground here!

'We've got to stop them, Mort.' Baxter started crawling backwards on hands and knees, Knight turned to say something, but to his horror his friend was already running towards the dip.

Chasing after Baxter, Mortimer realised he was headed, not for the cove itself, but towards the group of down-at-heel Nissen huts in the dip. Finally catching his colleague, the out of breath actor asked what he thought he was doing.

'There's no way of getting down there without being spotted; that doorway opened into the side of the cliff. There's underground workings here, tunnels perhaps; that whine we heard when the dog went mad came from beneath the ground. There has to be another entrance.' Grabbing his arm, Mortimer hissed angrily;

'And what makes you think there's another entrance?' Shrugging free, Baxter continued to the nearest hut.

'Simple; there's machinery of some sort down there; they didn't get it in through that single door, did they?' Reaching the tin hut, the two realised at once the rust and holes they had seen were in fact painted on. Someone had gone to a great deal of trouble to disguise brand new huts, just as the local children had said.

The doors to the hut were, unsurprisingly locked, but Baxter was determined to find a way in. There were windows lining the side of the hut, some with cracks in the glass, again painted on to provide the illusion of neglect. A quick look inside and Belmont put his cap against the glass and simply punched it through. A few seconds of heaving and grunting and he was inside, the door swinging open a short while later. Whispering, without quite knowing why, Mortimer asked why Baxter had chosen this particular hut.

'It's the nearest to the sea. Now look about for any clue as to how we can get down there.' Deeply worried, Mortimer nonetheless did as his friend had asked, but all he saw were rows of single metal-framed beds and lockers, a military barrack-room perhaps. There was, however, a partitioned-off area at the far end and this proved to be a single room, an NCO's quarters no doubt. The place was clearly occupied, a recent newspaper on a bunk, some socks and towels drying bore testament to that. There was no stairway leading down, no ladder to any tunnel, nothing. Maybe the second hut? But then, quite by luck, he spotted it.

The pattern in the linoleum floor gave it away. A chequered black-and-white, the floor was scuffed and worn, apart from one area of suspiciously new appearance. This was a large rectangle around the bed nearest to the door, next to the NCO's cubicle. On closer inspection, the locker was a sham; a hollow box with no actual door, just an etched line suggesting one and a 'keyhole' that was just an indent painted black. The bed was made, but the blankets and pillow were fixed firmly to the frame by hidden straps and cords.

'Why?' Mortimer wondered aloud.

'This is it! This must be the entrance; look at the proximity to the doors. This is where they bring in heavy equipment.' Kneeling at the wardrobe, Baxter started prodding and pushing everything within reach. 'See if you can find how it opens.' Mortimer could see nothing, leaning absent-mindedly on the foot of the bed-frame. It seemed to drop into the floor slightly. Experimentally, he pushed harder, but nothing happened. When he pulled it, however, two things happened; the floor swung up, the fake locker and bed rising with it – and Baxter was thrown onto the bed in a jumble.

The rush of air that came up from the tunnel was unexpected, a metallic, stale taste to it. The two went down the concrete ramp leading down into the ground cautiously; if anyone saw them they'd have a hard time explaining their presence here. At the bottom of the ramp, they found themselves in a concrete-lined tunnel some twenty feet wide, lit by bulbs behind glass and grilles. A railing rather like a single train rail hung suspended from steel supports at intervals, a foot from the roof and still easily above head height. The excavation work here must have been enormous; sub-tunnels branched off here and there and they could hear machinery at work, a generator most likely. Mortimer raised his hands and shoulders in an unmistakable gesture, so Baxter led the way towards the sea. After a short while they came to another branch, a sign declaring this to be *'Engineering Laboratory B - Ear Protection must be worn. NO unauthorised admittance.'* Next to that, a cheerful Churchill beamed down from a poster exhorting greater efforts to ensure victory. There were two sets of heavy doors leading to the chamber.

Moving closer to Mortimer, his voice a whisper, Baxter wondered aloud if this might be the source of the weird effects on the dog, Bobby. Nodding thoughtfully, Mortimer indicated they take a look inside. This decision was suddenly made for them as the sound of voices and boots came from the direction they were headed. Ducking inside the Engineering Lab, the two intruders looked for a place to hide. It was a strange kind of engineer that would use such a place; there were a few work benches at the far end, but also glass booths arrayed along one wall. The walls were covered with what looked like thick red rubber cones, the floor a grille-work with more of the rubber things covering the ground beneath.

'What the devil?...' Mortimer was inspecting the dominant feature of the room, a large circular metal cage suspended between floor and ceiling by a lattice-work of what looked to be elastic cords. Inside this contraption was some sort of device, a group of dishes, back to back forming a sphere. The electrical cable feeding down into the cage looked like it could power a tube train, the electrical sub-station in the corner appeared capable of generating a lightning spark. 'What *is* this thing?' Baxter realised there was no time to linger, as the outer door swung open.

'Quick! In one of those!.'

The two actors squatted in one of the booths, praying they would not be discovered. From the sound of it, two men had entered and were in a subdued, but furious argument of some kind, but the booth was almost completely sound-proofed, the debate muffled beyond recognition. Risking a glance, Baxter popped his head up and saw one of the men was Walton, and in a foul mood. The other man was bespectacled and quite young, dressed in a white lab coat; clearly a scientist. Taking a further risk, the actor pushed his knee against the door to open it an inch. The scientist was pleading with Walton not to take his work away, but the sailor was adamant he was clearing the place out today.

'It isn't safe here, Ennis, I don't give a damn what you say, we're moving the gear out starting with the sensitive stuff.' With one hand pressed to the side of his head, Ennis seemed to despair.

'But our work here is almost complete! In a few more weeks...'

'In a few more weeks Adolf Hitler will have the report on your work on his desk in Berlin. I've got my orders, and I'm carrying them out.' Walton stormed out, leaving the scientist alone with his surreptitious observers.

A sad, dejected and defeated air pervaded the lab now as Ennis sat at a work-bench, slumped, his head in his hands. By now several minutes had passed and Baxter was frantic to get out of there, Mortimer was seemingly just disgruntled with the whole affair, but too subdued for once to make much of it. Finally, with a defiant thump of the bench, Ennis rose and Baxter saw he was wearing some sort of headphone-apparatus and darkened goggles that covered half of his upper face. Belmont nudged Knight with his elbow as the scientist headed determinedly towards the electrical station.

'Not sure I like the way this is going, why do you think he needs all that paraphernalia on his head?' Mortimer didn't have a clue, but looking around the booth noticed there was a single set of the goggles and headphones hanging from a hook. Tapping Baxter on the shoulder, he whispered;
'Who gets those, then?'

Just one more test run; five minutes, no more... Charles Ennis was a man of science and hated warfare in all its forms, the weapon he had created was a mistake; he had intended it as a new form of radar, but the first tests had proven it had another, altogether more sinister application. Now he fired up the transformer array, determined to prove his Cyclic Ultra Low-Frequency Beam Oscillator Array would work. As the thrum of the transformer-coils filled the room steadily, the pitch lowering as each array came on-stream, he stood expectantly by the master control panel in its sound and vibration-proofed booth. Even with the protection this afforded, he was glad of the safety gear he wore. Turning a dial, the spherical device began to rotate, slowly at first then gaining speed. As it reached optimum revolutions, it became a blur, the dishes swishing through the air to produce the characteristic high-pitched scream that was terrifying to anyone without suitable ear covering, such as Baxter, now crouched on the floor of the cubicle with both hands clapped over his ears. That noise! It was as if a dentist's drill were going through his temples! Baxter had decided to give Mortimer the goggles and head-set, that way at least one of them would be safe from whatever this infernal machine did. He was regretting the decision already, and it was only to get worse. Far worse.

Engaging... Ennis flipped a series of switches, labelled *'Master-Circuit', Impulse Actuator'* and finally, ***'PULSE BEAM - DANGER!'*** The air in the lab seemed to ripple as the dishes

emitted their harmonic energy pulses, too low to be registered as sounds, yet devastating to the human ear. The 'sound' they emitted came as resonance, initiated in whatever the pulses struck, be it organic or otherwise. The idea had been to give an image of enemy planes, warships and even submerged
submarines in crystal clarity. The practice, however was infinitely more terrifying; the pulses caused any rigid structure to resonate sympathetically; metal shattered, hence the unique composition of the lab's interior. Tests on the unfortunate pigs the Admiralty had shipped in showed a horrific side-effect; the animals had become feral, attacking each other and the lab technicians with a fury quite alien to the species. Which explained why, at this moment, Baxter Bailey was quietly if intently strangling his best friend.

The test was another failure; the recording instruments had either shattered or failed in various ways. The beams were quite simply too powerful; they would have to relocate to a more remote location and try at longer range. Wearily, Ennis flipped the switches back up, turning the dial to stop the sphere's rotation. As he removed his head-protection, he thought he heard something. Yes! There was no mistake; a gurgling noise and grunting was coming from... but then Walton burst into the lab, accompanied by two of his sailors, both armed.

'We've got another breach; anyone come through here, Prof?' In response, Ennis made the 'shush' sign, stabbing a finger warily at the booth from which the sounds had come. Barely conscious of his surroundings, Baxter Bailey looked at the prostrate body of his friend and, shuddering, climbed off of him, just as the door to the booth opened and a revolver was thrust at his head.

'So that's why I nearly killed him?'

'You're bloody lucky we found the broken window and open hatchway when we did. Another ten seconds and this man was dead, for sure.' Walton paced angrily in the claustrophobic office. *Of all the days!...* another twenty-four hours and all this infernal stuff would be safely removed to the Falkland Islands. Walton's mind was made up, but he needed some answers. The Knight character was still groggy after nearly being throttled, so he addressed Baxter.

'You two could be shot for this, do you realise that? As it is you're looking at a long time behind bars.' Baxter had had enough, rising furiously to his feet to be knocked back into his chair by the burly rating standing next to him.

'Now listen, if you're going to murder us, why don't you do it instead of all this prancing about the place?' Cheeks flushed with anger, the actor continued his tirade. 'We're not the only ones, you know; your diabolical scheme has been uncovered and reported to London. It's a matter of time before the police get here.' Confused by this lunatic, Walton shrugged, turned and took out his pipe. Filling, tamping and lighting it, he took a few puffs to get the thing going and the air was soon thick with 'Ship's'.

'Now look here, what the devil do you mean, police? What's going on here?'

Walton listened as Baxter poured it all out; the Nazi plot to steal British secret scientific equipment, the Nazi spy at Cragston Hall, the hidden transmitter. The actor finished by repeating the threat of the authorities. Patience expired, Walton removed his pipe and said one sentence;

'There's just one flaw in your theory, *Sherlock* - I AM the bloody authorities!'

The two interlopers listened in grim silence as Walton explained it all. First, he swore them to secrecy under harsh penalty of imprisonment or even execution. Then he gave it to them. This was a top-secret Admiralty research station, chosen for its relatively remote location and access to the Bristol channel. He was a Lieutenant Commander in His Majesty's Naval Reserve, the E-Boat was a captured model they had previously used for the purpose of reconnoitring the approaches to the base to see if, as was suspected, it was vulnerable to an enemy commando raid. As it most definitely *was*, he had used his authority to begin evacuating the base. After all, the two actors had penetrated the perimeter fence with a small boy and a dog, it would hardly be enough to keep out German raiders. The plan was now to relocate the research to a remote island – he didn't mention the Falklands, for obvious reasons. As for Henry DeLacey being a spy, Baxter was quite right. He was a *British* spy.

Cragston Hall sat forlorn in the mist. The civilian Humber – a staff car would have drawn attention, rolled through the gates and up to the house. Walton's knock went unanswered, so, telling the two thespians to remain with the car, he strode around to the rear. After a few shame-filled minutes, in which the two fidgeted and said nothing to each other, the door was unbarred from within. Walton stepped out and beckoned them in.

'Something's wrong; Commander DeLacey isn't at home and the butler's wife has been murdered.' Rushing inside, the trio made for the kitchen. It was as he had said; Mrs. Harris lay in a pool of her own blood, clearly long dead. Feeling for a pulse anyway, Mortimer recoiled from the stiff corpse. Standing, he looked at Walton.

'Rigor mortis. She's been dead a while.'

'Where's the Butler?' Baxter's question sent the Lieutenant Commander racing to the field telephone by the main door. Ringing the gate-house produced no response, but perhaps Harris was on an errand somewhere?

The search of the house continued. Baxter mentioned Commander DeLacey's secret office, at which Walton strode through to the library. Following him, Baxter watched as the Navy man looked around, clearly foxed.

'Don't you know where the door is?'

'That's need to know. Until know, I didn't need to know.' Turning to face the actor, the Lieutenant Commander eyed him closely. 'You said you followed him in here. Where was the compartment located?' Baxter pointed at the right-hand corner and Walton set to work, prying and pushing everything in sight. Clearing his throat, Mortimer reached across with a single finger to push one of the spines, the volume tilting backwards with a mechanical *clunk.*

'How in Hell's blazes did you know which one it was?' Smiling, Knight indicated the other books with a wave of his hand.

'It was the only one not covered in dust.' The compartment swung open to reveal... a desk and chair, a radio transmitter sitting idly on the former. It was unoccupied.

'Where the hell is he?' Walton's thoughts were inscrutable as he stood, arms folded in a posture that suggested he was thinking it through. 'We haven't tried the basement yet.'

'You will.' The voice was familiar, yet somehow foreign. Harris stood at the door, a German machine-pistol in his hand.

'Of course; you're German.' Turning his gaze – and barrel onto Mortimer Knight, the butler nodded with a sneer.

'How did you guess?'

'You braked the car when that tractor pulled out, didn't sound your horn. I spent a summer in Dresden in '30; Germans give way to the right, don't they? An Englishman would have sounded his horn.'

'But still you did not realise.' Harris' voice was still the

50

same, flat Cockney, but with the cadence and phrasing of a German.

'No. Not until now, sadly.' Smiling triumphantly at having duped the English so easily and for so long, Harris shook his head.

'I was born in Bremen; I came here as a child, to London, but I have watched in dismay as your fools of leaders rejected the hand of peace offered by the Führer. I made contact with our Embassy here before the War and was accepted as a *Verborgen,* a concealed agent. My weapon and transmitter were dropped to me along with certain other more secret materials, by the Luftwaffe in 1937 on a routine maritime training flight. Now the time has come for action; in a few days, I shall be in Berlin with the contents of that laboratory. Who knows? The Führer himself may bestow on me the Iron Cross First Class for my actions here. I already have the inferior award for my, *work* here concerning movements of your Royal Navy and your Air Force.' Controlling the urge to spit at this creature, Baxter confined himself to a single question.

'And your wife? Was she to get a medal too? Or did she disapprove of having a traitor for a husband?'

'Be careful Englishman; I have no orders to kill un-necessarily, but I have had to humble myself before your foolish and stupid kind for too long. I warn you about your conduct for the only time. Am I clear?'

'As crystal. But why did she have to die?'

'She was suspicious; she knew nothing of my mission here or my true purpose and tried to warn DeLacey when she discovered the equipment I had been preparing. She was disposed of as an enemy of the Reich.' Unable to restrain himself any longer, Walton suddenly rushed at the Nazi spy, but the deafening report of the weapon chattering drowned out his bellow of rage. The Lieutenant Commander seemed to hang in mid-air as the bullets ripped through his body, finally falling, dead to the floor.

'You murdering bastard!' Baxter's hiss was met with the gaping, smoking mouth of the barrel.

'And I will be a murderer once again if you continue. Now move, to the cellar!'

The cellar was pitch-black, but Harris forced the actors down the steps with only the pale light from the house to guide them. Mortimer nearly fell, but steadied himself against the wall, Baxter's hand on his collar helping prevent disaster. At the bottom, they turned as the door was slammed and bolted from above. Neither spoke for a moment, then Mortimer asked his fellow prisoner if he had his matches with him. The answer came with a rustle and a rasp of match on box, the flare of a match startling in the darkness. Looking about, Mortimer seized on the nearest crate, wrenching the tarpaulin off to find it was full of old oil paintings. The match guttered and died. Knight had a sudden thought.

'Hang on...' *Oil...* reaching out into nothingness, his fingers came up against a wooden frame and he hauled it towards him.

'What's going on? What are you up to?; I've only a few matches left, you know.'

'Belt up, Belly!' The use of his old nickname stung Belmont into silence. The sound of thumping was followed by tearing and soon the painting was hanging in shreds. 'Right. That's the wick, now we need a, yes, this will do...' A shoe against wood, wood snapping and being broken up. Mortimer wound the strips of torn canvas around a piece of the frame as best he could, trying to keep them tight around the makeshift handle. 'OK, let's see if this works. I've made a sort of torch, but we'll need another match. When we light it, assuming all goes well, we need to make a better light from something. Who knows, there might be candles down here somewhere.'

The ancient canvas had once been soaked in oil and

prepared with wax; it burned fiercely and well. The light it threw, accompanied by a crackling and snapping noise, illumined the space around them and the two men were soon throwing tarpaulins aside in a rapid progression down the first chamber. Aside from more paintings, they found some old furniture and fittings obviously intended for the house, chandeliers with their ropes coiled ready to be installed, iron fitments for hanging paintings and the like. The torch was almost exhausted by the time they had returned to make a new one, lit that and made several more, destroying more ancient DeLaceys in the process. Passing the well in the second chamber, a faint sound reached the men's ears; an animal noise, muffled, coming from the wine cellar ahead. In a few moments, they stood over the bound and gagged form of Henry DeLacey. Baxter set to work to free him, with Mortimer holding the light overhead. Weak from thirst, Commander DeLacey had to be helped up to his feet. Gratefully he placed a hand on Mortimer's shoulder to steady himself. He had a nasty gash on his temple and had clearly suffered a serious assault, his face bruised and bloodied.

'Water...well...' Then he slumped back in collapse.

It took a while for the two actors to return to the crate containing the chandeliers, tie three ropes together, empty a precious claret bottle – some of it on the stone flags and then loop the rope around the bottle to form a cradle. Lowering it down, it took most of the rope until Baxter felt the bottle reach the surface of the water. Letting the bottle settle, he experimentally hauled the rope up an inch or two. Unsure if it had worked, he let the bottle down again. After repeating this fiddly process a few times, he could feel the bottle had some weight, so hauled it back up, rewarded as he was with a three-quarter full bottle. He took this to DeLacey, who drank like a Legionnaire staggering out from the Sahara. Finally, he wiped his mouth and spoke, his voice cracked and hoarse.

'Jumped me, no idea who; but then I came to to find myself trussed up like a brace of pheasants with Harris standing over me. Imagine my thoughts when he pointed that sprayer at me. Harris, an East End Nazi!' In sombre tones, Mortimer told the injured man of the deaths of Mrs. Harris and Walton, making sure to impart the latter's heroism in the face of certain death. Listening to this news in grim silence, Henry DeLacey shook his head and walked across to one of the last of the home-made torches, lighting it and striding back to the first cavernous chamber. Rummaging in the back of one of the crates he found a cardboard box half-filled with dinner candles. Lighting a few of these, he handed one each to his fellow prisoners. Mortimer was for finding something to batter down the door, but Baxter felt this unwise and the Commander felt their chances slim. The door was ancient, but solid oak and three inches of it. Besides, Harris was heavily armed. It was then that Baxter recalled the legend.

'So, what are you saying? That we rely on an old folk-tale? Just find the secret tunnel and walk out?' Baxter Belmont stayed silent a moment, then nodded.
'Yes. Think about it, Morty. Legends are sometimes based on fact. Sometimes.' Knight simply stared aghast at the idea, but Baxter's plan found unexpected support.
'We could always look at the painting.' Both actors looked at DeLacey as the Commander shrugged and walked across to the ransacked crate, turning each frame over with a clacking noise in search of one particular work. After a few moments of this, he looked bemused, then suddenly rushed towards the small pile of home-made torches. 'You bloody fools! You've torn it up!.'

Several strips of ripped canvas lay alongside each other on a 14th-century trestle table. DeLacey lined them up as best he could and set a lit candle either side. The painting was still visible, albeit ruined past the abilities of the best conservator. A disguised King Charles was seated on horseback with a woman riding pillion, Cromwell's troops behind searching for the King. The woman, Henry explained, was Lady Fisher, who had aided the fleeing King.

'So, this is a clue of some sort?' DeLacey answered Baxter's question with a shrug. After examining the torn artwork for a full five minutes, it was Mortimer who spoke.

'What's that she's pointing to?'

'That's odd; never noticed that before.' DeLacey peered closer; there was no doubt Lady Fisher was, indeed pointing rather surreptitiously towards the King's breeches, where *something* was poking out from his boot. Eyeing this closely, it seemed to be a parchment of some kind. 'If only we could read it.'

'Actually... I wonder... perhaps...' DeLacey went to the stack of pictures and once more went through them, coming up with a curious engraving. The image, also framed, was of an engraving, rather than a painting, showing King Charles II clad in armour, grasping a marshal's baton, his crown resting on a table behind. Behind him, a battle scene, his enemies sent fleeing by a vengeful angel, while Pegasus, the winged horse of myth, reared up on a cliff. It was the inscription below, however, which DeLacey pointed out. Although torn, the words were still decipherable.

Through providence did the King
defcend to safety, his Majefty
preferved from torment.
His fteps now fealed,
perchance revealed
when rebellion doft foment.

Charles II in 1651.
from the engraved portrait by
Hollar after Abraham Diepenbecke.

'Well, that's helpful.' Turning away, Baxter took his candle and started tapping at the nearest wall hopefully. Mortimer, meanwhile stayed at the engraving, staring at the inscription.

'You know this means something; it looks like nonsense, but there's meaning here.' Commander DeLacey turned his attention back from watching Baxter's exploration and regarded the ancient text.

Through providence did the King descend to safety, His Majesty preserved from torment.
His steps now sealed, perchance revealed when rebellion dost foment.

'I always assumed it just described his flight down here, to the cellar.'

'No, I don't think so. I keep being drawn to the second verse, it just doesn't make sense.' Shaking his head in confusion, the Commander absent-mindedly pulled out his lighter and packet of Players, offering one to the actors, Mortimer alone refusing.

'The use of the long 's' means that word 'fealed' is, of course 'sealed.' Why would anyone's steps be sealed?' Taking a draw of his cigarette, Henry again shrugged.

'To prevent them being discovered?'

'Exactly.' Tapping the ancient print with a finger, Knight frowned.

'*Perchance revealed – when rebellion dost foment...* so the idea was they could be used again in time of another rising.'

'With you so far, Mister Knight, but what the hell does it all mean?' Exasperated, DeLacey slapped down his hand on the table, making the picture jump. Mortimer shook his head slowly.

'I'm not sure... but what if we were wrong about the descent bit?'

'As in?'

'Well, as in perhaps the descent was *from* the cellar, not to it...'

The cover clattered down from the well as the Commander pushed it rudely aside. Going to the chandelier crate, he called Baxter across and soon the two were lugging a heavy piece of ironwork between them. Knotting all the ropes together, the Commander's seamanship was demonstrated with a swift and efficient piece of knot-work, the rope now anchored securely to a convenient iron ring set into the wall.

'Right, I'll stand on the chandelier, you two get the fun job; lowering me down. I'm only eleven stone soaking wet so it shouldn't be too hard on two big strong chaps like you, I hope.' Placing a candle in his pocket, Henry gave the two a nod and climbed up onto the stonework. Soon, he was being lowered out of sight, 'only eleven stone' seeming much heavier all of a sudden. After about ten feet of rope was used, DeLacey called up for a halt and the two braced themselves to keep him suspended. With a click, he lit the candle and the reflection of the flame showed up on the stones from above. A muffled rapping noise followed, with Henry calling up for a tool. Leaning forward, Mortimer called down;

'What kind of tool?'

'Well, a hammer would be ideal, but there's nothing like that down here as far as I recall, wrap the rope around the stronger of you and the other find something I can use for a hammer or a jemmy.'

As Baxter had once won five pounds in a drunken arm-wrestling match and played rugby for his college, he was elected to remain coiled in rope, straining manfully as Mortimer scuttled off in search of something useful. After a few minutes, Belmont called out that he was tiring and Knight settled on a large coach-bolt he had found in a pile of rusted fittings. Calling down to the Commander, he dropped it carelessly down to him, getting a loud shout of outrage in return.

'You stupid sod! You nearly brained me. Anyway, thanks...' This outburst was followed by a tapping, which grew louder with confidence in the substitute tool. All at once, there was the sound of pottery breaking. 'Hulloo! I've found something!.' Some furious scrabbling then the sound of pieces of something solid rebounding off of stone and an echoing splash into water. 'Right, lower me some more, please, a few feet will do it I think.'

By Mortimer's pocket-watch, a full twenty minutes had passed by the time they heaved Henry DeLacey back from the well. All three were quite exhausted, but the owner of Cragston Hall had news; he had discovered then uncovered a secret stairway, set into the stones of the well itself. Somehow, the steps had been concealed with earthenware, shaped as the surrounding stones and fired with a glaze to simulate them. By finding and smashing these, he had indeed *perchance revealed* the King's steps. Certainly rebellion was fomenting! There was more though; and it wasn't all good news. The tunnel itself was still there, open and uncovered, but thanks to the recent bad weather and rain, only the very top was visible above water. Gathering the candles up, the three took their turn on the rope, DeLacey going first, followed by a visibly nervous Knight. Finally, Belmont shimmied down, rather quicker than Mortimer had, and joined the others in the freezing water. It came up to his chin, and soon his teeth were chattering uncontrollably.

'Well, if you don't mind, let's get going.' Once more, Henry led the way, holding his candle high and carefully moving forwards slowly. For all he knew, the tunnel had collapsed and the floor may have even fallen away; this area was, after all, riddled with old mine workings.

Almost at once, Mortimer's candle went out, as he had neglected to keep it above water. The going was treacherous, slippery and uncertain. Several of the stones they could feel beneath their feet had shifted or otherwise come loose over the centuries and the whole thing gave the impression of being unstable. Indeed, some of the stones were missing from above and after fifty feet or so, twice the desperate little group had been forced to duck around and under tree roots that had grown through. The journey seemed to take hours rather than minutes and it was with sighs of relief that they emerged into a subterranean cavern. Re-lighting his candle, Mortimer gasped in disbelief at what he saw.

The chamber they had entered was about thirty feet in width, perhaps twelve tall. Within this confined space lay several trunks, the leather bands securing them musty and rotted. Against one of these lay a breastplate, a cavalier helmet on one of the trunks. To Baxter's disgust, several large rats scurried away at their approach to this unique scene, to a rusted iron portcullis door. Despite the urgency of it all, DeLacey could no more walk past these artefacts than he could float in mid-air. Calling to the others to open a crate each, he set about unfastening the nearest. Inside was some decaying fabric that fell away from his hands as he lifted it, leaving only metal buttons. Mortimer found more of the same, but also a wooden strong-box, whilst Baxter had found more items of armour and some weaponry, doubtless the forlorn remnants of a Cavalier's armoury. Holding up a scabbard clad in some sort of velvet, he drew the sword within, which was, incredibly, mostly unharmed by the damp storage it had lain in so many years. It was as it must have been when last sheathed.

'Dear God...' DeLacey was staring fixedly at the sword. 'Bring that to the light – quickly!' Bemused by the urgency of the order, Baxter did as he was bid.

By the light of the group's candles, the metal of scabbard and sword glistened and glimmered, a pure golden glow that sent a shiver down the men's spines. It *was* gold, both scabbard and hilt, pure gold. There was no doubt about it. Taking the sword, DeLacey wiped it on his shirt and read the inscription along the blade. *Carolus Secundus, Dei gratia, Rex Angliae, Scotiae, Franciae et Hiberniae rex, fideique defensor.* Mortimer asked,

'What does it mean? My Latin's shaky at best.' Without looking at the actor, DeLacey spoke, his voice reverential;

'Charles the Second, by the Grace of God, King of England, Scotland, France and Ireland, Defender of the Faith'.

'You must be joking!' There was no mistaking, however

the insignia by the hand-guard; a lion rampant and a unicorn surrounding the quarterly of three lions passant, the harp, *fleur-de-lis* and Scottish lion. This indeed was the sword of the King.

'Why didn't he reclaim this? He returned to the throne after his exile...' DeLacey's question could never be answered; perhaps the sword and the King's other possessions were simply forgotten, the guardian of this Royal secret killed or dead of the plague, or one of many other diseases stalking the land at the time. Such a treasure would be enough in itself, but there was more; Mortimer had found the key to the box.

Handing the key to DeLacey, Mortimer Knight stood and watched with his friend as the presumptive baron opened the box. The lid, however, simply broke away when he lifted it, the hinges rotted away. Inside, a leather roll and a small mouldered velvet bag. Henry took this tube out and uncapped it, upending it for a scroll of parchment to slide into his hand. It was sealed with wax, which crumbled away as he unfurled the document to reveal it was written in Latin.

'This is a Patent of Baronetcy. We'd best leave this stuff here and get moving. We've wasted enough time already.' Baxter wondered if it would be better to take the sword, or one of the other ancient weapons each.

'Trust me – I can do better than swords and axes.' Henry went to the portcullis and found it stuck fast. There was some sort of mechanism to raise it, but the ropes had rotten away and the counter-weights involved had fallen onto the stone flags at some time in the past. It took all three, heaving with all their might to shift it a foot or so, where it simply stuck and refused to budge an inch further. Scrambling beneath the gate, the three followed the fleeing rats along this new tunnel, which turned into one of chalk. There was a bend up ahead... and light. They came out halfway down a sheer cliff face, the sea beating the rocks below.

62

'Don't be such a faint heart! Get up there!.' Halfway up from the tunnel exit, Mortimer clung to a clump of grass with his eyes tightly shut.

'I – can't – move...'

'Right.' Henry had had enough of this; the man clearly wasn't good with heights, but time was not on their side and he had to stop Harris before it was too late. Reaching down, he grabbed a handful of collar and called down to Baxter, still in the mouth of the tunnel. 'Right then, listen in; if this man doesn't start climbing when I heave, *you* are to push him onto the bloody rocks, that's an order by the way!' It worked; the panicked Mortimer scrabbling at the cliff-face with hands and feet, somehow finding a purchase and, aided by the straining Commander DeLacey, he found himself level with the grassy summit. A push from below; Baxter had wasted no time in following. Soon all three men lay gasping for breath on the grass, but Henry was quickly back on his feet and urging the others to follow.

The walk back to Cragston Hall took them past the coastal path and their old friend Toby, chasing his dog. Bobby the collie bounded up to the three men and, barking playfully, dropped his stick at Baxter's feet. Despite the seriousness of the day, Belmont found time to throw the stick, the dog scampering after it. Henry went up to the boy.

'What's this, Toby Fairweather? School finished early today?'

'Yes Sir. I mean no, Commander, I mean...'

'That's quite alright; Mum's the word, *Cave*, eh? Listen, we've had a bit of an adventure, Sherlock and Watson and myself and we need a bit of help. Do you think you can run to the post office and have Mr. Borland call for the police and the Home Guard at Barnstaple? Can you remember that for me, Toby?'

'Yessir; Police and Home Guard. Come on, Bobby!'

Snapping off a child's salute, the youngster sprinted off, followed after a moment by his dog, who gave his saviours one final look before bolting after him. It was almost as if the animal knew he owed them his life.

The house was deserted, save for the corpse of the housekeeper. Running through to the library, the Commander found his radio transmitter smashed beyond repair.

'Damn and blast! Come on, to the gun room!' The keys to the cabinets were in the drawers below, DeLacey opening one then smashing the others with the butt of the Webley he had selected. With a boyish grin, he said 'Choose your poison, gentlemen.' Mortimer pointed at a twelve bore shotgun by James Grant, a beautifully crafted antique in walnut. Throwing Knight a box of cartridges from the drawer, Henry's smile was even wider; 'May I compliment Sir on his taste in firearms?' Baxter hadn't shot anything since a blank-firing blunderbuss on stage and not much before, but one weapon had caught his eye, what appeared to be a double-barrelled shotgun, with massive, over-sized barrels.

'I'll have that one, if it's all right.'

'Ah; that's the .600, not sure you really want *that*...'

'I'll take it.' Ruefully, Henry handed the actor the rifle – a .600 Nitro Express by Jeffery and Co. and his father's gun, one of perhaps only twenty ever made. Baxter took the bag of cartridges and his eyebrows rose significantly at what he found inside. The cartridges inside resembled over-sized ladies' lipsticks, the bullets having ominous domed heads. *This would do...*

The Alvis lurched and smashed its way through the fence, coming to a halt in the compound with a final burst of steam from the cracked radiator. Opening the driver's door, Commander DeLacey grabbed his rifle and made sure the Webley was secure in his jacket pocket. Rather more shakily, Mortimer and Baxter climbed out, weapons in hand. Soon all three were charging down the tunnel towards the lab. They were too late; Ennis lay dead by his creation, which had been riddled with bullets and then totally destroyed, probably by a grenade judging from the mess. Worse, DeLacey announced the vital schematics and associated papers were missing. Onwards to the boat dock, then, where more bodies lay. The E-Boat itself was gone; Harris had fled, taking with him the greatest secret of the War! One of Walton's men, however, was not quite dead; a groan alerted Mortimer and he cradled the dying man in his arms as he managed to speak a few, final words;

'He took the boat, five minutes, maybe more... tell Daisy for me, *tell her!*.' With that, he was gone.

'Chief Petty Officer Cartwright. His wife. Daisy's his wife.' Knight looked up to see a terrible fury forming on Commander DeLacey's face. Grimly determined, he dashed from the room, the others in his wake, as he ran down the tunnel towards the sea.

Thankfully, the Nazi spy had not had time to destroy the equipment in the communications room, though he had shot the sailors manning it. Grimly pulling a dead rating from his chair, DeLacey flicked some switches, turning a dial to adjust the frequency. Pressing the 'transmit' button on the desk microphone, he began speaking in rapid, clipped tones.

'All stations, this is Admiralty Research Base X-Ray, this is an emergency, repeat emergency. This base has been attacked by a German agent, I repeat, this base attacked by German agent. Believed heading for European coast in Admiralty E-Boat 107, request any maritime air patrol to assist, code word is 'Damocles', repeat 'Damocles'. Sitting back, he rubbed his neck wearily. 'Well, that's that. Now all we can do is wait.'

'What's that about Damocles?' Before Henry could answer Knight's question, the speaker crackled into life.   'Admiralty

X-Ray from Albatross, we are a Sunderland on delivery flight over the Irish Sea, state your co-ordinates please.'

'Sunderland Albatross from Base X-Ray, we are at 51.217994° West, 3.982759° North. Repeat my last.' While the navigator on the flying boat repeated the co-ordinates of the secret installation, Henry quickly answered Knight;

'You asked about Damocles; that's the code word giving me priority; I'll get him to attack that... wait! I've got a better idea.' Grabbing an Admiralty map-book, he flicked through the pages until he found the right one. Quickly estimating ranges and distance, he pressed the transmit button again. 'Sunderland Albatross from X-Ray, land at our co-ordinates, the tide's in so you'll have enough draft.'

'Base X-Ray, Roger. Received and understood. Approximate time of arrival twenty minutes, Albatross out.' Although he hadn't mentioned it to the others, the Commander knew something they didn't; Harris wasn't alone. *He couldn't be!*

The mighty roar of the four Bristol Pegasus engines rose to an overwhelming crescendo as the massive Sunderland swooped down from the sky and came down on the water in a spray of foam. Oars churning water furiously, the little dinghy made its way out to where an RAF crewman stood in the hatchway.

'This the party for the day-trip?' Smiling, DeLacey brought the boat expertly alongside, folded oars and started passing up the group's odd-little assortment of firearms. Seeing the .600, the crewman let out a whistle. 'Off shark-hunting, are we?'

'Something like that. Up you go, boys, I'll hold her.' The two actors clambered up into the open hatchway while the Commander held the boat fast, then Baxter reached down to help haul him up, the dinghy drifting away slowly. Hauling the hatch shut, the crewman turned to his new passengers.

'Who's in charge, may I ask?' DeLacey waved a hand casually. 'The skipper wants you up front, Sir. You other gents best accompany me to the wardroom, there's a brew and some sandwiches for you there.'

Climbing the metal stairs to the upper level, Commander DeLacey presented himself to the pilot, who introduced himself as Flying Officer Hoey.

'What's all the flap about, Commander?'

'Take us up first, please; we need to go South-West along the coast. I'll explain as we go.'

'Okay Wally, you heard. Fire her up, course 240 please.' One by one the thousand-plus horsepower engines coughed explosively into life. Soon the noise was indescribable, Commander DeLacey having to shout to make himself heard.

'There's a German agent aboard an E-Boat we captured earlier this year; he's probably headed for the French coast. He has vital top secret plans for a new type of weapon. I have to stress on you the secrecy of this mission; we have to stop him and recover the documents in his possession.'

Ruefully, the pilot shook his head at this news.

'Now look, Commander, I'm not about to risk a brand-new aircraft and the lives of my crew to get some papers back; we'll sink the blighter.' The pilot went to turn away, but DeLacey grabbed him. 'Get your bloody hands off!' The navigator stepped forward to intervene, but a shake of the pilot's head held him where he was.

'I'm sorry, but you're listening whether you like it or not; these papers are the only way we have to re-construct the weapon, the boffin who dreamt it all up is dead – murdered.' Again the flying officer tried to shake loose, but the grip held firm. 'This weapon must not fall into enemy hands; the Germans will win the bloody war! We have to recover the papers.' Relaxing his grip, the Commander apologised for his roughness. Staring at him with cool detachment, the pilot finally nodded. 'All right. But you and your men can do the recovery. How many crew has he?' His face grim, DeLacey's response was simple;

'Two, at least, plus himself.' Leaning over between pilot and co-pilot, the Commander scanned the sea ahead for any sign of the fleeing E-Boat. 'I really must apologise for all of this. The station was being evacuated when the bastard struck.'

'Is that how you got that?' The pilot was pointing to the gash on DeLacey's temple. In all the excitement, he'd forgotten about it. 'Go below; see Corporal MacDonald, he'll patch you up. If we see anything I'll send for you.' Gratefully, Henry clambered down below as the huge aircraft made a surprisingly graceful arc around a headland. Surely the swine couldn't be far ahead now?

In the cramped wardroom, the Scots corporal cheerfully whistled while he cleaned up and dressed the Commander's wounds. The tea and sandwiches went round and the three men consumed this repast eagerly. Looking over at the corporal, Mortimer asked what armaments the Sunderland carried.

'None, none of her own, that is; we're taking delivery of this aircraft after trials; she's to be fitted when we get to the squadron. What about the German boat?'

'I'm afraid she's fitted with a two-centimetre flak gun.' Henry DeLacey spoke as he entered the wardroom and took a mug of tea, declining a sandwich. The corporal looked at him aghast.

'Why didn't you remove it when you captured it?' Sipping his tea, the Commander considered his reply. 'Well, she's technically an Admiralty vessel, so she carries arms, and, frankly, we didn't anticipate this in time. My information was the Germans intended photographing the, well, the equipment and probably any documents relating to it. Initially, an outright assault was considered unlikely, it was only a certain – and sadly, Late Lieutenant Commander Walton's initiative to test security at the station that led to the flap. We realised we needed to evacuate and... hullo?, what's this?.' The Sunderland was banking sharply and dropping fast into the turn.

Using the bulkheads for support, Commander DeLacey made it back up to the flight deck in time to see the first bursts of flak from the E-Boat's gun exploding as angry black clouds through the cockpit window. Instantly, the pilot opened up the throttles and pulled up sharply, into a corkscrew turn the Navy man wouldn't have thought possible. He was forced to grab the back of the co-pilot's seat to prevent himself falling backwards. Screaming out of the turn, the Sunderland banked level with the boat and flew around in a wide circle, careful to give the heavily-armed craft a wide berth.

'Missed us; we won't be so lucky next time.' No sooner had Hoey spoken when the 20mm flak opened up again, having reloaded. In what seemed like no time at all, sixteen of the twenty explosive shells ripped through the port wing and fuselage, a crewman calling up there was a casualty. DeLacey thought fast; the way this was going the Sunderland would be left with no choice, but to pull away; the vital plans would be lost, along with years of research. He HAD to stop the boat! Shouting his instructions to the flight crew, he dashed back down the ladder. There was only one chance to get this right...

In the wheelhouse of the *Schnellboot*, Harris knew he was in the right area for the pick-up. The craft bounded in leaps through the ever-worsening waves. Heavier seas meant they were nearer to their goal. Everything had gone according to plan, except, of course, the massive white flying boat appearing from the coast behind. Fortunately, the aircraft hadn't opened fire, or worse, dropped its depth-charges. Perhaps they had seen the white ensign flying from the stern and were confused by it; the British fools! True to his nature, he had followed his instructions meticulously, used the coastal features and compass as instructed by Karl, one of his *Abwehr* naval agents, who was expertly manning the flak gun with the same cold detachment he used to kill the personnel of the British base. The *Kriegsmarine* engineer down below was coaxing every last knot of speed from the racing craft.

As the gigantic Sunderland swooped back around, Harris could see the open doorway in the side of the fuselage, what looked like... a man lying prone inside. There was the glint of steel and a puff of smoke, then Karl's chest simply exploded in a spray of shocking red, the Abwehr man falling backwards into his death.

'Cor! Blimey!' In his shock, Harris fell into the language of the land that had given him a home for so many years. Meanwhile, in the deafening rush of air streaming through the open doorway, Henry DeLacey rolled to one side to reload the massive Nitro Express rifle. The steel-domed pellets had been his Father's idea – a crazy scheme to bring down German fighters over France in the First War. Now, Colonel Vyvyan Trelors-DeLacey's son was using his gun for almost the exact opposite purpose; to stop a German craft *from* the air.

Aiming carefully at the engine compartment, DeLacey took a deep breath, then partially expelled. *Just like on the range at Hythe...* squeezing the fore-trigger gently, progressively his reward was a kick in the shoulder a mule would be hard pressed to better. Before breathing out further, he had squeezed the rear trigger and blasted the E-boat with a second massive slug. He could see the two holes he'd made, but the boat kept on its course, *away* from land now. Risking a look ahead, he was forced to shield his eyes from the wind rush, but saw a glimpse of land out at sea. Lundy? Yes! It must be the Isle of Lundy, but why head there?. As he rolled aside to reload, he saw Baxter Belmont looking down at him with a cheerful grin that didn't quite convince; clearly the poor man was airsick, but trying to be of some use. Snapping the breech shut on two fresh shells, Henry returned the grin and went back into the aim.

'Herr Kapitän Leutnant! Hydrophon - Effekt mit 80 Grad; Hochgeschwindigkeitspropeller, möglicherweise ein Torpedoboot!' The hydrophone operator leaned out into the passageway and waited for a response to the contact report from the control room. Kapitän Leutnant Von Herder reacted in an instant; At last! After all this frigging around! Rapidly he gave orders to the helmsmen for periscope depth. Sweeping around, he saw nothing but water and the island of Lundy, a rocky crag jutting out of the edge of the approaches to the Bristol Channel. A second sweep with the sky periscope, however, told him all had not gone to plan; one of the hated British Sunderlands was swooping around something perhaps seven kilometres distant. Another look through the high-power scope and he could just make out an indistinct shape that had to be the E-Boat. *Scheiße!*. They were in trouble, just what he'd hoped to avoid. This was meant to have been a simple pick-up, risky enough in daytime without the enemy taking an interest. Snapping the periscope handles up he stood back as the steel shaft lowered smoothly into its well housing.

'Vorbereiten für Oberflächenwirkung! Flak - Besatzungen in Standby.' Von Herder knew the importance the High Command had attached to this mission; the radio signal diverting him from his Atlantic patrol had been triple-encoded,

from Dönitz himself. He had no choice in the matter. The sound of the U-Boat blowing tanks came with a great surge of upwards motion, the Flak gunners crowded around the conning tower ladder in readiness.

The volley produced an immediate effect this time; a plume of smoke from the engine that billowed out from the holes the Nitro Express rounds had punched. Just as well; Commander DeLacey had only five more of the special rounds left. He doubted the shotgun or the Webley would do much damage to the large boat. Firing his last double for good measure, he left the last three rounds in the bag and pulled himself back from the hatch; he had some bad news for the pilot.

'You must be stark, staring mad, man! There's no way we can set down and take off again in this chop; we need calm waters to do it, not the bloody Atlantic!' Flying Officer Hoey was adamant on the matter. He could not and would not attempt a 'landing' in such rough seas. Only a gun to his head would change that, DeLacey knew. So he drew his Webley and did exactly that.
'I'm sorry, but I have the authority of the Prime Minister behind me – and this revolver in front. Please believe me I have no other choice. You either land, or I shall be forced to shoot you in accordance with Emergency Regulations.' The co-pilot looked back, his eyes signalling his fury at this outrage, but knew there was nothing he could do about it. The madman had the authority to carry out his insane threat, so the co-pilot took the decision to remove it; he lowered flaps and turned her in for a rough water landing.

'When we get alongside her, open up on the cockpit with that twelve-bore and then follow me across if possible. Mr.

Knight, you cover me from the hatchway with the .600; you've only got three rounds and she kicks like a horse. For God's sake aim it away from Mr. Belmont and myself. We'll only have one chance at this; that boat's still underway and, if we cock this up, we're in the drink and no mistake.' Having briefed his makeshift boarding and assault party, Commander DeLacey gave an apologetic shrug to the watching airmen and went back down to the nose of the aircraft, followed by Baxter clutching his shotgun, his own face shiny with sweat and quite grey in colour.

'Blasen!' At Von Herder's order the tension in the U-boat seemed to dissolve, the flak-crew already swarming up the conning tower ladder as she shuddered and rose clear of the water. The first man had opened the hatch and a shower of water cascaded down onto the others as they raced to their positions. The Kapitän Leutnant and his *Wachoffizier* were next, making it onto the bridge as the crew were ripping the covers from the dual 20mm cannon on the so-called 'Wintergarten,' the structure aft of the conning tower. This would make short work of the British flying 'Porcupine'! At the same instant that the submarine had broken cover, the flight-crew of the 'Albatross' were bringing her down onto the heaving sea, the Sunderland banging and crashing through the waves with a heart-stopping series of jolts that had the whole airframe shaking and reverberating to come abaft of the E-Boat. The co-pilot just had a glimpse of a pale face in the wheelhouse as he rolled back the throttles to equalise his speed on the water, the aircraft smashing its way through the peaks and troughs for which it was never designed to handle.

Assisted by a crewman, DeLacey pulled back the sliding nose turret cover, grateful for the excellent design of the Sunderland. This left the mooring compartment exposed and the Commander was granted a perfect three-quarter rear profile of a

German U-Boat as the flying boat came alongside. Despite the tremor of fear rising in his stomach, he yelled at Baxter to brace himself. The co-pilot cut the port engines and revved the starboard as, unseen behind him, a crewman threw a canvas drogue out of the port galley hatch; this had the effect of turning the albatross sharply to port – heading straight at the E-Boat. In a miraculous piece of manoeuvring, the Flying Boat cut across the bows of the Schnellboot and rammed hard into it, sending those in the mooring compartment hurtling into the bulkhead. Baxter was badly winded, his ribs broken, but Commander DeLacey was over the side in a flash and leaping down onto the bows of the stricken E-Boat. In the wheelhouse, Harris let out a stream of curses, grabbing his machine-pistol and racing forward to meet the threat just as the twin 20mm cannon on the U-Boat opened up and all hell broke loose.

Unlike the cannon on the E-Boat, the submarine's twin flaks were loaded with a mixture of tracer, high explosives and incendiaries; in theory capable of firing four hundred of these lethal shells a minute. The *Obermaat* in charge of the gun crew was a veteran and knew his job; the gunner was a crack shot, bracing himself against the shoulder pads and letting fly, using the battle sight seemed pointless at such close range as the forty mixed shells blasted into the defenceless Sunderland. The explosive shells punched their way through the aluminium alloy frame of the aircraft as their incendiary counterparts set alight anything that could burn. The co-pilot was hit in the head, his skull smashed in half by an explosive round travelling at 900 metres a second. Unbuckling himself, the pilot only just managed to duck in time as the entire instrument panel exploded inwards, ripped away by the sheer force of the twin cannon that were, mercifully, being reloaded now.

Down on the lower deck, Mortimer Knight took one look at the carnage and grabbed the nearest crewman. 'We've got to get out!' The RAF man merely gaped at him, his face white where the blood had drained from it in shock. Bursting through to the wardroom, he found the casualty being tended by the Scots corporal. The man had lost a lot of blood and looked close to death, but Knight knew they'd all die if they stayed aboard, yelling at the Scot to help him get the man out. Which is when the infernal flak guns opened up again.

Bracing himself against the bulkhead besides the flying bridge, Harris waited for the Englander *schwein* to appear. There was no sight of him. To reach the bridge he should come through the hatch between the torpedo tubes and the liferafts, but he had... the movement at the corner of his eye alerted the traitor too late. The barrel of the machine-pistol turned as he swung round, but the Webley spoke first, a short, flat **KRAK**; the first bullet taking him in the throat. Suddenly it was all very wrong, very distant and hazy. As the finger curled round the trigger of the German weapon, the British revolver had the final word, straight to the heart. Harris died seeing the sky darkening over the Western approaches to the land he had betrayed and hated so bitterly. Clambering over the bulkhead, DeLacey dropped to the deck heavily as the flak guns started up for the second – or was it the third time?

On the bridge of the U-Boat, one of the lookouts had spotted the brief fight on the bridge of the *Schnellboot,* reporting it whilst keeping his binoculars trained on the scene. The *Wachoffizier* seemed concerned at being surfaced for so long in such dangerous waters.

'Herr Kapitän Leutnant, vielleicht sollten wir die Deck-Kanone?' The Commander turned slowly to survey the face of the younger man. Use the deck cannon?. Perhaps he wasn't as solid as his file indicated. Shaking his head curtly, Von Herder returned his gaze to the vital E-Boat.

'Nein, das Stachelschwein ist unbewaffnet; Seltsam, warum würden sie senden ein unbewaffnetes Flugzeug? Dennoch ist es zerstört. Bringen Sie ein Gummiboot und zwei Männer, bewaffnet; Wir werden sehen, was los ist , wir müssen etwas vom V- Mann erholen, ob er tot oder lebendig ist.' ('No, the porcupine is unarmed, strangely; why would they send an unarmed aircraft? Nevertheless, it is destroyed. Bring a rubber boat and two men, armed; We'll see what's going on, we need to recover something from the V-man, whether he's dead or alive.') After the briefest of pauses to change the double magazines, the twin-flak let rip again. The Sunderland was beginning to break up.

The survivors were abandoning the doomed flying boat. The pilot and several of the crew had managed to get into an inflatable raft and were paddling away from the dying Albatross. Mortimer Knight, however had found a 'Mae West' life-jacket and was using it as a float to splash his way across the shockingly-cold water towards the E-Boat. With the slowly settling Sunderland between him and the German submarine, there was little chance he'd be spotted. The only thing worrying him was the weight of the Nitro Express, the rifle had already dipped into the water several times despite being supported by the life-vest and he wasn't sure if these things worked after a soaking. He would find out soon enough.

One of the engines was badly damaged, the casing cracked by the projectile that had exploded through the roof and struck it. Oil was spraying everywhere until Franz, the Kriegsmarine engineer shut it down. The sudden impact of the collision had sent him sprawling across the deck and gingerly he picked himself up, checking for broken bones. He was bleeding from the mouth, an exploratory finger finding two teeth missing. Spitting blood and curses, he made his way up to report and to find out what the hell was going on. He had his orders; if the English *Verräter* had fouled this up, he was to liquidate him and complete the mission. Drawing his Walther PP from an inside pocket in his coveralls, he headed for'ard. Sure enough, Harris lay dead on the main deck, in a pool of his own blood. Franz could see a shape in the wheelhouse, bent over furtively. *DeLacey...* he should have eliminated him when he had the chance the other night. Looking back, he saw what he had feared most. Karl was dead, still at his post. *Armer Karl !; er wird gerächt werden.* Now it was time for that revenge. Grabbing a piece of waste-cloth from a pocket, he waved it three times left to right at the bridge of the U-Boat, then crept forward, intent on avenging his friend.

As the door to the wheelhouse opened behind him, the sudden inrush of air and noise alerted Commander DeLacey, who turned to find the ugly mouth of an ugly little pistol aimed squarely at his chest. The man holding it was both familiar and foreign - literally. 'You killed Karl.' The statement was calm, and not a question.

'He was a German Agent, just like you. What is your name, if I may ask? It isn't Reverend Cholmondley, is it?.' Franz could see no harm in telling the Englander before his death.

'Franz Waldbaum. Of München.' Cursing himself for laying his Webley down on the instrument panel, Henry tried to stall for precious time.

'Thank you. Do I have time for a last cigarette?.'

'I should think not. I'll take those papers now, though.' As DeLacey stooped to reach for the all-important sheaf of documents, the glass behind Waldbaum erupted, as did his stomach.

Picking himself up from the deck, the sodden Knight shook his head to clear it from the shock of unleashing a .600 cartridge. If he'd been surprised to see Charles Jones, the vicar's nephew lying dead on deck, the sight of the Reverend Cholmondley himself holding a gun on Henry DeLacey was stupefying; the reverend was a German agent? Still, his eyes weren't lying to him. Slowly, he had raised the massive rifle to his aching shoulder, bracing himself for the appalling kick of the recoil and praying he would be forgiven for shooting a vicar, even a false one.

Forcing himself up to peer over the lip of the mooring compartment, Baxter Belmont found himself looking at the twin barrels of the submarine's flak-cannons. All he had against this beast was a twelve bore and a handful of shells, but he was damned if he'd die with them unfired. Shaking from shock and his injured ribs, he hauled the shotgun up and onto the parapet, squinting along the sights as he took careful aim. He fired, both barrels at once. He had no idea what shells he'd loaded, but hoped it wasn't something useless like bird-shot; by a stroke of luck, it wasn't. The Eley-Kynoch LG (The suffix standing for 'Large Goose') contained six 0.36 inch soft lead slugs, originally intended to control and kill deer. The buttocks of *Obermaat* Pedersen were no match for two barrels' worth.

Clutching his ruined backside, the *Obermaat* fell to the deck, a bellow of surprise and pain issuing from him. Startled, the gunner wheeled the flak-guns around to bear on the nose of the stricken Sunderland, where a man could be seen struggling to re-load what looked like a shotgun, of all things. A shotgun against a U-Boat? The gunner burst into laughter, as did the loader. Even the Commander, Von Herder, let out a chuckle at this

78

development. Then the barrels came up and the smile vanished. The second volley from Baxter's shotgun spattered against the steel coaming of the conning tower, sending a pellet hissing off the side and missing Von Herder by inches. Yelling down to the flak-crew he gave the order; *'Töte ihn!; Schießen, verdammt!'* Baxter Belmont was a doomed man.

Seeing the plight his friend was in, Mortimer Knight ran forwards to a bulkhead that afforded a better firing position; this gun was a back-breaker. Snapping the breech open, he ejected the spent casings and fished out the last of the monstrous shells. With the last two loaded, he took aim at the flak gunner. The Nitro Express barked twice, slamming him in the shoulder. The first shot whistled past the target... and the second also missed, but it crashed into the breech of the flak cannon, sending a shard of steel whirring through the air and into the gunner's face. Instantly blinded, the man fell soundlessly to the deck.

Recovering from his near-miss, Commander DeLacey wasted no time; with the bow of the E-Boat wedged against that of the Sunderland, there was a risk of the gradually-sinking aircraft taking the boat down with it. The immediate danger, however was the U-Boat; at any second they'd realise what was going on and open up on him. Already he could see a bright yellow rubber boat paddling towards him, a sailor armed with a carbine in the stern of the tiny, almost comical, craft. He knew the Admiralty had removed a pair of the torpedoes from the craft for examination purposes, but two had been left aboard; indeed, Walton had told him they had re-loaded the tubes in case of attack by U-Boat. Now he hoped against hope that information was correct. The starboard torpedo tube was damaged beyond repair – it was a miracle the torpedo hadn't exploded in the tube when the Albatross crunched into the side of the bow, but the port tube lay clear.

The only problem was, he had no idea how a German torpedo was fired; there were panels all over the cramped little cockpit, with labels in German, naturally; although he spoke fluent German, the meaning of some of these eluded him, not being a submariner himself. Flipping a few switches produced results; a series of dials and lights were now illuminated, the firing-circuits and torpedo-aiming reckoner active. What all this meant he wasn't entirely sure. DeLacey's speciality was Naval Intelligence; however; there was no mistaking the purpose of the innocuously-modest lever he saw mounted on the side of one of the boxes. Heart in mouth, he pulled it, not realising he had fired his only torpedo *unarmed...*

Over 23 feet of G7 torpedo broke from the E-Boat's port tube with a hiss of compressed air, the slim, elegant weapon leaping into the choppy water with a splash. Almost instantly, a stream of bubbles rose, marking the remarkably swift progress of the torpedo two metres below the surface. From the conning tower of the U-Boat, Von Herder watched in helpless terror as the lethal 'Eel' sliced through the sea, speeding unerringly towards the hull directly below his sea boots. Bracing himself for the inevitable, he closed his eyes involuntarily. *KLANG!* With a sickening impact, the unarmed torpedo struck the outer casing of the U-Boat at 81 kilometres per hour, over a ton and a half of metal punching straight through to hit the inner, pressure hull. 18.5 millimetres of steel was no match for the brute force striking it. Almost instantaneously, two things occurred; the submarine began taking on water and the torpedo exploded.

Despite being unarmed, the sheer kinetic forces involved

in the impact had caused a partial detonation that then became an inferno of fire and steel; 280 kilograms of high-explosive Hexanite discharging its energy in a single, fatal instant. Because of the uneven nature of the blast, the explosion rippled through the submarine, its internal hatches open, a fatal instance that condemned most of the crew to a fiery death. The control-room crew died instantly, the conning tower watch a second later. The last thought Von Herder had as the fireball erupted up from the open hatch was that he would never see his beloved Germany again. At once, the wrecked U-Boat began to break in half, the for'ard section dipping below the waves with startling suddenness, the remaining flak crew swept off the casing into the sea.

With tons of water rushing into the stern half came the inevitable. Not a single crewman made it out alive from that section, though a pair of heads bobbed up from the for'ard torpedo compartment, an almost miraculous escape. Nor did the two men in the rubber boat escape harm either. The shockwave pulsing out through the water knocking both men clean out into the sea. In moments, this became a rescue operation; Henry and Mortimer working together to heave the two rubber rafts that had been lashed between the E-Boat's torpedo tubes into the water, one for each set of survivors. With a last screech of metal on metal, the Albatross slipped back into the water and began her lonely final journey, pulling sharply at the Schnellboot, the craft lurching alarmingly to starboard. Mercifully, the wreckage of the Sunderland broke free, the flying boat graceful even as she sank beneath the sea, falling in a slow spirals to bump to her rest not sixty yards from the remains of the U-Boat.

Postscript; *The Admiralty, Two Weeks later.*

Sitting in the small, smoke-fogged ante-room outside Room 39, a nondescript door in a nondescript part of the building, Mortimer Knight and Baxter Belmont sat, waiting, waiting, waiting. Finally, the door was opened by a tall man in the uniform of a Commander in the Naval Reserve. Well spoken, he would have been raffishly handsome had it not been for the nose, doubtless broken on some playing field or other. With knowing eyes, he ushered them into Rear-Admiral Rushbrooke's office, the Commander left them with a few quiet words of caution.

'Don't take him too seriously; he's still fuming about the whole affair.' The man facing them was perhaps in his early fifties, whippet-thin with a long, sorrowful face. Seated opposite him was Commander Henry DeLacey, a boyish grin on his face; it was if he were in on some private joke they knew nothing of. 'No interruptions, Fleming. Sit down, gentlemen.' The voice was not *entirely* without warmth. As the reservist left the room, the two did as bid, there being only two chairs, Commander DeLacey ceded his to stand in the corner.

Clearing his throat, the Rear-Admiral glanced down at the buff-coloured folder on the desk in front of him, before abruptly signing his name in the margin and closing it with an air of finality, as if he were glad to be done with it.

'Commander DeLacey has briefed me thoroughly on the events of which you were involved. I can only commend you; as civilians you assisted the Commander in a dangerous and *reckless* (this last word was aimed at the figure in the corner) venture which recovered vital documents of national importance. Moreover, you helped destroy a U-Boat and even helped the Commander to take several prisoners.' Standing, he straightened his tunic, brushing an imagined speck of dust from the cuffs and strode around to stand behind the two men, forcing them to turn awkwardly in their seats. 'The matter has been referred to the Prime Minister and his first thought was to have you two interned...'

'Now look here...' Mortimer's protest was stilled by a palm raised in admonition.

'You both saw highly sensitive equipment while trespassing on Admiralty property; for that you could both face the gallows...' Now the Rear-Admiral had both palms up in a calming gesture, his voice grave as with the weight of responsibility. 'It is thanks to Commander DeLacey here that you are to be taken from here... to a building near here where you will be thanked accordingly.'

Baxter gasped aloud, while his friend merely stared at Rear-Admiral Rushbrooke as if he had lost his mind. Commander DeLacey broke the spell first;

'You'll have to sign an undertaking not to reveal the things you have seen and done, of course; the Official Secrets Act.'

'And if we refuse to sign?' Baxter's question caused the Commander to miss a beat, but only the one;

'It's binding whether you sign or not, actually. It's not a request; however you may refuse to add your signature if you choose. Thinking of publishing a memoir?' This last came in a jocular tone, which broke the rapidly forming ice a little. Shaking his head, Baxter smiled.

'No. Some things are best left unsaid. What about the families of the dead Sunderland crew? What will you tell them?' Rushbrooke fielded that one.

'Officially, they perished at sea on a flight to deliver the aircraft; no wreckage or bodies recovered, although some survivors were recovered by a Corvette that *happened* to come across a life-raft adrift in the Irish Sea.'

'And what about Harris' wife? What of her?' The lined face

turned to regard Mortimer's for a moment before replying. 'She died in a car crash. Next to her husband. Her next of kin have been duly informed.' Clearing his throat, Commander DeLacey indicated the time and the two actors rose to be given a firm handshake each. As if by some unseen signal, the young RNVR Commander re-appeared and ushered the party out.

After a few minutes, the Reserve Commander re-appeared in his superior's office.

'Well, Sir?'

'What? Oh, I suppose they'll play by the rules; they've little choice, I suppose. Who'd believe a tale like that?'

'Might make for a good novel at that...' Seeing the frown of disapproval this produced, the Commander hastily added; 'I mean, the whole thing's so absurd, sir. That's what I meant.'

'Well, forget it ever happened, Commander.'

'Funny though, a man playing Sherlock Holmes investigating a Nazi plot against England, don't you think?.' Irascibly, the Rear-Admiral frowned at the junior officer.

'What's funny about it?'

'Well, a fictional character investigating such a thing, that's what I meant, sir.' Wordlessly, the older man opened a drawer and rummaged inside, producing a faded photograph in a simple wooden frame. In it, a youthful Edmund Rushbrooke stood next to a tall, rather stooped man in old-fashioned morning coat and holding a top hat in one hand. Seeing nothing of significance, the Commander leaned closer; there was an inscription, in ink, made pallid by the many intervening years; *For Young Edmund, with appreciation for assistance, Sherlock Holmes...* Startled beyond words, the Commander merely stood silently as the photograph was replaced in the drawer.

In the Blue Drawing Room of Buckingham Palace, the

two men sat, acutely conscious of where they did so. Even as they had approached the building, in a drab green staff car, even when they were led through a side door and through the kitchens they hadn't quite believed it. Baxter noticed a section of peeling regency wallpaper in a hallway and that the carpets seemed quite worn in places, but he was quite simply in a state of shock. Presently, an equerry appeared, in a suit rather than the more familiar livery and took them aside.

'Gentlemen, time is short so if you please... you are to address the personage as 'Your Majesty' initially, subsequent to that you may call him 'Sir'. You do not approach the personage, you stand when in the presence and never, *never* allow your back to face him. When His Majesty enters, you will bow, like this...' The aide demonstrated a brief, formal nod from the neck up, the chin touching the chest briefly. 'Any questions? No? Very well, it is time.' At that moment, the imposing double gilt doors swung open...

A light wind played at the eaves of Cragston Hall, the staff car rolling to a halt outside. Hopkins, the new butler opened the door to admit the two actors, Baxter struggling with a wooden box containing some rather valuable presents from His Majesty the King. Henry DeLacey was there to greet his guests in the main hall, where a furled banner hung expectantly. At their approach, he sang out a 'Ta-Daaa!' and pulled a rope to drop the banner, the embroidered silk unfurling to reveal a magnificent Armorial.

'It's official! You are in the presence of Baron DeLacey!.' The ancient document they had discovered in the forgotten chamber had confirmed it; a baronial patency conferring the honour on the DeLaceys *in perpetuum.* Handing over the box, Baxter grinned;

'A little something from a rather well-stocked house in London; I'm told it was originally from Napoleon's own cellar.'

'Well, we shall judge the Emperor's taste for ourselves.

Hopkins is a *Cordon Bleu*, so we will have a meal fit for such rare wines!.'

'Better than Baxter's cooking.' joked Mortimer; 'His should be cordoned off!' The friends laughed together and walked towards Baron DeLacey's dining room. A shout from the driver caused them to turn.

'Ere, wot's this for, then?' Indicating the shiny new bicycle he was holding, Mortimer called back.

'Leave that there, please; it's a present for a rather brave little friend of ours.'

The Detective Who Wasn't There

'The patient has not regained consciousness?'

'No, sir, he has not.'

'Then we have wasted enough precious time discussing it.'

Sir. Trelawney Addison-Hope, known universally behind his back as 'Last hope' stepped down from his carriage and bristled through the side doors into a dark hallway, Dr. Henry Fox hurrying to keep pace with the noted surgeon and neurologist as he strode onwards into the bowels of the labyrinthine building. In his second year at Barts, Fox had taken the liberty of sending for the elder man at his club.

Under the formidable gaze of an elderly matron, Henry Fox stammered and blushed his way through a brief description of the patient's injuries, but when he attempted to discuss the circumstances in which the injured man was found, Addison-Hope merely fixed him with his legendary stare. This was not the time for abstractions. Bending over the prostrate form on the bed, the eminent figure took in the injuries in one long glance. Turning to the matron, his look was grave.

'Prepare this patient for surgery at once.' Although the junior in the room, Fox felt this was rushing things.

'But surely, sir, there aren't the sufficient indicators of sub-dural haematoma for a craniotomy...'

'As two things seem to have evaded your attention, *Doctor* Fox, allow me to supply these deficiencies.'

Taking the younger man's hand roughly in his own, the surgeon pressed it against a point on the base of the skull. At once aghast, Henry Fox felt the unmistakable signs of an injury to the occipital region. Feebly, he removed his hand and attempted to regain some of his fast-draining composure.

'I had not yet had time to examine the patient fully, sir.'

'Neither had I. However, as time is indeed an element we both sorely lack, shall we retire to the dressing room without further wastage?' Head bowed, the young doctor followed his superior along the corridor to the room where the dressers were already waiting, alerted by the matron's formidable bush-telegraph.

'Oh, I almost forgot, sir. What was the second thing?.'

'Hmm-what?' Earnestly, the youthful doctor persisted. 'Well, you said there were two things...'

'Oh that. Only that the patient is to be hanged if and when he makes a recovery.'

Things rarely turn out as expected, however and it was after nearly three weeks that the patient, having regained consciousness was transferred at Sir. Trelawney Addison-Hope's insistence to a convalescent ward at a nearby hospital favoured by the discreetly rich. This was not without its problems, however, Inspector Bradstreet had been given charge of the injured man and, as he was now awake and upright in his bed, a constable had been assigned to watch him in case of escape. Further, there was the not insubstantial issue of identity, for the man had none that he was able to recall. Put simply, the man in Bradstreet's care was unaware of who he was and where he had been when he sustained his injuries. It was on a sunny Monday when Bradstreet wheeled in, red-faced and somewhat out of breath, to find the constable engaged in a game of chess with the patient, whose features were largely obscured by the bandages around his head.

'Feeling better, is he?' Bradstreet waved the constable back down then cast about for a place to settle his tall, stout frame, settling on the adjacent bed, which was unoccupied.

'Yes, sir. We were just, that is to say, I was just...'

'Engaging the patient's brain in an attempt to ascertain his particulars?'

'Well, something like that, yes, sir.' The Constable smiled at his superior. Bradstreet being a favourite with the new men on 'F' Division, whence he had recently been transferred due to the 'promotion trap', that oldest of police problems where a man due for promotion cannot find it due to the available posts all being filled. Now with his new Division, it was expected Bradstreet would rise to Chief Inspector and then move on towards a well-earned retirement some three years hence.

The fact the man was a murderer and would hang was of lesser importance to Bradstreet than establishing who he was and why he had done it. The whole country had read of the burglary and murder of His Lordship, the Earl of Aldrington at his Knightsbridge home. The Earl, a notorious hell-raiser and gambler turned statesman, had been found face-down in the fire in his vast study, burned beyond recognition, the remnants of several charred papers found beneath the body when the shocked staff finally broke down the door the next morning. It had been a groundsman who had found the unconscious murderer – for surely he had been responsible, lying below an open second-floor window. The police had been called and Inspector Bradstreet had immediately sent for a police surgeon to examine the body, though the cause of death was fairly obvious; the ornamental paper-knife sticking from the Earl's back.

That first day, the comings and goings at the house, tucked away in a discreet corner near Montpelier Square, included everyone from servants to high-ranking police officers and several well-known faces from the Home and Foreign Offices.

Indeed, it was said afterwards that the Prime Minister did not attend only due to the forthcoming Conference on the European Problem. Finally, the house was sealed off, the servants paid off, and only a skeleton staff would remain until after the funeral.

One unseasonably cold day in April, the Earl of Aldrington was buried in the family vault at Highgate Cemetary. The Earl had not found success with his three attempts at marriage nor had his wives provided him with heirs, so it was a comparatively modest affair, a few senior servants and a great aunt or two in attendance. From the government, however, a veritable plethora of famous names were present, and this included the first Lord of the Treasury, the Lord Privy Seal and the Secretary of State for Foreign Affairs. A smattering of minor members of the Royal Houses of Europe completed the list of mourners.

It was early in May when Sir. Trelawney Addison-Hope arrived to visit his amnesiac patient for the final time, bringing with him a specialist, a young Doctor Lutz from Heidelberg to examine the man. Lutz was a disciple of Freud, the Viennese neurologist and would attempt to restore the patient's memory using hypnotic techniques. For these, the constable waited outside so as to avoid any undue effects. It was to no avail; after twenty short minutes the door opened and a regretful Addison-Hope informed the policeman that the patient was an incurable and as such, could be removed to Newgate prison to await trial and, inevitably, execution. So it was then, that an un-named man was placed in a tiny, dark and fetid cell awaiting a day in court then certain execution. All for reasons of which he was entirely unaware.

So much you have already read, but when I tell you that the man was neither found guilty nor hanged you may find yourself asking why; the short answer is Alphonse Bertillon. For no sooner had the bandages been removed than Inspector Bernard Edgar Bradstreet's orderly mind stirred into action. The Bertillon system of identification was being trialled at Scotland Yard against the method of taking prints from the fingers. The finger-printers claimed their system infallible, but the measurements of facial features have their merit and it was by using these late that Monday night, Bradstreet was able to show that the mysterious and nameless patient was, in almost certainty, one Jack Cooper of Newham in the East End of London. A well known confidence-trickster, Cooper's other speciality was 'skylighting', the burglary of dwellings by, as the name suggests, climbing the walls and entering through the attic. As, however, no ropes or hooks – tools of the skylighter's trade, could be found at the house, Bradstreet was baffled. There was only one thing left for him to do; he would consult with Sherlock Holmes.

Baker Street, that most busy of metropolitan thoroughfares was unusually hectic that glorious Tuesday morning. Bradstreet made his way through the throng avoiding the paper-sellers and the flower girl, threw some copper down for the blind Afghanistan campaigner with the highly polished campaign medals and strode briskly up to the bell-pull of 221. After a minute or so and a second ring a flustered spinster opened the door to send a cloud of dust billowing out into the street, followed by a harassed and scolded salesman clutching his hat in one hand and a Gladstone in the other.

'Electrical Beater he says! And us still fitted for gas!' Turning his attention from the departing pedlar Bradstreet raised his hat.

'Good day Madam, I wonder...' but the door had been slammed shut in his face.

After a furious round of bell-ringing and hammering on the door, a crimson-cheeked Inspector was finally admitted to the living room on the first floor. There he found Doctor John Watson rising from a chair with a copy of *The Lancet*.

'Good lord! Bradstreet isn't it?.'

'Doctor. It's been a while.' Gesturing with his index finger, Watson furrowed his brow.

'The Blue Carbuncle! Why it's been ten years!'

'Will the Inspector take tea?' At Bradstreet's eager nod Watson gave a nod to the landlady, who went to prepare some. Waving his guest to the familiar wicker chair, Watson lit his pipe and waited while the Inspector followed suit. Soon the air had the convivial quality as befitted any gentleman's establishment and it was with some reluctance that the doctor broke the silence to enquire as to the nature of Bradstreet's visit.

'I am here to consult Mr. Holmes on a matter of some importance. It concerns the recent death of the Earl of Aldrington.' Leaning forward awkwardly, Watson gave out a sigh.

'Ah. I'm afraid Holmes is on urgent business in the Western Isles of Scotland and will not be persuaded to return.'

'This is most distressing, Doctor. Most distressing; I had hoped for an audience with him. This case may turn on one of those queer little observations he is wont to make. I confess myself at an end in my own effort and cannot see a way to clear a man of murder.'

At this unexpected turn, Doctor Watson looked up from the re-lighting of his pipe, a cloud of whitish smoke fuming from the Arcadia tobacco.

'Did you say 'clear'?.'

'I did.'

'Then you think the amnesiac innocent of the crime?.'

'You have read the reports in the newspapers then.' Watson waved this away with a hint of irritability, indicating the Inspector continue. Just then, the landlady bustled in bearing the promised refreshments and the Doctor rose to show her out and to pour the tea. Bradstreet stood and took a cup, blowing on his tea to cool it in the careless manner of his ilk. Watson returned his attention to his pipe and the matter in hand.

'Surely it is a proven case; the man was found badly injured outside the house, but in the grounds and the Earl was clearly stabbed, falling into the fire, perhaps on his way to the bell-pull?.'

'I had thought it possible until I discerned the identity of the man. His name is Jack Cooper. His antecedents are of the worst kind. He is a confidence-trickster and swindler, but it is his abilities as an amateur Alpinist that set this business in its proper light.'

'He is a climber, then?'

'Of sorts.'

Deciding his tea was sufficiently moderate, the Inspector sipped and then slurped at it noisily while his host regarded the mirror on the mantle as if it contained something in the nature of inspiration. Wiping his lips with a sleeve, Bradstreet explained himself.

'He is a 'skylighter', that is to say he climbs up to force high windows and suchlike to gain entry to premises and robs them.'

'Then how is he innocent?'

'Simply this, Doctor; Jack Cooper retired some seven years back when his wife fell under a carriage. Since that day he has looked after her in his own way and a more devoted and reformed character I have yet to know...' Clearly, Doctor Watson was yet to be convinced, so the policeman dealt what he felt was his most secure hand. 'Of course, what clinched it for me was that since his retirement Cooper has not only forsworn all criminal activities, but promised his beloved Claire that he would only break his oath to her for the man who saved him from the *last* burglary charge he was on.'

Watson sat bolt upright as the meaning of Bradstreet's words sank in.

'Sherlock Holmes.'

'Indeed, Doctor. The very same. So, my question to you is; what was a retired burglar doing robbing a house for Mr. Holmes?'

Waiting until after Inspector Bradstreet had left by hansom for Scotland Yard, Doctor Watson grabbed a book of telegram forms and hurriedly filled one out, ringing down for the houseboy and giving him both 8d and a silver sixpence for his trouble, sent him off to the telegraph office in the Strand, this being the closest open at such late hours. Knowing the boy would be loath to part with any of the sixpence for a cab, Watson came downstairs to hail and pay for one himself. The message despatched, he decided to turn in for the night.

The sleeping man writhed in his bed, tossing and turning as the gale howling outside sent a low moan through the brickwork of the prison. Flashes of vision, fragments of imagery lanced through his deep subconscious mind. He saw a man, holding a pipe that would not light, wind blowing the match out. Spontaneously, the match re-ignited, but again the wind extinguished it. *And again, and again and yet again...*

It was during breakfast the following day that the corresponding telegram found Doctor Watson, a terse missive stating simply;

VITAL RETRIEVE DOCUMENT COOPER STOLE NOW IN HANDS DR. LUTZ OF BOHEMIA ESSENTIAL MOBILISE IRREGULARS - HOLMES.

It seemed an impossible task, to find a Bohemian doctor and get hold of some document from him. The telegram left no clue as to the nature of the document in question, but Watson knew Holmes better than to question him. Clearly if it had been important, it would have been mentioned and the first thing was to find this German doctor, whoever he was. It seemed clear the man must be in London to have gained possession of the paper and for the Baker Street Irregulars, that most unofficial branch of the Baker Street detective force, to be required. Perhaps the *Times* would provide inspiration? By unmatched good fortune, this indeed proved the case.

It was there on the page before him; an illustration of some of the most illustrious minds in science, gathered together at the Medical Society's annual dinner and a Doctor Theodor Lutz was to be introduced by no less a figure than Sir. Trelawney Addison-Hope! Watson had been fortunate enough to meet this pioneer of neurology on no less than two separate occasions, and he still recalled the acerbic wit and sharp tongue 'Last hope' was famous for. The article concluded by saying Doctor Lutz would give an after-dinner account of the value of hypnosis as a diagnostic, with special reference to his work on amnesia. This was it! Clearly Holmes was on to something. The man he named in his reply was a specialist in the field of memory loss! It was time to act. Finishing his toast, the Doctor rang down for the boots.

Wiggins arrived with the usual cacophony and shouts of feminine outrage from the landlady, the leader of the street Arabs bursting into the familiar lodgings with two of his lieutenants, 'Lame Leg-Lenny' and a sharp-faced boy named 'Smudger.' The urchins stood, eyeing the remnants of Watson's breakfast hungrily. It occurred to the Doctor that these boys probably had not had any sustenance, so he gave them each a thrupenny piece and a brief, but well intended lecture on the merits of a healthy diet that was delivered against a faint, but unmistakable waft of gin when 'Smudger' let out a surprisingly deep and resonant belch. To business, then; Watson gave the boys the information he had; that tomorrow night Doctor Lutz would be at the Medical Society building just off Cavendish Square and that his place of residence needed to be established. Sending them off with the promise of a guinea for the boy who came back with the correct address, Watson went to dress for his day tending patients as a locum at a friend's practice.

That same morning another man had arisen to a rather different breakfast. Newgate Prison, for long centuries past the terror of the London underworld was now used only for those awaiting trial and for the condemned. The abysmal execution cells and a walk over the unmarked graves of countless unfortunates led only to the gallows. Although he still could not remember anything of recent events, Jack Cooper woke to the sound of the key in the lock and the kindly face of Deakins, the warder.

'Up you get, Jackie-boy. Slop out and grub up.' Cooper did as he was told, picking up the soil bucket, but had no idea why he was in such a godforsaken place or what he had even done to warrant his incarceration. Perhaps the chaplain would know.

The only times a Newgate prisoner could see other inmates were during meal times or during exercise and as conversations were mostly forbidden it was unlikely anyone

96

would know or care about Jack's predicament. There were visits, of course, but these were unlikely for an unknown. However, Inspector Bradstreet had visited Claire Cooper at the hovel she shared with her common-law husband and arranged for her to visit. During such visits, conducted through a grille, no contact was allowed, but through that forbidding ironwork hope yet flickered. Claire had told her husband of his name, of their family, of their son (also named Jack) and of their life together. Almost instantly, the prisoner had flashes and sparks of illumination; memories, images flitting across the brain towards that area where memory lives. All too soon, the visit was over and Cooper returned to his cell to await the ever distant and fleeting exercise period in the yard.

There was one exception to the isolation; the Newgate Chaplain in Ordinary, Reverend Merrick had taken a sabbatical leave to study organ music at Winchester, but the Reverend Hemlock, a vicar from Derbyshire had agreed to take on the position for the duration of the chaplain's leave. A quiet, thoughtful man, the Reverend Hemlock was always keen to visit prisoners in their cells and had made a point of seeing Cooper every day. As the man was clearly amnesiac, it seemed cruel to compound his situation with isolation and the reverend was himself an advocate of prison reform. Today, he called upon his charge at eleven in the morning and patiently listened to the hapless man's complaints. After Cooper had finished his list of grievances, the Reverend Hemlock smiled and nodded thoughtfully.

'My dear chap, you have suffered most outrageously. Perhaps, however, you might recall our other discussions where I addressed the possibility, even the *probability* of your guilt?' At the prisoner's nod, the reverend continued where he had left off the day before, with an appeal to Cooper to try to remember the events of that terrible night. As before, Cooper struggled to regain his memory, but as before when he came to the death of the Earl his mind was a blank. Never mind, said the temporary chaplain. There was still time...

The night of the dinner saw Doctor Watson in a cab bound for the Medical Society building, the invitation in his breast pocket secured by his doctor friend, himself unable to attend. Dressed for the town, he hoped Sir. Trelawney 'Last hope' would remember him as he wanted to try to secure an introduction to this Lutz fellow. As he alighted onto the pavement and paid the jarvey, a ragamuffin raced past, chased off by a red-faced and liveried doorman. Recognising the scruff as 'Smudger,' Watson turned to present his invitation, in time to see a brougham pull up, the doorman hurrying forward to open the door, upon which was emblazoned the crest of one of the great houses of Europe. Standing back, he saw the crown prince of one of the Austro-Hungarian principalities sweep imperiously through the doors that were held open for him by flunkies. Waiting until this personage had entered, Watson made his own entry through the doors, detecting the hint of a sneer as he passed the doormen. His card was checked against a list and returned to him by a grinning footman whose smile didn't reach his eyes.

With dinner set for eight sharp, Watson had forty minutes or so to commingle and cast about for any sign of either Lutz or his illustrious sponsor. Accepting a glass of sherry from a waiter, he stood near the entrance to the main salon where the assembled guests, the cream of European medicine amongst them, chattered gaily about the latest developments in their respective fields. Social gatherings and pomp were never to Watson's taste and soon, he found himself drifting away to the main hall, crossing to a smoking room for what he hoped would be a quiet cigar when he noticed a flunky leading an older gentleman of distinguished aspects along a side passage that had been roped off to the general throng. Curiosity piqued, he abandoned his smoke to loiter as unobtrusively as possible to observe the passage and, sure enough, after perhaps five minutes another guest was ushered past the silken rope. However, this time, Doctor Watson was able to observe something that might prove relevant, the man had shown his invitation to the servant, but he had *already* done so at the entrance. Why twice?

Taking out his own card and examining it, Watson could see nothing unusual or out of place, but perhaps the speakers had different invitation cards and were simply being led to a dressing room? But, of course, you don't spend any amount of time with Sherlock Holmes and see the innocent everywhere! Girding himself, Watson strode across as the footman returned from the passage, producing his card with a flourish that he hoped would signify authority. Half-expecting to be told he had made a mistake, the Doctor was taken aback when the man glanced at his card, stared coldly at him and pushed him back to re-attach the rope barring his progress.

'What the... I say! What do you mean by this? This is an outrage!' The reply came in a quiet whisper with more than a hint of Cockney menace.

'Piss off out of it, pallie, or I'll stick you one... got it?.'

There was no point in making a scene. Clearly whatever was going on here right under the noses of the medical profession's finest was occurring with some organisation behind it. Obviously, Holmes' instincts had been proven right once more! With nothing for it, but to return to his evening, Watson went for that cigar, but first he availed himself of a large whisky with the connivance of a rather friendlier waiter. He would attend the dinner and slip away during the address, but one thing was certain; that offensive Cockney would find himself grateful of the proximity of so many doctors before the night was done.

As with all such dinners, the food at this one was mediocre, hardly better than those served at Repton, the school that, thanks to a modest inheritance Watson was able to attend. The grilled Dover sole was rather lifeless, the potatoes rather cold and the syllabub lacked lustre. All in all, it had been somewhat of a let-down, but the air of anticipation around the dining hall as Herr Doktor Lutz stood to begin his talk was scintillating. Although surely now was the best time to slip out, as the waiters hurried to clear the plates from the long tables and a few overfed guests went to use the gentlemen's WC, Watson decided to stay for the first part of the talk, which his card had adverted as *'A Discussion on the Application of Hypnotic States as Therapy in the Treatment of Amnesiacs.'*

Taking a sip from his glass, Doctor Lutz cleared his throat and stood for a moment, looking around the room. Despite his youth, this was a compelling figure and even from the table near the doors to the kitchens, Watson had an impression of piercing blue-grey eyes set in an aquiline face with high brows and cheekbones beneath a shock of black hair worn daringly long even for the times. In a clear, resonant tone he began to speak, his voice meticulously legible with a marked accent.

'My friends, colleagues and Fellows of the Society, I must thank you for inviting an unknown (This caused a ripple of polite laughter) to address you, but first I should express gratitude to my gracious host in London, Sir. Trelawney Addison-Hope. Waiting for the applause to die down, Lutz embarked on a fascinating speech on the efficacy and ethics of hypnosis, from the work of Mesmer to Reichenbach's theories on somnambulism and then to Dr. Braid's towering research in the field of ideo-motor theory.

Along with three hundred others, Watson sat spellbound as the youthful Bavarian doctor expanded on his own work, theoretical and practical, on the applications of hypnosis. He then turned to the main doors and held out a hand in welcome as an elderly, be-medalled man was shown in and led to a seat set out for him between the long tables. Lutz began clapping and instinctively the audience joined him as the old fellow took his seat. It transpired this man had suffered with amnesia of the retrograde variety for years following an incident where he was wounded in the Second Opium War and developed typhoid fever. On his return to Britain, he was found to be suffering with amnesia.

Turning to his patient, Doctor Lutz addressed him directly.

'Mr. Anderson, I have worked with you for how many days please?'

'We've never met before today, Doc, first time I sees you is this morning when I comes to your surgery, like.' With a smile more suited to P.T. Barnum opening a new exhibit, the young doctor faced the audience as he phrased his next question in his immaculate English.

'And what is your first childhood memory?'

'Oh, *that,* well it's a bit daft, like – not sure all these fine folk will be interested.' Lutz turned his smile on his subject as re-assurance.

'Alright then, it was Daisy, me sister. She gave me a paper hat. She'd made it out of an old newspaper, see? Like an admiral's hat it were...' The assembled guests gasped at this, but Lutz raised a finger in caution.

'Yes, interesting indeed; however, amnesia can take many forms. Who is to say that this man can recall recent events with such clarity?'

'Well, you give me a guinea and a slap-up luncheon today, sir, so I'd say I was cured.' This time, the audience was on their feet, the hall resonating to the sound of their thunderous applause.

The building was a large Regency affair and the echoes of Lutz's acclaim followed Doctor Watson as he made his way through the deserted hallways and passages towards the back of the kitchens. It had been relative child's-play to slip through unobserved and he soon found himself in a high-walled courtyard that led to a mews-block. There was an iron stair-case to the rear that led upwards and, with no other way to go, he chose this, climbing up to the first floor to find the door there firmly locked. It was the same with the second and then the third. It seemed there was nothing for it, but to return down in defeat, but then he looked up to see the ladder.

Clambering up onto a flat expanse of roof, Watson found he was out of breath, cursing his lack of regular exercise and the syllabub that sat heavily with him. From where he stood now, he could see and hear the great city around him, a waxing moon hidden behind scudding clouds. Looking about, he saw he could move virtually without hindrance almost the whole length of the roof to where it rose sharply to a knife-edge running the entire width of the edifice. There were several large skylights, some brightly lit and to the first of these went the Doctor, careful to keep the sound of his steps to a minimum. Peering down, he saw a stairwell, going down to the ground floor. It was a dizzying sight and he moved on to the next. This turned out to be a large chamber of some sort, lustrous royal blue velvet carpet covering the floor with a large table at each end just visible from his vantage point. A conference room, perhaps. The next two lights showed similarly uninspiring chambers, the third another staircase. It occurred to Watson there might be more of these skylights to the front of the building, beyond the imposing angle of tiles rising to the centre.

Bare-footed, his shoes tied around his neck, John Watson inched his way up the treacherous incline. Twice he slipped back, but each time he managed to claw his way back up, until he found himself at the capstone and was able to look down to see the ornamental balustrade running the length of the facade. There were, indeed more skylights and the moon that now peeked out from behind the clouds reminded him time was fleeting. Glad for the absence of rain, he allowed himself to slide gently down towards the nearest skylight. Or would have, had he not suddenly lost his grip and slipped, shimming down at an alarming rate and sliding off the edge of an attic window coping into dizzying space. For a horrifying moment it seemed as if he would fall into the skylight directly below. Which is exactly what then happened.

Exploding into the darkened room in an incandescent spray of glass, Watson plummeted down to crash off of something metallic and into something hard, then the unmistakable soft-hardness of a plush carpet on a solid floor. But by then, he was unconscious.

The rays of light came through the thick mist and seemed to hover for a moment, then turn away as if hesitantly, before apparently changing its mind to return, the beams playing over Watson's upturned face as if underwater and not in fog. The light became a point of an unbearable intensity and at once, he awoke to find himself in excruciating pain. Tentatively putting his hand to his head, he found it wet with what turned out to be blood. Looking up he was rewarded with a jolt of pain from his neck, but by the clarity of the moonlight he could see his path downwards had taken him through a gas-light fitment and then he must have hit the table above him with the result he was sent spinning into the carpet. He was lucky to be alive after such a fall and spent the next five minutes slowly feeling himself over for any signs of further injury. Apart from a badly twisted ankle, a bruised elbow and what were almost certainly two cracked ribs, his only other injury was a small gash to the cranium which would require suturing.

With his head bandaged with a piece of shirt-tail he cut with a piece of broken glass (Gaining another slight injury when the shard slipped) and leaning heavily on his good ankle, Watson made his way haltingly from the room, finding a deserted hallway that led to some stairs. His immediate thought was to return downstairs and seek medical help. However, the man who had once walked five miles to the regimental aid post with a Jezail bullet lodged against his subclavian artery is made of sterner stuff. He continued his surreptitious exploration of the building. There was, however, nothing of interest save that one of the rooms was both locked and completely dark inside, despite the fact there should have been at least some light visible through the keyhole, as it was clearly situated beneath one of the skylights.

Moving carefully down the velvet-covered stairs to the second floor, Watson turned a corner to the main floor, but had to pull back quickly lest the thug – there was no better word, stationed at the central doors along the hallway saw him. After a moment, he risked another glance and saw that the man was indeed guarding what looked to be the only room on that side of the floor. Clearly, this was a sizeable chamber, therefore important. The walls, however, were both thick and impermeable to sound, so Watson knew he would have to do better if he were to penetrate the barriers surrounding whatever secrets were being kept here. *If only Holmes were here!* Doubtless the man would have a clever guise and a carefully forged invitation bearing, well, whatever it was that gained people admittance... that was it! *Admittance...*

'Sorry I'm late.'

The brutish guard turned his head to see a cheerful, clearly well-oiled doctor approaching at a lurch, his top-hat perched jauntily on his head and a bottle of what looked to be champagne tucked under one arm and using a walking-cane more as a balancing aid than anything else. The latecomer continued talking as he approached.

'Got talking to Chadswick and one thing...' Watson made the universal 'drinky-drinky' sign '...led to another. Quite a few others, in fact.'

'The meeting has started. No-one comes in once the meeting's started. Orders.' Unperturbed, Watson kept up the patter and the jollity.

'Oh, I know *that*... tschaw! rules, eh?. No, I thought you could help me finish off the old shampers...' he held the bottle out invitingly by the neck so the guard could see it was, indeed, Roederer, the 1864 vintage to boot, not that that would impress this dull fellow.

A massive forehead was by now wrinkled as the sluggish brain within ground slowly along.

'No drink. Orders.'

'Pity. Seems a waste.'

'Wot does?'

By way of answer, Watson brought the bottle crashing down on his head as hard as he could. By some happy miracle the bottle did not break, but the ruffian dropped like a stone, Watson quickly catching him as best as he could to reduce what sounded like the most appalling racket.

It took Watson, still aching from his fall, some five minutes to haul the insensate thug back to the stairs. There being no fortunately-placed rooms or nooks to place him, he simply left him out on the iron stairs he had used to scale the building in the first place. A light breeze brought with it the first hint of rain, which might revive the man, but Watson had no other choice. Sweating, bleeding from the wound he had concealed beneath his 'topper,' he stole back to the doors and bent to the keyhole in an attempt to discern something of the clandestine meeting therein. Amazingly, this schoolboy effort bore fruit, of a kind.

From his perilous listening-post, Watson could hear several voices, but one in particular stood out for the principal reason that it seemed to him to be familiar, as if he had heard it somewhere in the past. Authoritative, British, the man spoke in an upper class accent with the self-assurance that only the finest public schools can provide. Knowing Holmes would doubtless quiz him on it, he attempted to infer a trade from the speaker, to narrow down that commanding tone. *Army officer?* Perhaps so; the man spoke as if used to having his words obeyed, but was there a hint of genteel living? A touch of the gentleman's clubbery so prevalent in society London, perhaps? The words would be important, of course, so Watson did his best to memorise:

...events have moved even more swiftly than we had foreseen
...must take painful measures without reference to conscience or outmoded thinking
...vital our actions are timed to the hour, minute and second if we are to achieve our aim and liberate the peoples of Europe.

After this, another voice spoke, perhaps an older man, with an unmistakable Western European trace that hinted at Paris or perhaps Belgium;

Monsieur Chairman, still there is nothing regarding the Unenlightened One, always we are told there will be found such a man and never is he revealed to us...

A clamour of voices then, all seeking to be heard at once, falling away as if stilled by... a raised hand? Certainly, Watson noted the abrupt silence as significant; perhaps the original speaker was the *Monsieur Chairman,* but whatever, the assured Englishman replied to the Continental, in tones that brooked no further argument or dissent.

*The matter is in hand. We had hopes for a suitable candidate, but he had the bad grace to attempt to inform the police. His body was found hanging beneath a bridge, which is the fate awaiting **any** man that does not offer us his immediate, unyielding and boundless fidelity.*

It seemed the meeting was breaking up. The sounds of chairs being pushed back beneath a table and general conversation alerted Watson that he had, at best, just seconds to make good his escape. The missing guard would be instantly noticed and who knows what these people would do to an eavesdropper? Indeed, the door swung inwards suddenly and a shout went up at the sight of the injured Watson hobbling away down the hall. Taking the stairs as quickly as he could, he made it to the first landing and turning for the next set of stairs he saw a thin man aiming a pocket revolver at him. The shot probably wouldn't be heard by the guests downstairs, and Watson knew he must take a chance. Hurling himself forwards, he vaulted the banister rail and dropped down to the next set of stairs, landing badly with a sudden lance of searing, shocking pain up his leg. To the sounds of commotion and alarm from above, he rolled over the final rail to tumble all the way to the marble of the ground floor. Almost at once he was aware of a pair of polished shoes before him and with a weary fatality, he looked up.

It was the footman, the one who had coldly rebuffed him and threatened to 'stick him one.' Holding up a hand, Watson allowed the man to heave him roughly to his feet. The man looked past Watson to see the armed pursuer quickly pocket his pistol and point emphatically at the injured man. The Cockney knew what this meant and made to grab Watson, but paused in confusion at the invitation card that was being held up in front of his face. Watson's other fist crashed through the card, breaking the man's nose with a sickening sound of gristle crunching. Dropping the now bloodied card on the slumped figure, he stumbled desperately towards the double doors that held his only hope of salvation.

A shocked gasp arose as the doors banged open and a dishevelled and bloodied figure staggered into the dining hall. His head wound bleeding freely, the pain from what was almost certainly a broken ankle overwhelming him, John Watson's gallant croak of 'Is there a doctor in the house?' was followed by his collapsing onto a table. Immediately, the nearest physicians rushed to his aid. He was safe. For the time being.

It was not the first time Wiggins and his gang proved their mettle. Standing on the worn carpet before Doctor Watson, the urchin was unable to suppress a giggle at the sight of him in plaster cast. This earned him a frown of reprobation, but the leader of the Irregulars was unaffected by such things and grinned broadly until Watson held up a guinea as a reminder of his assignment, snatching it back from the grubby hand that darted out for it.

'Righto, Doctor. 'ere goes then; Devonshire Place. Nice posh house too lahdy-dah, you know; fancy carriage in the mews, snooty butler and all sorts.' This made sense; Doctor Lutz's sponsor, Addison-Hope did indeed reside in Devonshire Place, a mere ten minute's walk from Baker Street. Surely, however, such an eminent physician would have nothing of a plot like the one he had uncovered? He tossed the guinea and, with the dexterity of his calling, Wiggins had snatched and vanished the coin in an instant. Unfortunately, a ten-minute walk was ten minutes more than Watson could manage.

It was some three days later when Inspector Bradstreet called early on Watson at Baker Street. His broken ankle rested on a pile of cushions, Watson greeted his visitor with a cheery 'Hullo.' However, Bradstreet's face was grave.

'I arrived before the papers, Doctor. In fact *with* them.' This said, he tossed down the morning's dailies onto the arm of the settee next to Watson's chair. Something about the Inspector's manner left Watson in no doubt that he should consult the broadsheets and without delay. *The Express* was first to hand and he saw it straight away; *SHOCKING MURDER, POLICE SEEK GANG.* Reading further, Watson's heart sank into his stomach as he read of the savage murder of his friend Doctor Harold Price by beating and then, a knife to the back.

Harold had indeed been Watson's friend, so much so that he gave him his own invitation to the dinner that fateful night. With a thrill of horror, Watson realised that the group had mistaken Harold for him. They must have tracked him down through the address the card had been sent to. Without a word, Bradstreet handed the convalescent Watson *The Times* and, once again, he went through the hideous article. It seemed Mrs. Price had heard a loud noise and then a stifled cry and had hurried downstairs to find her husband dying in his study, the broken blade of a dagger jutting from his back. Looking up at the bleak features, Watson was lost for words. The Inspector broke the moment by seating himself unbidden on the sofa and producing his battered and much-travelled briar. Without speaking, Watson threw over a pouch of 'Ship's,' the disreputable tobacco he was wont to favour in difficult situations such as this. Nodding in recognition, Bradstreet took a fill and passed the pouch back before tamping and lighting his pipe.

Through a cloud of pipe smoke, Inspector Bradstreet regarded Watson thoughtfully. Clearly this fellow had suffered an accident of some sort and when he had enquired as to the nature, the Doctor had become evasive. Pointing the stem of his briar at Watson, Bradstreet asked him where exactly Sherlock Holmes was, raising a finger in admonition to add 'The Western Isles' would not do this time.

When Watson named the island in question, Bradstreet nodded to himself as if confirming a suspicion. Suddenly, a thought struck Watson. How had the Inspector known of his connexion to the unfortunate Doctor Price? It had been Mrs. Price; when the police were summoned to the Price residence, his widow had mentioned her husband's generosity towards Watson.

'So here I am again. And you with a broken leg.'

'Ankle. It's my ankle that's broken, Inspector.'

Drawing his chin into his neck, the detective raised his eyebrows and turned his head to scratch at his head.

'And where, exactly did you break your ankle, Doctor Watson?.'

'The subtalar joint, to be exact.'

This was too much and Bradstreet leaned forwards to jab the stem again.

110

'Don't joke with me, *Doctor,* a man's dead and you have both association with him and an injury, and I want to know this instant, *where,* *how* and *why* you got that injury... or we can continue this at the station.' Watson's cheeks had coloured with anger at this, but he retained control of his temper enough to reach for his own pipe and begin filling it.

'I broke it attempting to escape from a man with a revolver. Let me fill my pipe, Inspector and I shall tell you everything I know.'

Bradstreet listened as Watson spoke then, pausing occasionally to send a cloud of 'Ship's' into the fug of the room. When he had mentioned the secretive cabal and their sinister confabulation, the Inspector extracted his notebook from his pocket, read something written inside, then frowned and crossed something out with his pencil before adding some new note. Doubtless Holmes would have a method of discerning the nature of that inscription, but Watson was none the wiser and far too polite to ask. Finally, the notebook was replaced.

'That is all very – interesting, Doctor. However, I would be remiss in my duty if I did not demand an account of your own whereabouts last night...' Holding a finger up to stifle his host's indignant response, the Detective quickly added 'Of course this is just a formality and I shall not expect anything to come of it, you understand.'

Watson did indeed understand. He also understood these were, as his friend had often remarked 'deep waters' and he was out of his depth alone. It was time to send for Holmes.

Some three hours before the Inspector's visit, Jack Cooper had opened his eyes to the grim surroundings of his cell. The day started early in Newgate Prison; the warders came round unlocking the cells and the gruesome process known as 'slopping out' began. Next, it was time to gather mug and bowl to collect breakfast, an unappetising gruel with a chunk of bread and, as he was yet to be tried, a mug of tea. Eating it in the privacy of his cell was one of the few privileges afforded to Cooper in this dank hell. That day passed as slowly as any other, with only his time in the exercise yard and a brief, but welcome visit from Deakins. Against all the regulations, the sympathetic Warder lit a cigarette and handed it to the open-mouthed inmate. Taking it with a nod of thanks, Cooper took of his first tobacco since his incarceration began.

The Reverend Hemlock visited again, spending almost an hour with Cooper, again doing his best to rekindle the spark of memory regarding the hour before the skylighter had met with his accident. Again, however, little if any real progress was made. Sitting on his bunk, Jack Cooper simply could not recall the events of that night, however hard he tried and however skilfully the chaplain tried to coax the memories from their hiding place. Standing by the window of the tiny cell, the Reverend sighed.

'I am afraid I have bad news for you. It seems that your trial is to be held soon, Jack. You cannot hope for acquittal without any evidence against that of the police.'

'I'm sorry, Reverend, I wish I could say it was coming back, but all I get are flashes.'

'Flashes?' The chaplain had turned to face his captive parishioner.

'Well, I'm not sure as you'd call them even that, just what I see in my dreams more.'

'Oh?'

'Well, I see a man, like. Holding a pipe, trying to light it.'

'And?'

Apologetically, Cooper shrugged his shoulders.

'And it won't. Light, you see. It keeps blowing out, don't it?' The Reverend Hemlock shook his head, perplexed. This was impossible!

That night Jack Cooper's sleep was tormented by dreams. There was that damnable pipe again, as ever refusing to light. But there was more this time... something was blocking it, stopping the tobacco taking light... He dreamed of his Claire, waiting for him at the gate, banging on the famous Newgate knocker, but instead of reply, the gates swung inward to show her a gallows. *He wanted to cry out, to warn her not to watch,* but it was too late; the floor dropped away and there was only blackness.

The reply Watson received to his urgent missive was brief and to the point;

CANNOT RETURN BAKER STREET - IMPERATIVE YOU RETRIEVE DOCUMENT! - BRITISH EMPIRE ITSELF IMPERILLED - HOLMES.

From the newspapers that day Watson had learned of the trial of Jack Cooper for the murder of the Earl of Aldrington. It was set for that Thursday and there could be no doubt the man would indeed hang the very next morning. That left two days in which to retrieve a document that could be anywhere by now and with a broken ankle that caused him excruciating pain if he so much as moved it. Things were bleak, to say the least. There was only one person to whom he could turn in all London. And he was ringing the bell downstairs.

'How on Earth? How could you possibly know I was intending to consult with you?'
'Because, my Dear Watson, there is no-one else to whom you could possibly turn.'

Mycroft Holmes seated himself in his brother's chair, impervious to the indignation this intrusion provoked. 'There is also the fact that I read the telegram he sent you some twenty minutes before you received it.' This was an outrage! To read a man's private correspondence! Watson said as much, but knew of Mycroft Holmes' position with the government. Although unofficial, the man had access to state secrets far weightier than anything in a simple telegram.

Waiting for the doctor to regain his temper, Mycroft examined the ceiling for a long minute, as if it contained some interesting feature. Watson had done this himself recently and recognised the tactic. At length, the elder Holmes returned his inscrutable gaze to Watson.

'You are, of course aware that nothing I tell you may leave this room?' At Watson's abrupt nod, the elder Holmes continued. 'My brother is, as you may be aware on important business, though God alone knows what outweighs matters concerning the Empire. In point of fact, there are moves abroad to create a British Commonwealth out of the Empire itself, not that that directly affects us here. Now, do you have any inkling of the nature of this document my brother refers to?'

'None whatsoever, only that it is clearly of extreme importance and urgency. That suggests the conference regarding the European crisis.' This elicited a tight little smile from Mycroft, more a compression of the lips than a smile of pleasure.

'Indeed so. Doctor, your writing fails to give you credit; clearly Holmes chose well when he chose you as colleague.' This was base flattery of course and Watson snorted in derision.

'Well, that only confirms it. Very well, I shall take you fully into my confidence, Doctor. It is in part because you have refrained from adding many of the more pertinent details to your illustrations of Sherlock's adventures and therefore can be trusted with this momentous secret, partly because my choices are limited, to say the least.'

'Then tell me what it is about those papers that was worth two men's lives and my broken ankle.'

Watson listened with growing horror at the explication Mycroft Holmes gave. The document was a formal proposal of stratagem concerning the rising tide of international Socialism that was threatening to sweep European governments aside. The danger, it was recognised, was that by proposing methods to defeat the communists, the way would be open for other radicals to conquer whole swathes of the continent, unbalancing the current, fragile, order of things and endangering the British Empire itself. The proposal outlined in the stolen papers was itself revolutionary; a plan to acknowledge the Socialists and even allow then a limited access to government in European nations. The danger for the British government was obvious; should such a plan be made public, it could cause widespread panic in the populace and instability in the banking houses. Worse, it could cause the powerful nations of Germany, the Austro-Hungarian Empire and Russia to consider Britain an active threat to their own stability and result in a horrifying and devastating European war.

'The sad fact is, Doctor, that war is almost a certainty. These are enlightened times, but we have seen events in Europe moving on an unprecedented scale and all we can do, that is to say, all the government can do, is to try to prevent each incident from blossoming into a crisis.'

This was profoundly shocking to Watson's sensibilities, that the solidity and immutable constancy of Empire could be destroyed by something as abstract as ideas and ideals! Pulling himself together, he reached for his stick and began to get up, dismissing Mycroft's offer of help with a wave.

'It seems to me, then, that this Doctor Lutz is, in fact, a German agent?'

'Quite so. He is both a foremost member of his profession and an agent of the German Secret Service. We believe he was sent specifically to obtain this very document, with the purpose of sabotaging the impending conference in Paris.'

'Then he must be stopped.'

'Just so.'

'But surely...' Watson limped to the settee to steady himself there. 'Surely he has already sent the papers to his masters in Berlin, or wherever these people are.'

'The Wilhelmstrasse has received neither original nor copies. We have methods of determining this that I cannot divulge. There are, however... complications.'

'And what might they be?'

Turning, the corpulent mandarin let his gaze wander around the room before replying.

'The British government cannot do or say a single thing regarding the theft of the papers without revealing their existence and thus confirming their intent. Put another way, we are totally and utterly powerless.'

'Which is why you came.' This time the smile that came across Mycroft's face was genuine.

The effects of one-sixth of a grain of morphia, injected subcutaneously are swift to be felt, but even in his somnial state of bliss, Doctor Watson's ankle was still causing him some discomfort; hardly surprising as the hansom conveying him through the streets of London did so at a fast clip. He had a long journey across town and a short time to make it; he had promised the jarvey a good drink if he made it under the hour. The horse was lathered and its ears pricked as it surged east along the

Marylebone road. Settling back in his seat as best he could, Watson let his eyes close, drifting in and out of a fragile sleep.

Although the horse's hooves were flying, the driver cracked his whip to spur it on into the East End. At length, Watson was shaken from his stupor outside The George and Dragon public house on Hackney road. Consulting his watch to find the jarvey had excelled himself, he paid him and gave him instructions to wait. Taking the horse around to the stables for a well-earned drink and some feed, the driver touched his cap and took the reins to walk the sweating animal off.

There was a thrum of conversation that became a positive roar as Watson opened the door. Inside, he found he needed a moment to adjust to the dim lighting, the smoke making it hard to see across the place. The pub was fairly packed with patrons, even at five-thirty in the afternoon. Market porters vied with sooty boiler men and local toughs for the attentions of the barmaid, a suitably busty girl with a winning smile and short temper that seemed dependant on the amount of leering she had to endure. Thinking it best to buy a pint, Watson shouldered his way in, wincing in agony as a local bumped his ankle, now tightly strapped in place of the bulky and impracticable cast. Reaching the bar, Watson ordered a pint of India Pale and casually, as casually as you can when forced to shout, asked after Jim Dodds.
'Nah. Never 'eard of 'im, Squire. Try the Star and Garter, Roman Road.' Watson sighed, but she was already serving another customer, a girl of perhaps ten darting past him and dashing out from the public bar into the snug.

Finding himself a seat wasn't easy, but a space at the end of a bench became available and Watson sank into it, grateful to be able to reduce the pressure on his damaged ankle. Next to him, a loud type was busy extolling the virtues of some liniment or other and all around him were busily enjoying their free time in a noisy, good-humoured manner. The exception being the two men who suddenly appeared to either side of Watson. One, a heavily scarred and dangerous-looking man of about fifty reached across to yank the liniment advocate clear from his seat, moving towards his prey at which the mood of the place changed dramatically.

'Not in 'ere you don't! You gonna do 'im, do it somewhere else.' Somehow the barmaid's words provided scant comfort. Preparing to hurl his pint at the nearest adversary, Watson's attention was caught by the entrance of a newcomer from the direction of the snug, the small girl tugging at his sleeve and pointing with her head in the direction of the unfolding ruckus.

Wiry, perhaps only forty, the man stood, thumbs in belt and a broad smile across his crafty face.

'Thanks boys, this is a pal.' At his words, the two thugs looked at each other uncertainly, suddenly unsure of themselves. 'Go on, the pair of yer; go see Mary, there's gatta for you both, on me.' Without taking his eyes off Watson, the grinning man raised a hand and pointed at the pair, who went gratefully to the bar for the beers that the barmaid hurried to pour for them. Clearly, the man carried weight here. Watson decided to proceed with more caution. Helping the linament man back to his seat with the gentleness only the truly powerful or meek display, the man cocked his head to Watson.

'Come out to the office, feller; we can talk better there.'

Jim Dodds, for indeed it was he, sat in his customary space in the snug, one of only five or so people there. It seemed however busy the place, the snug was reserved for a higher – or lower, class of patron. Risking a handshake, Watson sipped the surprisingly good ale and wiped his mouth.

'I was told I would find you here.'

'Ah. Were you, now? Let's see; you're a bit of a toff, no offence mind. Nothing too lahdy-da, so that puts you in a profession, I'd say...'

'Doctor.'

'Ah. *Doctor...* and *whom* might I ask, sent you, Doctor?' Leaning forward, his voice low, Watson told him. At the name of Mycroft Holmes, Dodds' features assumed a serious, sharper aspect.

'Best keep that between ourselves, Doctor. I'm a well-respected man and have to keep my, *associations* discrete.' Such talk from a rough-looking Cockney was unexpected, Watson making a mental note of the man's intelligence of speech.

'So what's the problem?.' Over the rest of his pint, Watson told him. Over several more, the two formed a hasty plan.

Dodds himself had been in Newgate twice, for burglary and robbery, but his area of expertise was locks. Beginning life as an orphan, he was found asleep in a smithy and became a blacksmith's apprentice, taking his name from the Smith, a kindly man long since passed. One day the two were called out to fix a jammed lock on a gate and, to his surprise as much as anyone's, Jim had opened it at the first attempt. From there, any time a lock needed work, old Dodds would send Jim out and it would be fixed. After the old man died, Jim tried to keep the business going, but a cruel and ruthless landlord foreclosed and the smithy was gone. On his own once more, the young Dodds took the first set of picks and keys he had forged and went out into the world, earning a living by thievery and craft. It was said there wasn't a single lock in the whole of London that hadn't felt the touch of Jim Dodds' picks. These, he now made at home in a small workshop. He made sets for the master criminals of Europe, had even made a set for Sherlock Holmes. No safe, either was safe from Dodd's touch, including a model Alfred Hobbs, the famed American safe-breaker had failed to open. Although he hadn't been 'up West' awhile, at the mention of Mycroft Holmes he had immediately agreed to help.

Devonshire Place was a wide, airy place by London standards, Number Two, Devonshire Place was a large building set within the Georgian terrace. The early-evening crowd was mainly hurrying home at this hour; the odd carriage clipping its way along the street. To anyone passing, the crippled hawker selling his *Evening News* with his medal proudly displayed on his chest was just that; a war veteran with one leg up on a footstool. From Watson's lowered perspective, the street was laid bare before him and he was able to see everything without being observed. No-one passing would have suspected that he had merely bought his stock from other vendors a half hour previously and was busily reselling them. In this fashion, he saw the patrolling constables and noted the time it took them to pass by and how often, the evening routine of the footmen and carriage drivers as they brought or took their charges from the mews behind and the comings and goings of London society. More than once, he had to cover his face with a paper to avoid recognition; the beard he had borrowed from Holmes' disguise bag was not a guarantee of anonymity to colleagues. The street was home to many eminent physicians and surgeons of his acquaint, plus the odd quack.

Finally, he saw it; Addison-Hope's carriage was coming around the corner to wait outside number Two. Presently, the door opened and Watson observed a distinguished lady and a younger woman leaving the house, followed by an abrupt Sir. Trelawney, who paused for a harsh exchange with a servant before joining his companions in the carriage. With a few hours left, Watson settled back to watch, observe… and try to recoup his losses as London's newest newspaper-seller.

Jim Dodds had arrived as planned at ten-thirty, taken one look at the front door, let out a soft chuckle and opened it in somewhat under ten seconds with a pick he produced from the lining of his flat cap. From there, he led the way inside, the false-bearded Watson limping along on his stick behind, careful to make as little noise as possible. Once, a manservant walked right past the intruders, straight into the parlour. By some stroke of good fortune the man had not seen them and Watson was able to breathe again. Dodds quickly identified the study and opened the door, which had been locked, before waving his hobbling accomplice inside. Placing his mouth up to Watson's ear, Dodds spoke in a whisper.

'Lean against the door, *hard,* I'll try to find the safe.'

No cracksman, however talented, is of use without a safe and, try as he might, Dodds found none in the study. The room was in darkness until he lit his bullseye, a 'present from a copper' as he told Watson. By the light of the lamp, they could see the study was panelled, with portraits of medical men lining the walls and a bust of Hippocrates on one of the two large bookcases that ranged along two walls. There was a mahogany desk and a green leather chair, a matching sofa but no sign anywhere of a safe.

Undeterred, Dodds took to prying and pushing at the books, moving pictures and the like in an attempt to find a hidden safe. After ten minutes or so, he perched himself on the corner of the desk and let out a long sigh. Watson waved him over to where he stood at the door.

'Well? What now?' He was not heartened to see Dodd's

shrug of reply.

'What about the desk?.'

'If these papers are important, Doctor, he won't have 'em in a poxy desk, now will he?' Watson had not told Dodds the nature of the document, only that it was essential to retrieve it. The East-Ender knew better to ask; where Mycroft Holmes was concerned, questions could lead to trouble. Still, he went to it, opening the main drawer, which was unlocked, to find the usual impedimenta of a gentleman. The drawers to each side, however, were all locked and, one by one he was busy opening these when Watson let out a start. The front door! All at once, there came the sound of busy feet, excited laughter and gaiety. Addison-Hope and his party had returned.

While Dodds frantically re-locked the drawers, Watson risked a peek, inching the door open to see there was no way out. The voice of Sir. Trelawney came booming down the hallway, stating his intention to smoke before retiring. He was striding towards his study. They were trapped.

It has often been said that of the Holmes brothers, Mycroft was by far the smarter. This, if it needed to be, was proved yet again by what happened next. A loud banging at the door was followed by a commotion; a drunken Irishman, from the sounds of it, mistaking the house for his lodgings. Nor was he alone; a few passers by, seeing the unfolding fracas, had stopped to gawp and interject with their own advice. Despite his predicament, Watson could not resist it, taking a look down the hallway as one particularly genteel old fellow began
admonishing the drunken lout, receiving a swift backhander across the face for his trouble. In an instant, a brawl had developed on the doorstep, a manservant rushing to his master for advice. Addison-Hope wasted no time in giving it, ordering the servant to send for the police at once.

'Nice show. Shall we be on our way, Doctor?' The sound

of Dodds' voice broke Watson from his surreptitious observation. He had a pick in his mouth and a look of mischief in his eye that somehow did little to quell the unease in Watson's stomach.

When the coast was clear, Dodds, bold as brass, opened the study door and shoved his colleague in crime out into the hallway. In a trice, he had locked the door and, placing an arm under Watson's, marched *towards* the stairs. When the mystified Doctor attempted to wrench himself clear, Dodd's grip merely intensified and he increased the pace, forcing the limping to become a hopping.

'I say! You there! Stop at once!' The unmistakable voice of Sir. Trelawney Addison-Hope cut above the brouhaha and there could be no doubting as to whom it was addressed. Instead of halting, however, the cracksman kept going, propelling his charge along towards the stairs and depositing him on them, hissing at him to *'Sit and keep schtum.'* Turning to face the baffled surgeon, Dodds took off his cap in a gesture of deference.

'It's his ankle, sir. Broke it, see? Got the nurse to strap it for 'im, but when that lot started mafficking, my pal 'ere, 'e goes in. Says 'e won't stand for it, not a decent house like this, sir. Veteran, see? Afghanistan. Any chance you could send for a Doctor, like?' Gazing down at the diminutive Cockney, Sir. Trelawney's brow was furrowed in both annoyance and confusion. Could these scruffs have tried to defend his household? It seemed unlikely, yet as a surgeon he could not leave an injured man untended. Gruffly, he waved a hand at Watson's ankle, addressing Dodds directly.

'Bring him into my study. I happen to be a doctor.' Unlocking his study, the surgeon turned to his manservant, who was hovering nearby.

'Rawlings, send round for my carriage, would you? I shall

attend to this fellow myself, it shouldn't take more than ten minutes. Oh, and a glass of water, please.'

Hardly able to believe Dodd's cheek, Watson let himself be helped back into the study he had been intent on burgling so recently. Easing himself onto the sofa, he put his injured ankle up for examination. Sir. Trelawney took one look at the spotless and professionally applied bandages and raised an eyebrow.
'Neatly done. It doesn't seem that I can improve on this. I can give you something for the pain, however.' Before Watson could object, the surgeon had gone across to a ship's medical cabinet and taken out a small bottle of pills. Rawlings arrived with a glass of water and Watson took it, with a rough show of thanks that he hoped fitted with Dodd's characterisation of them as street louts. Handing him the bottle, Addison-Hope advised him to take two immediately and thereafter every time he felt pain and to have the ankle examined in a week's time.

It had been a disaster. By the time Watson pulled himself up the stairs to 221b he was exhausted and empty-handed. Sir. Trelawney had, as promised, provided a carriage home and, loathe to reveal his true address, Watson had let Dodds give his own address, a seedy room above a pub. Finding a cab in Spitalfields at one in the morning was no easy task and by the time his head had hit his pillow, it was nearly dawn. Falling into a deep, but troubled sleep, Watson was assailed by dreams of far-off plains and mountains, of walnut-skinned men with prominent noses and muskets, of fire and blood. He woke to sweat-soaked sheets and a wave of agony pulsating from his ankle. Damn Holmes! Where *was* the man?.

The massive pipe loomed before him – desperate now, he

reached into the bowl of the pipe. Suddenly, he overbalanced, falling into the gaping maw – falling-falling...

That Wednesday saw a pale sun washing across the grey rooftops of London. At the same moment Jack Cooper was roused from a troubled sleep, his Claire was doing the laundry for a well-to-do family, her long day starting early. Since Jack had been arrested, she had had to take in extra to make ends meet, but try as she might she could make no sense of it. For every week since his accident, a dirty little scruff had pitched up, banged on the door and without a word of explanation, thrust a guinea into her hand, touched his cap in a cheeky salute and then ran off. A guinea! It was more than she could hope to see in a week even if she worked round the clock!. Claire Cooper was a woman of unshakeable morality, brought up to believe never to steal, a belief that had brought her and Jack to the brink of separation more than once in their early days together. The money was not hers, not earned and so the guinea joined the others behind the loose brick in the yard.

Sunlight now streaming in across the breakfast table, Watson sat with his tea and a steaming bowl of Mrs. Hudson's porridge. A family cure-all, she had advised him. The papers were full of the European situation; things looked grim. With a sigh, Watson set aside *The Times* and took a tentative spoonful of the porridge. It was excellent – the native meal of the Scots proved a remarkable morale-booster and nobody makes it like that fiery Celtic race; stirred clockwise with a good pinch of salt. The landlady had told her tenant that the Hudsons had their own recipe, with a secret ingredient that tasted suspiciously like brandy. By the time he had finished his repast, Watson found the pain from his ankle was remarkably duller.

Deakins showed the Reverend Hemlock into Jack Cooper's cell and went to complete his rounds; he made a point of checking all the cells on his landing every half hour. The Reverend had brought ominous news; Cooper's trial the next day was to be heard by Justice Hodge, a notoriously keen advocate of the death penalty. There were, it seemed no grounds for hope, no base upon which to build an appeal. If he could not recall events, perhaps the Reverend could try? Bleakly, Jack nodded and listened as the chaplain spoke.

'The accounts, from what I read in the press, all seem to centre on the murder of the Earl. It seems clear that you entered his property with a view to larceny... please, my dear fellow, pray allow me to continue.' Subdued, Cooper forced himself to relax and give an encouraging nod, despite the flush of anger the Reverend's words had provoked.

'You may have acted in self defence... perhaps the Earl disturbed you and attacked you?.'

'I don't remember any of it, Reverend.'

'Not even what you were there to take? You must have been in the Earl's study. Not much silver to be had there methinks, so money or papers, perhaps?'

Bemused, the Cockney scratched his head and clapped his hands to his knees in a gesture of frustration.

'Can't remember papers; they say I had no money on me when they found me there, sir, so it looks as if old Hodge will have another one for his rope. Suddenly, the chaplain stood and bent over his charge to grab him by the lapels.

'Cooper if you don't remember you'll hang!. Don't you see? There was something in that study. You took it. You *have* to remember!'

'What's all this then? Everything all right Reverend?' Reverend Hemlock released his grip to see the gentle-natured

Deakins in the doorway.

'I – I'm, yes, yes – everything is indeed fine, thank you.'

The warder saw the chaplain out with a touch to his cap and produced a flask from his hip pocket.

'Just a nip. Keeps the chill out, you understand.' And then Deakins took a long pull at the flask before wiping his mouth and offering it to Cooper.

The Old Bailey was, in those far off days rather a different creature to the sombre and stately edifice that both reassures and intimidates the citizenry of today. The day of Jack Cooper's trial dawned overcast and rather muggy, the ever present threat of rain in the pale hazy air. Due to the trial of the notorious blackmailer, Lemay, courtroom number one was unavailable, the rather less imposing courtroom three being set aside for Cooper's trial. In this cramped chamber were crammed the lawyers for both defence and prosecution, the jury and a small crowd composed of sightseers, well wishers and, barely visible amongst these was Claire Cooper, a slight, pale woman with, unsurprisingly a look of anguish and distress on her face. Suddenly, a murmur arose from the packed room as Jack Cooper was led up into the dock, flanked by two burly warders. At some unseen signal, a clerk called out:

'All rise.'

Hurriedly, Mr. Justice Hodge swept into the courtroom and took his seat. A portly man, short of temper and ruddy of face, he had the unmistakable cauliflower nose of the habitual drunkard and a decidedly ominous mien. It was almost as if he felt the trial an unnecessary impediment to a hanging. At his impatient signalling of a flick of the hand, the clerk stood, cleared his throat and read the charges against Cooper. As well as wilful murder, he was accused of burglary and theft. Once seated, the clerk nodded to the lawyer for the prosecution, a Mister James Garron, to begin his case. As there was no lawyer for the defence, it was not expected to be a problematic one. As so often, however, fate is capricious and fortune fickle...

'Jack Alfred Cooper, it is alleged that on the night of Tuesday March the 13th of this year, you did enter, with criminal intent, the dwelling of the Right Honourable Carlton Trevithick, Earl of Aldrington. There, you did wilfully murder His Lordship and stole items unknown from him.' At this, Claire Cooper broke down and had to be supported by friends among the spectators. Mr. Garron then called as a main witness a servant by the name of Broom, who stated he had brought his master a cup of cocoa as was his habit before retiring. He had found the body and raised the household, apart from the laundry maids who had been hard at work even at that late hour. He had, he said heard a scuffle and a shout of 'Murder!' He then saw Cooper's prostrate body outside in the grounds. At this, Jack Cooper was seen to shake his head, as if to clear it. Clearly puzzled, he would have spoken, but for the strong arm which one of the warders had thrown across his chest.

The servant Broom dismissed, the next witness called was a sergeant of police who stated he had been among the first officers on the scene. This man gave it that Cooper had been apprehended attempting to flee the scene and was quickly dismissed. Several more servants and a constable followed before the prosecution rested its case. Somewhat distracted, Mr. Justice Hodge seemed not to notice the absence of any developments and was only roused from his torpor by a discreet cough from the clerk. Looking across at Cooper, the judge asked if he had anything to say in his defence. Which is when events took a turn for the unexpected.

'Milord, I shall be conducting the defence, if it pleases the court.' Heads turned and Hodge's florid features jerked up as if he were a marionette on strings. His beady eyes struggled to focus through the haze afforded by this morning's first bottle of port, finally settling on the sombre, austere and rather overweight form of the man now standing in front of the defence bench.

'And who, Sir, might you be, eh?.'

'My name is Mycroft Holmes. Forgive my lack of punctuality, but I have been at the Cabinet Office and only just had leave to depart.'

'And what, pray, gives you the gall, the impudence even to enter my court and assume the defence of the indefensible?'

'This.' With that simple reply, Holmes held out the leather tube he had been holding behind his back, to the side, eyes fixed on the rotund figure seated beneath the royal coat of arms. At length, a junior clerk took this from his hand and with an air of increased nervousness, began to fumble with the straps binding it. A parchment was withdrawn, bearing a wax seal. At a nod from the clerk of the court, the younger man broke this and unfurled the scroll. After a moment's reading, however, he began to stammer out incomprehensibly and, irritably, the chief clerk went across and took it for himself.

A minute passed, with the only sound a buzz of excited conversation from the gallery. By now himself ashen-faced and sweating noticeably, the clerk approached the bench.

'Milord...' he began, then tried again. 'Milord, this is an arrest warrant. Signed by the Home Secretary and the Lord Chief Justice... Milord... it's – it's...'

'Oh damnation man! Spit it out!, what's the matter with you?' Mutely, the clerk handed the warrant to Justice Hodge. A moment or so later, Hodge's face assumed a pallor that suggested the vapours or a fit of apoplexy. Struggling to stand, he was forced to lean on the armrest of his chair as he fought for breath. As one the crowd gasped and the clerk of the court, now recovered of his powers to act, summoned his subordinate with the instructions to fetch one of the warders down from the dock and to seek a constable without delay.

A POSTSCRIPT BY JOHN WATSON, M.D.

By now, of course, the facts have all been set out in the press. You can hardly fail to have read of the arrest and subsequent trial of the key conspirators in the matter; Sir. Trelawney Addison-Hope was, of course, acquitted of all involvement in the affair on the evidence supplied by Sherlock Holmes to his brother Mycroft. That Addison-Hope had, however inadvertently, provided lodgings for the German spy Lutz was a reflection on the man's generosity of spirit and not, as some had thought any dubious motive on his part. Lutz himself, of course was deported and later killed in the Great War in the fighting at Ypres. As for the shadowy organisation that I stumbled across that far distant night, there remains no trace. That is not, to say however that there were no repercussions. Certainly, Mr. Justice Hodge did not face trial for his part in the conspiracy; his death from a stroke has been well-documented elsewhere. It seems he was to have removed the last link between the malefactor, the originator of the plot to steal the government papers and the man who had tried and so nearly succeeded to recover them.

Who, then, this mysterious malefactor? This kingpin of the group that set itself against the British Empire and for the German? None, but The Right Honourable Carlton Trevithick, Earl of Aldrington himself. Far from being a victim of robbery and murder, it was the Earl who had planned to offer the papers for a price, to the highest bidder. Through the auspices of the still nameless collaborators, Lutz had agreed to buy the documents for a veritable king's ransom. That he was sold a set of forgeries is only now to be revealed and only then at the express stated request of the Late Sir. Mycroft Holmes, KG, Companion of the French Legion of Honour, who obtained my oath that I would not reveal or publish any details of the case until twenty years or more had passed. This oath I have upheld and now discharge myself from.

Forgeries? Just so! They were exchanged for the original on the night of the Earl's death. Although he could no longer recall it, Jack Cooper had indeed been retained by Sherlock Holmes to break in to the Earl's house and exchange the forgeries for the original papers which he kept in a small safe, hidden in the floor beneath his desk. It was while he was replacing the rug covering the safe that Cooper was disturbed by the Earl. Enraged and convinced he was about to be robbed of his stolen papers, the Earl attacked the intruder with a poker. Forced to defend himself, Cooper, who had already sustained terrible damage to his head from the blows raining down upon it, was left in a state of semi-consciousness upon the floor. Panicked, the Earl began taking papers from his desk and throwing them into the fire. Who knew whom had sent this burglar? Perhaps the authorities! Desperately, he began to destroy the traces of his own involvement with the sinister group, including papers guaranteeing him substantial sums and estates in Saxony if he betrayed Her Majesty's government who had entrusted him with the vital papers.

Reaching up a hand to pull himself up onto the desk, the badly wounded Cooper had turned to see the poker flashing towards him. He grabbed the first thing to hand; this turned out to be an ornamental paper-knife. On seeing his victim armed, the

Earl panicked and turned to the wall to take down one of the swords hanging there. Cooper's blow was not immediately fatal, the Earl staggering away and falling, expiring face down in the fire of his own deceit. Servants had, however, heard the commotion and with no other way out, Cooper had opened a window and climbed the outside wall, scaling it in a matter of seconds. Once there, he had cast about for a place to hide the government documents, did so, but then slipped on a mossy slate and fell hard, being found near to death some moments later.

Of course, the conference on the European Problem was a triumph for Her Majesty's government. It was said that the advantages afforded to Great Britain by the retention of the crucial papers enabled the government to ensure peace on the continent for some fourteen long years afterwards. How then, was Sherlock Holmes able to recover them? We may never be certain, for, alas Holmes died last summer. As his friend and scribe, however, I have my own theory. As I write, I have often looked over at the battered old prison Warder's cap I found amongst his belongings after his death and can only conclude that it was in fact he, in the guise of the friendly Warder Deakins who eavesdropped on the other fraudulent personage as he visited the hapless Cooper in Newgate. Of course, the Reverend Hemlock was none other than Doctor Lutz, hoping to the last to persuade Cooper to reveal the whereabouts of the papers, yet too afraid of retribution from his masters in the Wilhemstrasse to report the switch for the forgeries which set back the Kaiser's cause so badly.

Holmes never did reveal the method by which he discovered the hidden documents. They were, of course lowered down a drainpipe and secured there by the rope which Cooper had first used to scale the house, (he had indeed entered by a skylight as was his habit) which explains the lack of any climbing tools found at the scene. It is my belief that in the guise of sympathetic Warder, Holmes overheard Cooper's recollection of his dreams and correctly ascertained the significance of the constant pipe imagery; thus smoking pipe became *drain* pipe.

And what became of Jack Cooper, the housebreaker? He was pardoned, in secret of course and to this day lives on a farm in Norfolk with his beloved Claire and, I am delighted to report, their two grown sons. That the farm was originally part of the estate of the Earl of Aldrington, dissolved after his treachery was uncovered cannot have failed to delight him in his happy and peaceful retirement.

The Unlikely Detective

I have had some strange experiences in my time, but none stranger than those that began the day in September 1990 when, at a car boot sale in Findon in the county of West Sussex I came across a large leather wallet stuffed with old papers. A quick look through showed me a Masonic parchment and some cards from old lodge dinners. Being a keen collector of ephemera, this appealed and, as he was calling it a day, the old man selling the wallet was happy to take a fiver. Off-handedly, I enquired as to the origin of the contents and was told he did house clearances – he was a retired 'knocker' as the trade calls it, going from house to house offering to take unwanted items. He'd taken a box full of old things, a 'proper gentleman's box' in his parlance, from the attic of a house near Arundel, not that many miles to the West. The place was being demolished, to make way for some banker's idea of Shangri-La. I asked if he knew anything about the occupants, but they were long gone. All that was left was a wooden sign, which he had taken from a pile of bricks that had once been a gatepost. It was for sale, too, he assured me, but I'd spent my twenty quid that day and declined; though it was clearly an antique the sign itself seemed a bit shabby, with a home-made quality about it. It read simply *'Sinopia.'*

It was only two days later that I found it. I'd thrown the wallet down on the coffee table with the vague idea of going through it properly – my late father was a Mason and I thought I might learn a bit more about the Order from the contents. Sitting down with a coffee, I put the telly on in the background and turned out the contents. As well as the parchment and the cards there was a small book of rituals, old hat really as I had my dad's book and they were nearly identical. The book was for instructing brothers in the various degrees and nothing sensational. The parchment was similarly uninspiring, although the date given was interesting; the *Anno Lucis* or Year of Enlightenment was 5877, which meant 1877 by the Gregorian calendar. Initially, the name of the brother being raised to his third degree meant nothing; *Mycroftium Holmes* was the Latinised Masonic name given, but the plain English was also there on the faded and stained heavy paper; *Mycroft Holmes*.

It took a moment for the significance to sink in; I had read the Sherlock Holmes stories as a boy, of course… but surely this was coincidence? After all, neither Holmes nor his equally eccentric brother had ever existed. Had they? I was about to put the papers away when, on impulse I picked up the wallet. The leather was old, untreated and cracked and already the leather thong that had bound it was lost and it needed a good soak in dubbin to bring it back from the brink. I was always tinkering with things and restoring old objects in my spare time, so this wasn't unusual, but for some reason I put a finger in the wallet and immediately felt paper. Looking inside, I saw an envelope was stuck there, held, it turned out by the wax seal which had presumably been impressed and inserted whilst the wax was still warm.

Digging the envelope out all but destroyed the seal, leaving only the fragment of a coat of arms and a motto; a wreath on a field of *barré*. (Perhaps I should point out I was given a book on heraldry for my twelfth birthday). There was even a motto, which I could just make out; *Justum et tenacem propositi*. I'd been to a prep school as a boy, and my time at Sompting Abbotts hadn't been entirely wasted – the Latin translated to 'Just and firm of purpose.' Opening the envelope carefully with a butter knife I pulled out the paper inside and a small, round key fell onto the carpet. Retrieving it, I found it was an unusual type, one I'd not seen before. I set it aside and read the letter. I've included a photocopy of the original on the following page, so you can judge for yourself and see just what I became involved in;

From the desk of Sir. Mycroft Holmes K.G. O.B.E. Chev L.H.

Dearest Brother,

If you are reading these words please accept my felicitation and sincere apology for what passed between us during the latter stages of the recent European conflict. I have no exculpation for my actions save that England was at peril. If it were possible to ameliorate the anguish you will have felt, I would say that the loss of your friend and our agent Janssen was unavoidable given the circumstances. He died so that Sweden may be free and I can say no more.

Now to business, as it were. By now you will have learned of my own passing from the usual sources - I trust Messrs. Goodman, Cowle and Sweet have read the will and my appalling cousins will have dutifully wept by my grave whilst plotting to steal the other's share of the lolly. It follows, then that you are cognizant of the fact the whole lot went to the Society for the Furtherance of Esperanto. Of course, I had only a passing fancy for the language, but if it served to piss on their chips it was money well spent. However, I have rambled on, Brother mine. Forgive me I beg of you. I never was much for small talk until now and not up to much as a brother. Allow me, belatedly, to supply a deficiency.

The key is, of course, for a deposit-box. Against all the Service regulations drummed into me, I shall name the bank. It is, naturally Courtts. All will be explained when you open it, but, Dear Sherlock, I must urge you to take all those precautions you were so famous for in those funny little stories; the contents of the box will settle affairs between us as surely as they will be of interest to the potentates of a dozen countries, some more hostile than other. Make no mistake on the matter, that nondescript key holds the answer to many questions. Wield it as carefully as if it were the Sword of Damocles.

I really was your superior in many things, but for with-holding that which was rightfully yours, I am truly derogate. My last act towards you is of Cephaleptic nature and the scales, I hope have found balance at last.

I remain, in death as life, your Brother.

Mycroft Holmes

This was definitely odd, like something from a novel even. Folding the letter, I put it and the key back in the envelope and thought no more of it. It was only much later, in February of 1991 when I was going up to London that I remembered the envelope. I'd been saving for a camcorder, always wanted one and finally had the cash, so long as I didn't mind a 'grey import' as they were called. The shops along the Edgeware and Tottenham Court roads were famous for cheap electronics and I had £800 burning a hole in my pocket, all in fifties and twenties.

February that year was freezing. As I was getting my coat, hat and gloves I remembered how cold the trains were that time of year and quickly filled my dad's old hip flask with brandy, taking a quick nip for the journey, as it were. On an impulse, I grabbed my old Fuji camera from the drawer – I didn't get up to 'the smoke' often and thought I could take a couple of snaps. As I opened the drawer, my eye fell on the leather pouch resting on the kitchen worktop and I thought back to the letter. Finding it amongst the usual bills and clutter in another drawer, I opened it and pocketed the key. Maybe this Courtts Bank was still in business – I could always ask when I was up there.

The train rattled and creaked from Worthing station and I settled in for a long ride with a much-thumbed copy of *Tinker, Tailor, Soldier, Spy* and the odd nip from my flask. From the corner of one eye I saw West Sussex slipping away as I tried to concentrate on my book. One by one they fell away beside me; East Worthing and Lancing stations, Shoreham all in their turn and then the funny little places went by; Fishersgate and Aldrington, places that seemed in my mind to exist only as train platforms. (To this day I have found none of these; every time I think I have, it turns out I'm somewhere else entirely) Jim Prideaux was holding his car club rally as we stopped at Hove,

138

but by the time we'd made Three Bridges there were 'three of them and Alleline' and a carpet of snow to either side of the tracks. By the time the train shook-shuddered to a halt at Victoria's platform two, Peter Guillam was stealing files for George Smiley and I was seriously in need of stretching my legs. I shoved and barged through the ticket check at the concourse with the rest of the herd and fought my way through to find a cab. At once, the taste of London was between my teeth; that film of leaded grit that you only remember too late once you arrive after a break from the city.

On a whim I decided to try the bank mentioned in the letter. This was before the age of the Internet, remember, but I did the obvious and took a taxi. Courtts Bank turned out to be an anonymous slab of sandstone tucked away in a little side street just around the corner from Trafalgar Square. You wouldn't have known it was there unless you'd happened upon it. Even my cabbie had frowned at the name, but luckily he'd had a fare there once before and had that encyclopaedic memory essential to a London hackney cab driver. A modest brass plaque evinced this to be simply 'Courrts'. Inside the revolving door I found myself in a time-warp of a place; all mahogany panelling and portraits of Worthies, probably the founding members. The whole place reeked of Empire, of discreet wealth and power and it took me a while to compose myself enough to approach the girl at the desk. If her name had been Moneypenny I wouldn't have been surprised, but a badge showed she was *'Annabelle Hawthorne, Clientele Adviser.'* Although she was stunningly pretty, her look said she was thinking of thumbing an alarm button, but I was clientele and I needed advising, so I smiled and asked if I could see my deposit box.

His name was Lambton, but he had to tell me that himself as he didn't wear a badge. Smartly turned out, he could have stepped from the pages of one of those posh magazines you find in doctors' surgeries. Expressionless, he listened as I told him I'd 'inherited' a key and wanted to use it. It was clear I wasn't going to be seeing any deposit boxes, the air was becoming distinctly cold as it became evident I wasn't a 'genuine' customer. And then I produced the key.

The change couldn't have been more pronounced had he offered me his wife for the night and to use his toothbrush afterwards. I found myself being ushered down a plushly carpeted hallway and into an elevator. Here, the Olde Worlde charm gave way to the electronic swipe card and down we went. The basement vault was exactly like the ones you see in the films, you know; the ones where the amnesiac hero finds he owns a box full of passports, money and a gun. A security guard stood ready to admit us through a heavily barred gate and Lambton showed me through to a surprisingly narrow room, the walls of which were top to bottom with metal boxes. Exciting wasn't the word – I nearly started biting my nails. The best was still to come though, as we went through the room to a curtained off area, which waited down a set of curved steps. This, my guide explained, was the original vault. Here, the fortunes and secrets of kings, dukes and tycoons had quietly rested. At least, that was the impression; Mr. Lambton stayed silent from the moment we entered this hallowed chamber, a plain and solid looking door set into the wall below the steps behind us.

Whereas the upper vault was all polished stainless, these boxes were of a dull hue, iron perhaps. Every other box bore an embellished 'C.' Taking my key out, I waited to be told which box was 'mine', but Lambton did the oddest thing, going to one of the 'C's at the far end, which he unlocked with a key on a chain he produced from under his jacket. From this, he took a cylinder of metal and held out his hand, rather like a waiter hoping for a tip. Foolishly, I took an age to realise he wanted my key, handing it over sheepishly. He inserted it into the mysterious cylinder, without turning it. At once, a loud **snick** sounded and another key popped out of the other end. Seeing my mystification, he half smiled, half sneered as he told me it was a 'safety measure.' Only when the box key was returned to the cylinder could I recover mine.

Clearly Lambton thought I was 'below the salt.' For a moment, I had visions of wiping the arrogance off the man's face with some exotic and priceless jewel from my box, but then reality kicked in and I asked 'What next?' By way of reply, he stepped backwards to jauntily tap the box next to the one the cylinder lived in.

'You open your box, sir. I shall wait upstairs at your disposal. There is a privacy room behind that door. When you have finished, simply lock the box and I shall retrieve your key for you.'

Great… I felt more of an idiot than ever… I was in another world, it seemed.

My box proved reluctant to budge. At first I thought I hadn't opened it correctly, but the thought of Lambton's smug mug gave me the courage to give the key a savage twist, at which the box sprang out an inch or two from its recess. Pulling it out, I had the feeling of being the first to do so for many years. Taking it to the privacy room seemed a bit over the top, but when in Rome…

The room itself was another surprise. Far from being a pokey affair, it was more like the sitting room in a gentleman's club, leather chairs and a green baize table, even a few more worthies on the walls, sconce lights around the room. A shaded desk lamp sat on the table, so I did what anyone would do and switched it on. The bulb blew instantly. Obviously, this wasn't a room anyone used much, though it looked as if someone came in to dust every week. Still, there was enough light from the sconces and I was getting impatient to see my new found and hardly-earned wealth. The villa in France, the Aston Martin and the super mega yacht with the helipad and the frolicking lovelies in the jacuzzi were in my reach as I opened the lid… to find an old book and a velvet bag. Going for the bag first, I emptied it into my palm, getting not the Akbar Shah or, for that matter, *any* diamond, but a rather battered signet ring.

Setting the find aside, I opened the book, half the pages falling out as I did so. It wasn't even much of a book as books go; a diary perhaps, leather bound and embossed, the sort of thing you could probably have bought at any posh stationers in the old days. I could see it was handwritten, so went to the first page, finding an inscription below the same crest I'd seen on the letter.

If found this book is
to be returned
to the Foreign Office
of the
British
Government.

A reward is payable

Justum et Tenacem Propositi

Explicatio in Libro

The bit about returning to the Foreign Office was intriguing, but the Latin more so; *The answer is in the book.* Clearly, something juicy was in this book, some explanation of a rift between the two perhaps. I was starting to believe that Mycroft Holmes had been a real person – which meant, of course that Sherlock Holmes had also existed. This was a turn up. Remembering why I had come to London, I checked my watch and saw I'd best get my skates on. I decided to take the tube from Charing Cross, so walked across the famous square, fishing out my camera for a snap of the Landseer Lions. You cannot go to Trafalgar Square and not be struck by the feeling you are at the heart of English tradition, power and influence. That was the idea of the place, I guess. Crowds of Japanese and American tourists were lapping up all that history, so I went round to find an 'unoccupied' lion. As I did so, I spotted a couple who seemed out of place somehow. They were young, my age, casually dressed yet somehow they weren't touristy. As soon as I noticed them I forgot about them and took my snap, pocketing the camera and heading for the tube.

About twenty minutes later, the train rattled and heaved its way into the Edgware Road station. Exiting with the crowd, I headed for the subway that would take me under the Marylebone flyover – I'd been here before. Walking through the tunnel there were fewer people and my mind was on the camera I wanted. It was a toss up between a Hitachi job and the Panasonic I really wanted, if I could haggle on the price. Cash was king on the Edgware road, so I was hopeful of a good result. Normally I'm fairly alert as a person; we were always being warned about the IRA leaving bombs and I felt I was a fairly observant type, but I failed to notice that by now the only people in the underpass were two people coming the other way and the two behind me. It happened in the blink of an eye.

One of the two men in front of me asked me the directions to Regent's Park and I was shoved hard from behind in the same moment. The woman who had bumped into me apologised and made a show of brushing me off. Suspicious of this being a mugging attempt, I grabbed at the coat pocket where I kept my wallet and the envelope with my money in it. I felt a dragging sensation and wrenched myself away, at which I was pushed violently into the wall, falling to the cold hard concrete. Swearing in fear and anger, I struggled to my feet, but instead of attacking further, my assailants were simply running away in both directions. My first thought was to call for the police, but I decided to check the damage first. A mugging in London would hardly make headlines, and I was worried for my money. Oddly, all that seemed to have gone was the book, or at least *most* of the book, as the leather cover was still there in my pocket, with a few loose pages. I was furious, but my money was all there as was my wallet. Ironically I had only put my wallet there because I was worried about the pickpockets in London that targeted tourists. Apart from a bruised face and a broken camera I was OK. *Bastards*. My fingers were shaking as I opened my flask to take a swig. Definitely medicinal.

The rest of the day went normally enough; a very nice man named Karim flogged me a Sony Hi-8 video camera, a nifty little job which took small cassettes with incredible definition. I was 'made up' and couldn't wait to get home and use it. Karim had even thrown in an aftermarket high capacity battery pack and a telephoto lens that meant I'd be able to take action shots. Of what I wasn't sure, but the home video thing was big back then and this was my new hobby. Admittedly, part of me just wanted to make dirty videos, but I was a huge film buff and had visions of turning my flat into a studio filled with model spaceships and all sorts. Worthing's answer to George Lucas. It's as hilarious as it is cringeworthy, but that was me back then in those carefree days.

Before it all happened.

The train rolled in to Worthing a little after eight thirty –
if I were really lucky I'd make the chippy before they shut. Bloody
thing had been stuck at signals for the best part of forty minutes
outside Brighton. Sodding British Rail. Reaching for my ticket, I
realised I still had the remnants of the book and, without thinking,
ditched it in the bin on the platform. It was interesting, but with
most of the pages gone it wasn't worth the candle. Walking home
with my precious new camera I reached my place just as the first
snow started to come down. Putting my pride and joy on the sofa,
I was heading back out to get my dinner when I noticed the
cushion on my armchair was slightly out of place. So what? I went
for my large cod and chips. I was starving, my face hurt and it
was starting to come down heavily out there. Maybe I should go
and get some extra milk in while the Spar was open...

Half an hour or so later, I bumped the door shut behind
me, laden with both dinner and several cartons of milk, plus a few
tins 'just in case.' I'd even put a bit extra on the gas and electric
meters that week, so I was ready for the next Ice Age, should it
come. I shoved my cod and on a plate, still in the paper and
grabbed the wooden fork I'd snaffed at the chippy. Always tastes
better; *never* eat cod with a metal fork; ruins it. Mind you, Mum
(bless her) always said fish & chips didn't taste right on a plate;
she preferred newspaper, being a different generation. It was
when I went to plonk myself down in front of the telly that I
noticed the cushion. It wasn't out of position any more. That did
it; I jumped up and went into the kitchen, grabbing the pickaxe
handle I kept behind the door. Going from room to room, heart
pounding through my chest, I searched the whole place – well,
the bathroom and bedroom, which was pretty well it apart from
the places I knew were lacking in menacing intruders. There was

no one, of course there wasn't. What was wrong with me? Gingerly fingering the bruise on my face, I replaced the 'hickory butler' and went to eat my dinner before it got cold.

I woke up early, just before six. In those days I worked in the local Tandy; the UK version of RadioShack. As work didn't start until nine, I had plenty of time. After breakfast and a bit of Radio Four I threw on my coat and a woolly hat. The shop was in Tevile Gate, a sixties' concrete shopping centre dominated by a multi storey car park, some half a mile or so from my place. To get there, I had to walk past the train station and without really knowing why, I walked onto the platform to find the bin in the process of being emptied by a station worker.

'Excuse me, I dropped my book in there by mistake – couldn't just fish it out, could I?'

The bloke just shrugged, holding the bag towards me. Finding the book took a few seconds, after which I gave him a smile and a thumbs up before heading off to work.

I took a short break at eleven, a mug of awful instant coffee and a fag – I still smoked back then, on the back steps. Idly, I sat thinking about nothing for a minute before going back in to my coat. What I had been left with was a sorry assortment of a few pages and the cover itself. The frontispiece was intact, the inscription *Explication in Libro* still waiting for someone to find the secret. Whoever the idiots who mugged me were, it was unlikely they knew Latin. But then it occurred to me… what if it wasn't a coincidence? They certainly seemed a bit well turned-out for muggers. I'd never even *been* mugged before, now I get robbed just after finding this book? They hadn't even taken my wallet, or the money. Even the ring I'd found was safe at home in its little bag. I'd hidden it in a bag of sugar; a spate of local burglaries prompting me to take the precaution. Mind you, with my luck, I'd get burgled by some clown with a sweet tooth.

The remaining pages gave an account of Mycroft Holmes' life from August of 1891, when it seems he was working for the government in some capacity. His brother – Sherlock, of course, had left England to escape the attentions of a man named only 'M'. This, of course, had to be Professor Moriarty, the baddie in the Holmes stories. Once more, I was amazed to find that these people existed, *really* existed. Maybe the whole thing was an elaborate hoax, a wind-up, but whoever went to this amount of trouble? There was no way a hoaxer could have set this up; if I hadn't bought those Masonic papers, I'd never have known about any of it. It was time to get back to work, so I put the book back in my coat and went back to work.

At lunchtime I picked up where I had left off, learning that after he had survived a fight with Moriarty at the Reichenbach falls, Holmes had nearly been killed by someone with the initials 'SM.' I thought back to when I had read the stories, to when I was a kid at school. The school's copy of the Sherlock Holmes stories was a dog eared, shabby affair, held together with Sellotape. I had loved reading Conan Doyle's tales of danger and adventure, but couldn't recall which of the characters 'SM' might be. Anyway, fearful of his return to London bringing danger to his friend Doctor Watson, Holmes had spent three years or so on the run. Changing his name to 'Sigerson' he posed as a Norwegian explorer, travelling to Tibet, of all places. Mycroft wrote of how his brother had sent telegrams and letters to his London Club, the Diogenes.

It seemed Sherlock Holmes had kept himself busy during his travels, there were references to his 'sending items back for inspection' and a mention of the British Museum's subsequent interest in several of these. Someone; Mycroft, presumably, had gone to the trouble of sketching some of these. The next page was filled with these drawings, which showed a keen, if amateur eye. There were Tibetan daggers, a charm made from silver and some oddities such as a riding whip and a prayer bell of some kind. Turning to the next – and final remaining page I found a hand drawn map and a postcard. The map was clearly of some remote mountainous part of the country, while the card was more immediately intriguing. (Following page.)

Brother Mine,

The tobacco you sent was appalling – more please!. Events progress as they must; I trust you to take every precaution; some Continental friends called on me the other day. Who was it that said 'Io vado e vengo ogni giorno, ma tu andrai senza ritorno'?.

S.H.

Mycroft Holmes
c/o The Diogenes Club
Pall Mall
London
Great Britain

BAMFORTH & CO., PUBLISHERS (ENGLAND) AND NEW YORK. SERIES NO. 4573/1
PRINTED IN ENGLAND.

POST-CARD

This seemed like a clue; why else include it in the book? Handily, the manager decided I could have the rest of the day off. It was about three thirty, so I decided to go to Worthing library. Off I trudged through a light rain, to the large concrete block that is the town's library. It occurred to me that someone in the town council must have had a thing for concrete. At the front desk, a nice girl called Angela told me I wanted the Crime Fiction section, only I didn't. I wanted reference works. Patiently, she told me I'd need to know which books to order, which seemed a bit Catch-22 and, not sure at all I just asked for the 1891 *Who's Who*, anything on London from that year and waited at the desk while Angela trudged off to the lift. After a while she returned, with an armful and a smile. Thanking her, I took my haul to a vacant desk and started.

As if I needed any further confirmation, there he was; *HOLMES, Mycroft Eugenius, Chev L.H.* Advisor to Her Majesty's Foreign Office, Expert in Oriental Antiquities, British Museum (*Consultant.) b.* 1847 Address: 43a Pall Mall. On an impulse, I found his brother, learning that his middle name was Scott and he had been born in 1854. The address given was, of course, 221b Baker Street. So far so obvious. I needed more – I wanted to know what Holmes' postcard meant; *'Io vado e vengo ogni gionro, ma tu andrai senza ritorno'.* It sounded Italian to me, rather than Latin. I'd gone as far as I could with this. I needed to go back to London.

I'd never needed much of an excuse to take a day off; even less than ever, now. The Public Records Office at Kew was my destination. Another flask and I was good to go. The ticket-office was fairly busy; it was just after seven-thirty on a Friday morning, and I queued up to buy a return, gritting my teeth as I parted with the best part of another tenner. I waited out on the platform wishing I'd had a better breakfast; there was no way I was going to blow £1.25 on a bloody sandwich or 40p on a 25p pack of crisps. Except, of course, there was and I did, settling back down with a pack of cheese and onion, my blt in my pocket for later. At least if I was mugged again there'd be less in it for them, though as they'd not been after cash last time this was of little comfort. Unlike the knuckle dusters in my trouser pocket.

Borrowed from a dubious friend of mine named Gary, the dusters were part of an alarming collection of martial arts weapons he owned, along with an impressive pile of Bruce Lee and Jackie Chan videos, scenes from which he was always re-enacting in a fairly hopeless and clumsy attempt to become an adept without simply joining a karate club and doing some actual hard work. More than once I'd seen him with a black eye or split lip after another spectacularly ill-advised and brief punch up, but you had to hand it to the man; he wasn't going to learn at any cost.

The train pulled into Kew Gardens station at around a quarter past ten. Relieved, I was off quickly, looking around to find my bearings. A family headed off for the nearby gardens and I took a minute to check return times with the nice man behind the window. Oddly, I thought I spotted a woman I knew – or at least had seen somewhere, but this wasn't a spy film and I wasn't James Bond, so I just asked for directions to the Public Records Office. To his credit, the ticket bloke didn't actually call me a dickhead, just pointing 'out' and 'left' and smiling. A walk of no more than six or seven minutes along a suburban street of pleasantly-kept houses and across the South Circular Road and the massive concrete edifice of the Public Records Office was looming ahead. If Worthing Library looked like a pillbox this thing looked like Hitler's bunker on steroids. I walked over a wide walkway over a pond and up to the massive glass doors, half-expecting to find Hermann Goering hiding from the Russians. A plaque on a nearby wall told me a Right Honourable had opened the building somewhen or other and like every other visitor I forgot the name instantly and went up to the long wooden desk.

The people at the desk were fairly busy and I waited until I caught the eye of a matronly woman with dark, intelligent eyes. I always make a point with name badges and called her by her first name, Sarah. I told her of my interest and she looked surprised, telling me that under the rules the Census information for 1891 would be available in 1991. Helpfully, I pointed out it *was* 1991, but she shook her head as if I were being annoying.

'The information is being compiled.'

'Can I see the com-pile then, please?' Another shake. I couldn't. In a flash of inspiration I asked for 1890 only to get a look *and* a frown. Clearly, customers were tolerated and then only so far.

'The previous census would have been 1881.' She looked at me. I looked at her.

'And can I see it, then?'

'Yes, of course; it will help if you know specific details about the person. Holmes, you say?'

'Well, I don't have much to go on, a birth date and maybe when he died would be good.'

'That's not information contained in a Census; only the approximate date of birth is entered. I'm afraid it looks as if you need the General Register Office.' *Oh shit. I'm an idiot!*

Off I went on the District Line, the hopeful idiot on his travels. Somehow I hadn't expected all this and wasn't best pleased about it either. Sat in the tube carriage I watched the stations slide by, Stamford Brook, Hammersmith, Earl's Court… at least Sarah had taken pity on me and written the address down and how to get there. At Victoria there was a sudden rush and the carriage filled, people standing. A middle-aged woman was among them and, being polite I offered my seat. She glared at me as if I'd offered to show her some dirty pictures. The train was slowing for Westminster when I spotted them; a youngish couple, the man hanging off a strap and his girlfriend holding onto him. It was the girl I'd seen at Kew Gardens station; though she'd changed her coat, it was unmistakably the same woman. That in itself was odd, but the fact she was with this man made him suspect too. All at once I woke up; I was being followed. These people had already mugged me, taking the best part of the book. Criminals don't go to this amount of trouble for some bod working in a Tandy, so what was this about?

Stepping off the train at Temple I decided the best thing for it was to stay in public places. I had a shortish walk ahead of me to get to St. Catherine's House, then the home of the GRO. A light rain started to fall – when doesn't it? Thinking it through, I could see no reason for these people, whoever they were, to jump me again. After all, I had nothing they wanted. Perhaps they wanted to see what I was up to. But why? What possible interest could anybody have in my visit to the Records office? I walked, careful not to give any sign I knew about the surveillance. Walking casually; you should try it sometime. It's nearly impossible not to end up marching along like a robot. Once, I looked in a window and saw the reflection of the passers-by across the street, including the young couple. There was nothing for it; I went to the GRO.

This time, I had a result; the records were kept on microfiche and a nice man showed me how to use the viewer then left me to it. It took a while, but as I scrolled through endless birth certificates registered in Northallerton, the County Town of North

Riding in Yorkshire, I finally found one dated 12th February, 1847. There he was, Holmes, Mycroft Eugenius himself. Born to one Siger Holmes, occupation 'Squire' and Violet Holmes, *nee* Sherrinford. The Registrar was one William Pemberton. So now I had a date. All I had to do was work out the *Io vado e vengo ogni gionro, ma tu andrai senza ritorno* bit. And, of course work out what any of this had to do with anything. I was lost, this was beyond me. For a giddy moment I considered hiring a private eye then mentally slapped myself. Even if I could afford one, it was a stupid idea. I had gone as far as I could with this… or had I?

The British Museum had already turned up twice in this, whatever *this* was. That was my next port of call, but I knew I had to give whoever was following me the slip first, but how to actually *do* it was the problem. I reckoned if I did what the spies in the films did, switch cabs and hop on and off buses, I might manage it. With any luck.

As any luck would have it, a cab was dropping off across the road and, without even looking, I pelted across, just missing an irritable man on a racing bike. Mr. Tour de France gave me some advice I can't repeat here and I waved at the cabbie to indicate I wanted a ride.

'Where you off to in such a hurry then?. Nearly run you dahn, he did.'

'Well, I want to go to the British Museum, but I'd like to take a bit of a scenic route. You know; tourist.'

'Anywhere special?'

I fished out my wallet and showed him a few twenties which was virtually all I had.

'Surprise me.'

'Look mate, don't piss about. You want a mystery tour, I can take you to a place along the river; open top bus, not that you'd

155

want to go up top in this weather.'

'St. Paul's. I'd like to see St. Paul's cathedral.' We saw St. Paul's cathedral. All I learned is he must have been best mates with God. Looking through the back window I could see there were several cars, a motorbike and a bus. I didn't think they'd be on the bus somehow. The guy on the bike? All I could see was he was wearing leathers and a dark grey helmet. He had one of those smoked visors so I couldn't see his face. Looking again, I saw he wasn't wearing motorcycle boots, but what looked like hiking boots. He could have just been stuck in traffic, but as I looked he weaved past a couple of cars and drove past.

'We can't stay here mate; where next?.' Great. My knowledge of London was the polar opposite of this man's. All I could think of was Trafalgar Square.

Nelson looked down on me with his one good eye as I paid off my cabbie and he drove off, leaving me facing the famous square. Again. I did the obvious, walking across it, moving fast, keeping my head down. I didn't want my friends to know I was onto them; chances were they already knew, but why make it easy? Halfway across, I had an idea. Spotting some kids coming towards me, I pulled out a couple of pound coins.

'Sell me that Coke for two quid?' The girl holding the can looked at me as if I were a nut case, but one of her friends giggled and nudged her.

'Go on, let him have it. You can buy four for that.'

I was the proud owner of a two thirds full can of fizz. I had decided to mess about with my followers' heads. If they thought I was a spy or something sinister, drawing them out might be an idea. I walked over to the nearest lion and, looking around ostentatiously, reached up and placed it behind the paw of the bronze beast before walking off quickly.

Stopping inside the entrance steps to Charing Cross, I looked back and was rewarded with the sight of a man I hadn't seen before jumping up onto the plinth to retrieve my can. A moment later, my arm was gripped in a vice-like hold. Struggling for a moment, I turned to see a police warrant card and a friendly smile. The face doing the smiling could have belonged to a bare knuckle boxer and he wasn't easing up on the grip either, ushering me firmly down the steps.

'Come with me, Mark and I'll tell you what's what; we need to get you away from those people first, if you don't mind.' Down we went, him holding onto me as if we were friends.

Introducing himself as Detective Sergeant Booker, he told me everything. The people after me were from the Soviet Embassy – he waited for me to finish laughing and realise he wasn't joking, propelling me along towards the platforms. He told me Special Branch had been watching them for some time and followed them to Courtts Bank.

'Bit of a mystery that. Some old book, wasn't it?.'

'Er, yeah, it was a diary. Mycroft Holmes, if you can believe it.'

'I do. I don't know how much you know about us, but Mycroft Holmes worked with the Branch in the late nineteenth and early part of this century. One of the 'funnies'.'

'Funnies?'

'Spies, to you and me. They sniff 'em out; we nick 'em. No powers of arrest, your spook. That's where mugs like me come in; keeping people like you safe from thieving Russian sods like that lot.'

We'd reached the ticket office and Booker paid for two

travel cards. Instead of explaining, he handed one to me and winked. We went through the barrier and along to the Bakerloo line. There was another surprise – a second man was waiting there for us. This man couldn't have looked more like a plain clothes copper if he'd tried; I was waiting for him to bend at the knees and say 'Evenin' all.'

'Mark, say hello to Detective Constable Radlett. DC Radlett, say hi to Mark.' Radlett looked me up and down as if wondering if I were worth all the effort they'd been put to.

'Hi.' Not one for conversation, then. I had questions.

'So, why all this? Why not pick me up in a jam sandwich and take me to the nearest nick then?' I was grateful Booker decided to field that one.

'Because we don't want them latching on; if they know they're blown, they'll disappear. A marked car isn't exactly low-key, is it? The idea's simple – we bounce you around town a bit, shake them off, then we get you to the safe house.'

Safe house?. This wasn't in the brochure... a train was arriving, the gust of air preceding it down the tunnel.

'Safe house? I'm not a bloody Supergrass. What the hell's going on?.'

'You tell me. Or rather, you tell the Guv'nor when you see her.'

'Her?'

'Yeah. She's got tits. All part of the Met's new equality policy. Not my idea, but whoever asks the bus driver where he'd like to go, eh?.'

The train pulled in and we got on, along with several others. DC Radlett elbowed a city type out of the way and made it clear I should sit, with him and DS Booker standing to either side. I had my own bodyguards, courtesy of the Metropolitan Police Special Branch. The trouble was, I didn't feel any safer than when I was alone.

158

We changed at Oxford Circus. We changed at Green Park. We changed at Baker Street – the irony wasn't lost on me, and we changed again at Paddington. I tried to see any sign of my Russian friends, but saw nothing, just a whirl of humanity on and off the various trains. Just when I was expecting another change, we left the tube at Paddington, crossed the road where I was bustled into the back of a rusty old Transit van with Radlett. Inside, however, it was fitted with bench seats and when the doors banged shut, an overhead strip light came on. Radlett took the seat nearest the door and sat impassively. The door slammed shut and then there was an onimous click as it was locked. The van started up and we drove off, a panel sliding back to reveal Booker's battered and unloved face.

'Not long now, Mark, we'll be there in under half an hour.'

'So why all the cloak and dagger?'

'Well, we're more cloak, they're more dagger, to be fair. Just sit tight and relax.' The panel slid shut again and I was left to my thoughts and the sombre company of DC Radlett. The Transit rumbled its way through the streets of London, driving at speed for some of the time. Tossed about in the back I had no idea of which direction we were headed or how far we'd driven. Finally, to my relief we stopped. The back doors opened and I found myself outside a large Victorian villa. I looked around for a street name or some landmark, but it was a leafy street filled with what looked like similar houses. I had the distinct feeling I'd made a mistake, but Radlett and Booker were either side of me and I'm not a fighter, even with knuckle dusters in my pocket. Meekly, I went through the gate and up the tiled pathway to the house.

The 'safe house' looked like nobody had lived there in a

while. Going through the bare hallway, we went past a living room with bare floorboards and the single piece of furniture, an old sideboard resting dolefully against a wall. Going through the next door, however, revealed a different picture. This room was brightly lit and tastefully, if hastily furnished. I could see at once all the stuff in here was brand-new; not old enough to need dusting even. There was a comfortable sofa, some chairs, a coffee table and various other touches all designed, I suspected to make the place seem more homely and to put me at ease. It wasn't working. Still smiling, Booker asked if I needed the loo. I did. The bathroom I was taken to was a small downstairs job and I noticed at once the bars covering the whitewashed window. I wasn't feeling 'safe' in this house somehow.

Back in the sofa room, I asked for, and got, a coffee and a sandwich. I couldn't see a clock anywhere, but risked a look at my watch. Four p.m.
'She'll be here inside five minutes.' It was as if Booker had read my mind.

The woman that glided into the room was impossible to describe, one of those rare women words seam to cheapen. Blonde, tall, slim, she had the air of a movie star from the days when Bogart was king. At once inaccessible and bedable, this woman gave you the impression trying would be futile, but she knew you'd never stop trying. She wore a business suit – well, they did then; the impossible shoulders and trousers that never seemed to go with the heels. It helped that Booker was right; she had tits. Luckily, I caught myself before I melted entirely, eh? She spoke with a tutored voice just shy of Roedean; that public school privately tutored drawl money buys.
'Mark. Hi. Sorry about all this, but you've really been quite busy. We've had quite the run-around with you, I'm afraid.' Her

160

perfect features displayed concern and dismay all at once. Now I felt silly at not having stood when she walked in. Sensing this, she patted my knee and seated herself in a chair opposite.

The interview was about to begin. I half expected her to ask me for my references.

'Not sure if I can help…?' I did the face you do when you want a name.

'Oh, Natalie. Natalie Woods, Detective Chief Inspector, but you can call me Detective Chief Inspector… everyone does.' *Ha-ha.* This one had an awful sense of humour. I was starting to like her. It wouldn't last long.

It turned out that DCI Woods wanted to know my entire life story, but starting with the bit where I laid hands on that book. I told her about the car boot sale, but she seemed keen to get onto the book. I told her everything, about Courtts Bank and the safety deposit box, the mugging, my wasted trip to Kew right up to being followed that day. All she cared about was the book. What did *I* think the book meant? Clever old me, I told her that it was a diary written by Mycroft Holmes and it mentioned his famous brother going to Tibet. For some reason, the mention of Tibet seemed to bring about a change in the room, the atmosphere suddenly got tense. As if sensing this, Booker called time for a coffee break (Two please, plenty of milk) and cheerfully set about the kettle and bits and bobs set up on a side-table. As if conforming to a type, he even started whistling. It struck me that the tea and coffee making gear came from a hotel caterers, rather than a pint bottle, as he poured the milk from those little plastic containers you get that are never quite enough. Aware of my scrutiny, DCI Natalie turned on the charm, showing a lot more teeth in the process. Either this girl flossed obsessively or her dentist was expensive. I'd seen worse teeth at the zoo.

Coffee made, Booker set a cup beside the Guv'nor and handed me mine with a wink, as if to say 'Classy, ain't she?' DCI Natalie resumed the interview – she called it a 'de-brief', asking me about this and that, but I was waiting for Tibet to re-appear and I wasn't to be disappointed. As casually as anything, she asked if I knew anything about Tibetan antiquities. Truthfully, I answered that I didn't. For some reason, I kept back the part where Mycroft had drawn several of the artefacts. I wasn't entirely sure why, but I was having another one of my distinct feelings; I didn't trust DCI Woods or her colleagues. Then she changed tack, asking about the car boot sale and the man I'd bought the papers from. I fudged around a description, save that it was an old man and that he'd been in the antiques game. She seemed disappointed, but changed gears smoothly again after sipping quietly at her coffee.

'So, what's next?'

'Pardon?'

'What's next? Come on, you can tell us. What's your next move?' I only had one move left before I would have given all this up as a dead loss anyway; the British Museum.

You know those films where the bad guy has someone hostage and demands they tell them where the microfilm is, or what the combination is? The second they tell them; BOOM! They're a goner. So what did Our Man in London do when put in what looked to be the same spot? Yep; I spilled the beans. All over the carpet. I told Natalie about my idea the museum might hold the key to this mystery, but she seemed unconvinced.

'Well, whatever might be there – the museum has over seven million objects, can you think how we might narrow it down a bit?' She sat back and sipped her coffee. I followed suit rather more noisily wiping my mouth ostentatiously in a bid to cover up my reaction. *Where did* that *figure come from?* Either

DCI Natalie was a massive history fan or I was being played. Which meant, of course… these weren't the police. Unless the Met had decided they needed a Tibetan Antiquities Unit.

After going round in circles like this for another half hour or so I began to feel a bit drowsy. Noticing; nothing escaped him, Booker suggested we call it a night. DCI Woods agreed, getting up to leave with a smile and another tap on my knee that I felt in other places. I wanted to make a call, but was told the house wasn't provided with a telephone for 'security reasons.' Great. My bed for the night was a comfortable single in a first floor bedroom, like the furniture downstairs this was brand-new, as was the table and chair that made up the remainder of the furniture. There was an ensuite bathroom complete with hot and cold running bars on the window. Thoughtfully, someone had provided some men's toiletries and the bath was spotless. Why not? Closing the door on the ever silent DC Radlett, I half-expected to hear a key being turned, but I was left alone. So I undressed and filled a bath.

It was early in the morning, the first light of dawn. Waking up slowly, at first, I convulsed in a shiver and got a mouthful of ice-cold bathwater for my pains. Spluttering, I hooked the chain with a toe and yanked the plug, reaching forward with fingers like those of a melted waxwork to turn the hot tap. I nearly screamed in pain as the hot water fizzed down onto my feet. I'd been in the bath all night and must have dropped off there. I was lucky not to have drowned, but that wasn't much consolation at the moment. I was seriously cold; maybe even suffering from exposure. As the bath slowly refilled, I began working through the pain, joint by joint and limb by limb.

Finally warm, I yanked the plug again and rolled out onto

the cold floor, padding over to the towel rack where some kind soul had laid out a bath towel. This was clearly brand new like everything else, as I got bits all over me using it and it had none of the softness of a washed towel. I checked my watch; 4:17. Throwing my clothes on I went to the bedroom door and listened for a moment. Looking down at my trainers, I considered removing them, but figured socks wouldn't be that much quieter – besides, I might end up having to make a run for it. There was no sound from the hall outside. Risking it, I carefully opened the door and crept out, expecting to find Radlett looming out of the darkness. I was petrified, but still wondering if I was making a gigantic mistake. Somehow I didn't think Gary's knuckle dusters would do much good against these people.

The upstairs was empty. The downstairs was empty. However long you live you won't feel as much of a mug as I did that morning. The 'Special Branch' had cleared out. Suddenly I had a thought; I wasn't the most dynamic person – but falling asleep in a bath? If this was a film, it would be knockout drops in the coffee. So it was knockout drops in the coffee. I got out as fast as I could, walking quickly up the road to find out where the hell I was. I was on Carlton Hill, as it turned out. It was freezing, with a light rain that seemed to want to turn into snow. Turning to go into the adjoining road, I did a double-take; Abbey Road. I walked roughly southeast for several blocks until I was at the famous crossing. At least I was seeing the sights. I looked about for a taxi, but seeing none I thought 'Why not?' I did a 'John Lennon' - along with some Americans that were delighted at just about everything they'd seen in London and then spotted a cab pulling up outside the studios. Some musicians clambered out with their instruments. Classical, by the look of it and I quickly hailed the cabbie for the trip to Victoria and home. I was cold, PISSED OFF and wanted nothing more to do with any of it. When I got home, I was going to rip that sodding book into pieces and get my life back.

I got home about lunchtime, went to freshen up and change my clothes and went into my kitchen for a coffee. Seeing the book, I grabbed it and tore it to bits. And found out what *Explicatio in Libro* really meant. The cover had ripped awkwardly, the leather catching as it tore, revealing what had been hidden inside the binding. A dull metal key, almost identical to the first, with a card, now ripped in half with some holes punched in it. The explanation was, indeed, in the book.

Monday morning saw me on yet another trip to London, only this time by coach. My resources were dwindling like a candle lit with a flame thrower and coaches were cheaper; besides, the manager hadn't seemed impressed with my 'flu' excuse over the phone and it looked like I'd need a new job in the near future. It was a little after eleven-forty when we arrived at Victoria coach station, as some idiot had stuffed his transit into a car and the M23 had been a nightmare, but luckily our driver was able to throw in a shortcut and we were only slightly delayed thanks to his quick thinking. I slung my shoulder bag on and walked out of the station.

Then it was off to Courtts Bank again, only this time I walked, reasoning that I could see if I was being followed by raising my awareness, doing little things like looking both ways as I crossed the road. It was only when I got to the road leading past the Royal Mews that I thought I might have spotted a follower. There was a man walking across the road in the same direction as me; something made me think he might be one of 'them', whoever 'they' were.

I ducked into a tourist shop and spent a few minutes poring over the tat; toy black cabs vied with plastic guardsmen in tubes and piggybank letterboxes. All made in China. Amusingly, there were some Chinese customers in the shop, pondering which dust-gatherer to buy. All this way to buy something made just up the road. Maybe, however, I thought I could give my shadow a diversion; after all it had worked with the Coke can... So I blew seventy-five pence on a postcard of Buckingham Palace and, as the tight git of a shopkeeper wouldn't lend me one, had to spend another £1.99 on a crappy plastic pen which featured a tiny Sherlock Holmes floating in liquid. When you tilted it, Holmes revealed a miniscule picture of 221B Baker Street. Very apt. Quickly scribbling the words '*If you ARE Special Branch – I'm headed to the Bank'* on the card, I went outside and walked until I saw a small post box and posted my missive. The man was nowhere to be seen, so I carried on my merry way.

Buckingham Palace was swamped with the usual tourists and, for no real reason, I took some Hi-8 of the scene, panning around with my new camcorder to see if any familiar faces showed themselves. I had brought a baseball cap with me and put this on, hoping it might change my appearance a bit. Also inside the bag was a bright blue Pac-a-Mac. As it was raining again I put this on. With any luck I now looked identical to a thousand other tourists. I carried on down The Mall, heading ever closer to my destination.

Annabelle wasn't behind her desk this time, but an older woman was. Her name-badge showed her to be 'Cecilia Hargreaves.' I was starting to think the name badges were a wind up when she raised her eyebrows and smiled at the lunatic in the cap and plastic mac.

'Hi, I've come to look at my box, please.' I held up the key to stop her screaming.

This time Lambton didn't appear, instead it was another posh Charlie by the name of Townsend-Fitzgerald. Sounded made up, but I waved the magic key and down we went.

'Lambton's day off, is it?.'

'Sorry, who?' Double-Barrel seemed puzzled, so I just smiled and followed him down the curved steps.

After the cylinder rigmarole I was once again alone in the clubbish room, where I discovered the light bulb had at least been changed. This time my box opened to reveal – I was still poor. It was an envelope. Hooray. The seal was the same, so I opened it to find a hand-drawn map of some building plan, a largish house from the look of it. It was oddly familiar, but I couldn't place it. The shape maybe?. I knew I had seen something like it, but couldn't nail it down. An honest to God treasure map. It was like being in *The Goonies*. Without the pushbikes or the kid out of *Indiana Jones* with the hopeless gadgets. At least I knew what I had to do to be free of all this. Replacing the map in the envelope, I slipped it inside my bag.

Outside the bank, I spotted him almost at once; he was lounging against a wall reading a magazine, but I recognised the hiking boots. It was Motorcycle Man all right. Clearly, they'd opened the letter box and found my postcard. That settled it; this lot were the real McCoy. Without acknowledging him, I put my Pac-a-Mac and hat back on and headed off to find a cab.

Less than a quarter of an hour later, I was standing in front of the imposing and massive building, a gigantic Greek temple dedicated to knowledge. Even outside the British Museum, I knew they were here; the Soviets or whoever Woods and her fake Special Branch people were working for. Since 'Booker' had told me the people following me were Russian, it was probably Soviet Russia paying him and his friends. Either way, look around as I did, I couldn't be sure I was being followed by Evel Knievel or anyone else, but I was now sure he was a real copper or even a spook, as sure as I was of any of this. It seemed the best way to draw them out into the open was to go inside and hope the Tibetan stuff worked as bait. It was feeble, to say the least. I climbed the steps and went inside.

I shelled out more cash on a guide and a quick consultation showed me I needed to go upstairs to the Oriental galleries. The place was massive and it took a while, especially as I was genuinely distracted by all the incredible artefacts at every turn. Next time you are embroiled in a Russian conspiracy in London I heartily recommend it. I looked around for any sign of Woods or her friends Booker and Radlett, but saw nothing. Anyway, if these people were professionals I wouldn't, would I? I paused before a glass case with ceremonial garments, decorated skulls and ritual *Phurba* daggers. It struck me that I had had no real plan, just to draw Booker into the open. After that? Well, I just had to hope Hiking Boots and his shadowy associates were on the ball.

Just then, my thoughts were broken by the realisation someone was standing next to me. Looking in the glass, I could see the reflection of a tall, slim man with aquiline features, a rather prominent nose and piercing blue eyes. I began to turn, but he began speaking, his tone low.

'It would be best, I think, if you remain focused on these rather absorbing items.' I turned my attention back to the case, but risked a glance downwards. Hiking boots. And he had now discovered speech.

'My name is Thorn – that's not my real name, of course. If I tell you that I work for Her Majesty's Government and that the man seen taking you away last Friday is a disgraced former police sergeant by the name of Adam Howlett, currently believed to be in the employ of a counsellor at the Soviet Embassy by the name of Petrov, you may have some questions to ask. Mr. Petrov is, in point of fact, a former colonel in the GRU; Soviet Military Intelligence and one of the highest ranking KGB officers at the London Embassy.' The man spoke with an educated drawl and I realised he had produced a small black and white glossy, which he was holding discreetly. It showed a pale, hard-faced man I didn't recognise with thick black hair and the look of a man you didn't want to upset. Thorn waited for this to sink in. It didn't. It still hasn't, come to think of it. However, I just stared blankly at an ornate skull and waited for him to continue, while I worked out if I believed a word of it.

'Petrov has been, we believe, charged with locating a rather unique object that came from Tibet in the 1890s, but I think you already know that, plus that you are here to either find said object or perhaps to confront Howlett and his gang with the knuckle dusters you carry in your right pocket.' Seeing my look of confusion, the tall man smiled, scratching the side of his nose. 'No great mystery; I brushed past you on the way in. It's not hard to do a fingertip sweep with practice and you've been practically clutching the thing every time you think you see surveillance.' So that was it.

'O.k. then, say I go along with this; where do I come in? If you think I'm mixed up in something, why not arrest me?'

'Something I have been at pains to explain to my rather slower colleagues is that arresting you both shows our hand and almost certainly scares off the Soviets. We may never know what

169

it was they were after. But I think you do – or am I wrong, Mr. Sohn?' Thorn had turned to stare directly and I felt the heat of his gaze, penetrating and intelligent. I had the uncomfortable feeling of being scrutinised by an intellect superior to any I had encountered. Plus, he'd pronounced my name right, which was a first.

I looked back at my skull; my face reflected in the glass providing the unsettling illusion the Tibetan skull was wearing my face.

'I told them, about this place. But I didn't know what else to tell them; they mugged me, you see, got most of the book. I only got the bit I did because it was falling to bits anyway.'

'And yet here you are.'

'They're here; the Russians?' He nodded once, briskly.

'At this very moment they are heading for this gallery. I have made suitable arrangements.' No sooner had he spoken when a fire alarm went off, followed by others around the vast building. I was impressed. Raising my voice to be heard, I voiced a reservation.

'So they'll have to leave with everyone else. Won't we?'

'As I said, I have made...'

'Suitable arrangements. Yes, got that; so you want me to lead you to the mystery object. One; As *I* said, not a clue. And two, what could this place have that's worth all this... this, piss-arsing around?.' Again that piecing gaze.

'A meteorite. A lump of metallic rock from space.'

I never did understand all of it. 'Thorn' gave me a brief version as we walked alone down the magnificent gallery.

'Every year, thousands of these rocks fall on land, many more, of course, in the sea. You can do the mathematics yourself, but the total is in the trillions. Only a fraction of these have ever been recovered, of those only one has the metallurgic composition of the one falling on a remote area of Tibet, some five miles North of Bharatpur, should you ever plan a visit.' I was still none the wiser.

'So, it's unique; must be worth a bit.'

'Impossible to quantify. The properties of the meteorite themselves have been registered as an Official Secret by Her Majesty's Government; the very existence of the object is strictly deniable – despite the rather plain fact it has been, unknown to us on public view for many years.' This all sounded like hogwash, but for some reason I found Thorn to be utterly believable. Everything about him spoke of honesty and decency, but then I'd been fooled before of course, so maybe I wasn't the best judge of a person's character.

We paused by a cabinet containing what the labels told me were thokcha, little amulets and talismans crafted from what looked to be bronze, though some were, I saw made from metals found in *meteorites*. The penny dropped; one of these must surely be the one! As if reading my thoughts, Thorn tapped the glass to indicate a dullish flat disc, worked into a sort of random filigree.

'Sky iron, that's what thokcha means; sacred, magical objects used for protection from various ailments and spiritual harm. Fascinating.' The alarm abruptly stopped, at which he consulted his watch.

'We have four minutes, perhaps less. Here, take this.' He pulled a thick glove from a pocket and handed it to me. I stared at it then him.

'Well, put it on, man; it will protect you.'

'From what?.'

'The glass. Which you are going to break.'

I tried to argue, tell this odd man I didn't fancy a criminal record, but he just tapped his watch and made a 'tick-tock' noise. When that had no effect he impatiently asked if I wanted my life back, to be free of the Russians once and for all. Which I most certainly did. So I punched the glass. Thorn was holding his hand out imperiously and I realised he wanted his glove back. When I gave it to him, he reached in, snatched the thokcha and tossed it into the air for me to catch.

Thorn had grabbed me roughly by the shoulder and was marching me back the way we'd come.

'Oh bloody marvellous. Now I'm a thief?'

'Precisely. Now you make for the front exit, at some point on the way you'll encounter no less a personage than Petrov himself.'

'The KGB guy in the photo?.'

'The KGB guy in the photo. You will allow him to take the purloined thokcha, possibly after a minor fracas. Feel free to make use of your knuckle dusters, but for heaven's sake try not to incapacitate the man. It is imperative he escapes. Ah! Here's where I leave you – and good luck.' With that, he clapped me on the back, then was gone, dashing off along a side corridor and disappearing through a doorway marked 'Staff Only.'

I honestly was planning to go to the first security guard I saw and turn myself in. This wasn't for me, all this. Suddenly the life of a Tandy shop assistant seemed like a wonderful dream, and I wanted it back. Rounding a corner, I walked into a short, stocky man and automatically gave an apology, before doing a double-take. It was Petrov; there was no doubt. The man scowled at me for a moment, but then an unpleasant smile crept across his peasant's face.

'You have the object, I think.' He cocked his head and held out his hand, pushing me hard in the chest with the flat palm of the other. Suddenly, the anger of the previous days was too much. Forcing a smile I nodded and reached into my pocket. The dusters smashed into the leering face at the side of the chin and he went down like a sack of spuds dropped off a lorry. So much for not incapacitating… Gary would have been proud; his dusters had finally won a fight.

While I was wondering what to do next, Petrov started groaning and I started to panic. What next? What next was 'DCI Woods.'

'Oh shit. What have you done, you stupid bastard?'

I looked down at Petrov; it seemed fairly obvious what I'd done to me.

'Don't start that old crap up, love – I know you're with him.'

'Oh great, another genius. I must attract them. Who do you think swapped the K-2 in your bloody coffee? They were going to kill you; I made sure you were just out of it for a while.' There was a loud groan from the area of the carpet and the woman seemed to be weighing up her options. Seeing the knuckle dusters I was still wearing, she ran a hand through her fine fair hair. Despite the circumstances, I felt my mouth go dry and my heart quicken.

'Lend us those, will you?'

'What, so you can hit me?' She held her head at an angle and gave me a look that shot right down my spine.

'Don't tempt me, sunshine. Give.' She fluttered her fingers to hurry me up and I watched as she slipped her right hand into the brass knuckles. A loud *thud* sounded as the brass flashed down onto Petrov's temple. His head dropped onto the Axminster heavily. Quickly, she knelt on one knee to check his pulse. He was out for the long count this time.

I watched aghast as she pocketed the dusters.

'I'll keep these, if you don't mind. Can't have an idiot like you running around with an offensive weapon, can we? That reminds me, I almost forgot... hand it over.' Woods, or whoever she was, was holding out a perfectly manicured hand and it took a moment to realise she wanted the thokcha.

'You know this is just a lump of old iron, right?'

'So what? This is what it's all been for. What do you want; the Holy Grail?. Now be a good boy and piss off before he comes round.' So I did what good boys are supposed to; I pissed off. You wait a lifetime to meet a woman like that and then she tells you to piss off.

ONE WEEK LATER

Pausing by the muddy track, I pulled out a stud from the poacher's pocket of my Barbour and removed the card I had found with the key when I'd ripped the book in half weeks ago. It seemed like an age. Now held together with Sellotape, the paper was blank, save for seven carefully punched-out holes. I'd worked it out, but it had taken a while. By laying the card over the sketch map of the building plan I'd found at the bank, then lining up six of the holes with the corners of the building shown on the map, the seventh hole revealed the location... of whatever was hidden there. If anything. I knew the thokcha the woman calling herself Woods had taken was worthless – which meant if my guess was right, I'd find the *real* one buried or hidden here. At Sinopia.

It had taken two weeks to find the old boy, driving round the different car-boot sales until I found him at Ford, at the sale held on the site of the old wartime airfield. I asked him about the items he'd sold me, and the sign that he still had. *Sinopia.* He told me where the old house had been – at least he did after I paid him a tenner for the sign. All I could do was hope some yuppie hadn't built his house there yet. For the sake of the new owner's privacy, all I will say is the site of Mycroft Holmes' old house was near Amberley, in the leafy lanes of West Sussex.

It's hard to find a more English setting than West Sussex in spring. I rode through narrow lanes that wound through the gentle slopes of the South Downs and felt alive, free even. The day was bright, if cold, and I had high hopes as I pushed my motorbike into the track and looked for some solid ground to put it on the centre-stand. The bike, a Yamaha 750 was my present to myself. It would take ages to pay off the finance, but after the crap I'd been through, I felt like splurging.

The place was a building site, but from the local enquiries I'd made at the nearest pub, the work had been halted for reasons unknown.

'Builders, eh?' I'd said to the Landlord, a ruddy-cheeked man straight from a Central Casting catalogue. He'd snorted and topped up my Coke. And here I was. I could see the new structure taking shape, trying to ascertain the boundaries of the old building beneath. Luckily, the section where the seventh hole was didn't seem to be part of the new building, from what I could see it was around to the north side and part of what would presumably be the new back garden for a slightly smaller property than Mycroft's original Sinopia. As I rounded a half built exterior wall I could see I'd found the right spot. Because Thorn was standing there, by a freshly dug pile of earth.

I threw the folding shovel I'd brought onto the ground with an exclamation of disgust. All this way only to find I'd been beaten to it. Seeing my disappointment, Thorn's face was not entirely unsympathetic, a twinkle in his eye as he held out a hand for the card. He had pianist's fingers, I noticed.

'Ah, yes. Ingenious, don't you think? To anyone an innocent sketch of a house and a simple piece of card. Bring the two together, however...' Leaving the rest unsaid, he handed them back to me. I was calmer, somehow – perhaps the man had that effect, but I still needed answers.

'How did you know?'

'Oh, no great feat of the mind to line up the dots, so to speak. Mycroft Holmes was notorious in his day for the lengths he would go to in order to protect the Empire. Even his famous brother paled next to his intellect, they say. All I did was keep a quiet eye on you and quietly arrange to break in to your flat. All above board, with a Home Office Warrant, should you have doubts. We found the remnants of Mycroft's journal, photographed these and retreated to see where you were headed next.'

The man calling himself Thorn paused to light a cigarette, offering me one from a silver case. Somehow I wasn't surprised to see the crest on it was familiar. I declined.

'Quite right. Filthy habit, but I find it stimulates the thought processes somewhat. Any way...' Thorn waved smoke vaguely in the direction of London before continuing. 'There were a few possibilities, places you might try, but this presented as the most likely. After that, it was just a matter of location; if you recall there was a rather inexplicable postcard in Mycroft's book?' I nodded, recalling the odd lines on the card.

'Io vado e vengo ogni gionro, ma tu andrai senza ritorno...'

'Quite. I go and come, but you will not return.'

It occurred to me that simply digging up an Italian dictionary might have been the blindingly obvious course of action, but I pushed the thought aside. What comes and goes? And what did 'you will not return' mean? The answer hit me like a ray of sunlight... because that was the answer; the sun!

The old sundial was still there, albeit broken, dumped by a hedge. The brass of the sundial itself was covered in verdigris, but there was enough of the stone intact to read part of the motto. No prizes for guessing it. Turning back to Thorn, I pointed at the hole.

'It was under the sundial, wasn't it?'

'Something was. The boffins at the Ministry of Defence are hard at work examining it. I rather think they'll be in for a disappointment.'

'Meaning what?'

'Meaning someone – most probably Mycroft of Sherlock Holmes, if not both... realised the significance of the metal that Sherlock had discovered.'

I was about to speak, but he held up a hand to indicate he had more to add. Strolling over to the sundial, he stooped to brush away some of the muck that had accrued on the surface.

'Mmm – yes, anyway... it seems the metal had unique properties. I alluded to this at the museum, you will recall.'

'What type of properties would make it so valuable the Russians nearly drowned me just to get a sniff at it?' Thorn scratched at his large nose absent-mindedly before answering.

'Oh, it's light-weight, extremely resilient to impact and heat... almost impervious. In fact, the only way to even cut it would be with a tool specially fashioned from the same material. Tungsten drill-bits skid off its surface, so I'm told. Diamond bits simply shatter. Anyone able to synthesize or replicate it would be able to create shell-proof armour for tanks, planes that couldn't be shot down by conventional missile and submarines able to reach unheard of depths...'

'But you said the M.O.D. would be disappointed.'

'Because, my friend, the only thing in that box, the item which had to be specially despatched by helicopter at great expense to Her Majesty's Government, was an old horse shoe. It seems the Holmes brothers felt such a metal would bestow an unfair advantage in an uncertain World.'

It was getting dark. It was time to take my leave of this man and place. I still had unanswered questions.

'Woods. One of yours?'

'In a fashion, yes. The woman is quite remarkable; oh, not her looks, though I daresay she is quite attractive. All I will say is, she's leading us to Petrov and his network.'

'The man I chinned?.'

'The very same. Natalie – actually her first name, as it happens, has been operating under deep cover for some while now.'

'And you? who are you *really*, I mean?'

'Oh, no one of any great significance. Just the man who owns the house you're almost standing in. For my retirement eventually, though God knows how long it'll take to finish. I am building it myself, you see, in my spare time, such as it is.' With that, he began to walk away to the track leading back to the road.

I looked around. Even in this state, it seemed a bit rich for a policeman's blood. As if reading my thoughts, Thorn spoke over his shoulder.

'An inheritance. From a great-uncle.' It couldn't be... *could it?* I remembered something; the signet ring I had found. I was wearing it on my pinky. Removing it, I held it up.

'Yours, I think.' Smiling, he carried on his way.

'You keep it. As a memento, if you will.' Shaking my head,

I took a last look at the former grounds of Sinopia and followed Thorn around to my motorbike. By the time I rolled it out onto the road, he was gone. I never saw him again, but at least now I knew his last name; his *real* one.

The Tinseltown Detective

Author's note; the following story contains some language that may be offensive as well as some that definitely is. The story is set during a period of time where racist abuse of minorities, although regrettable, was commonplace. I have only included such language in the interests of verisimilitude and apologise unreservedly for any offence caused.

PROLOGUE

The solitary, slim figure stood on the clifftop as the dawn broke over the hills behind him and lit up the Pacific. Reaching into a pocket, he withdrew a small piece of enamelled metal, considering it carefully as a man does things that have some significance. Shaped like a Maltese cross, some two inches square, the metal felt sharp at the edges. Drawing back an arm, he threw the object as hard as he could, sending it into the caroming waves far below.

Two Weeks Earlier

Sometime after 11 a.m. the occupant of 10728 Bellagio Road in fashionable Bel-Air left his home in his 1940 Chevrolet convertible, perhaps a modest choice of automobile for a film star, but it was a joy to drive and he was no great lover of expensive status symbols. Not for Basil Rathbone the ostentatiousness of the Duesenberg or the other chauffeured land liners that the public craned their necks to see at the gates of the big studios. His wife, Ouida, was constantly nagging at him to buy a Rolls Royce or some such extravagance; then again she was constantly nagging him about everything these days. On his drive that morning in late 1941, he turned his radio on to hear news of the Nazis issuing an ultimatum to Norway; surrender or be crushed. The breathless announcer went on to Secretary of State Cordell Hull's description of Nazi attacks on U.S. shipping as 'piracy'.

Rathbone pushed a button and the sounds of Duke Ellington came through the speaker, blowing away the madness of the world. The eight miles passed quietly enough; Thursday mornings were never the busiest of times in Hollywood. As the little car rolled along Sunset Boulevard, the traffic that was becoming the curse of California living showed itself, the landmarks of the Sunset Towers, the Chateau Marmont and the Garden of Allah all sliding past in their turn.

Rathbone pulled into the parking lot beside the massive studio complex – NBC's answer to CBS's Columbia Square was certainly some statement, an Art Deco wonder. As he'd seen no fans hanging around at the entrance, he walked around and skipped up the steps. Lit by floor to ceiling glass, the cavernous space of the lobby was like a futuristic cathedral. Waving at the receptionist on duty, Rathbone walked along the zig zag patterned floor; a symbolic radio wave, to the soundproofed glass at the far end. The walk was dominated by the gigantic mural above; the Spirit of Radio, a genie holding a radio. Behind the thick glass was the master control room, the heart of the operation, visible to visitors in a clever display of architectural design. This was what it was all about. Rathbone knocked on the glass and waved impishly at the technicians, one of whom pulled a face and mimed puffing at a pipe while examining something with a magnifying glass. The actor's face stiffened imperceptibly before he smiled back. If he wasn't careful, he'd end up typecast, an actor's nightmare. It was time to get to work.

Striding along the hallway to the offices at the far end, Rathbone popped his head round the door of one of the furthest to give a cheery greeting to the girls hard at work answering the fan-mail. Every week the show got thousands of such letters, everything from requests for autographed pictures to marriage proposals. The latter were sent a stock reply lamenting the 'fact' that Sherlock Holmes was married to his work. He was just going to leave when one of the girls held up an envelope. She looked worried.

'Mr Rathbone – I think you should see this one.'

'And whatever makes you think so? Another lovelorn child who cannot tell the difference between reality and make-believe?'

'It's… different.' Seeing the girl blush, Rathbone smiled and took the envelope with a wink, ducking back out to walk along the plush corridor the way he'd come, pocketing the envelope absent-mindedly.

'And I told him so! Bloody fool won't forget me in a hurry...' An avuncular and rotund figure was holding court in the lounge, a modern and yet still comfortable space, around which the stars of the day were often to be seen rubbing shoulders with studio executives. Nigel Bruce was in good form today, regaling the assembled cast with anecdotes from his time at the Hollywood Cricket Club, the very heart of expatriate British society. On seeing his friend and co-star's arrival, he made a show of checking his watch.

'My, my… five o'clock already! Time for dinner!' Rathbone made a comic gesture, clutching at sides in mock amusement.

'You've missed your calling, Willie – you should have been a comedian… or an actor.'

'And balls to you too.' A harassed-looking producer

arrived and shooed the actors into Studio G.

Everyone had rehearsed their parts earlier, except Bruce and Rathbone. The stars got to rehearse in the comfort of their own homes. The cast assembled and the sound engineer signalled he was ready for a take. Several foley men gathered round a curious collection of objects, ready to create the sound effects millions of listeners would soon hear and thrill to. Knox Manning, the announcer, cleared his throat noisily. A technician cued a record – the show's signature music and finally, the producer nodded to Rathbone and Bruce, gathered around a single microphone. The record played; 'March of the Ancestors' and Manning spoke over the stirring music;

'The Adventures of Sherlock Holmes, starring Basil Rathbone and Nigel Bruce. The makers of Bromo Quinine cold tablets bring you another adventure of Sherlock Holmes, with Basil Rathbone as Sherlock Holmes with Nigel Bruce as Doctor Watson. Friends, when you're the victim of a cold, remember this...' Throughout the introduction, Rathbone and Bruce played around, the former flicking paper balls at the foley men and Bruce making his eyes cross absurdly. It was the third series and no-one took it seriously as the intro wound up, the scene set beside Watson's fireplace.

The script called for Manning to 'pay a visit' to Watson, who was preoccupied with America's latest gang shooting. As a foley man crackled cellophane noisily, simulating a crackling fire, Bruce recounted a tale from 1894 when Watson and Holmes were embroiled in a case in London. As the two exchanged lines, a distracted Rathbone pulled the envelope from his pocket. He had about fifty seconds before his first line was due, long enough to see what all the fuss was about. The envelope had already been opened, so he was able to slip the contents inside out quietly, as the music played to indicate his cue was approaching. There was a letter, of sorts and a glossy photograph. Two people on a beach, entwined. After a few seconds, he looked about him, startled. For a minute he considered leaving the studio mid-performance, but Bruce gave him a quizzical look beneath beetled eyebrows and, his face pale, Rathbone picked up his cue.

'Mrs. Hudson tells me that you've been having some difficulty with a lodger, Mrs, Mrs, err...'

After the show wrapped, the cast broke out the cigarettes, relaxed, happy. There was still another episode to be recorded that day, but Rathbone complained of a severe and sudden headache and left the studio. He drove out to the hills, before abruptly turning for the coast. He took the scenic route, following the curving ribbon of Sunset to where its namesake could be found, the beach at Inceville. He turned for Malibu, fishing a cigarette from a silver case as he drove. He knew this drive well; he had twenty minutes and about eight and a half miles to go.

Passing the pier at Malibu, Rathbone crossed the creek bridge and pulled over onto a dirt track leading down to the sea. Parking, he pulled a floppy sun-hat from the back seat and donned sunglasses; not much of a disguise for Sherlock Holmes perhaps, but it would have to do. Walking briskly down to the edge of the sand, he passed behind one of the more modest of the beach-houses on the thin strip of sand.

Names such as Ronald Colman, Gary Cooper and Clara Bow all had owned homes on this precious sliver of Pacific beach front. Many stars owned or rented a slice of private heaven here, like the one Rathbone now entered by a side-gate. Knowing no-one was likely to be home, he passed through a simple garden and around the house, the narrow pathway lined with fuchsia and wild rye. Finally, he found himself by the beach itself. There were few people about, which was a relief. What people there were, were likely to be film people, so with any luck he would escape notice – people in 'the trade' valued privacy. The last thing he needed was a fan. Not here.

Taking out the photograph, he turned this way and that to line it up, deciding the picture was taken from some way back to his right along the coast, to the west. Probably a long lens. A car? It fit; someone with a good camera and a steady hand might have sat by the road and... it was enough. He walked back, determination in his stride, but a feeling of hopelessness overwhelming him. As was happening more frequently these days, he thought of France, of the shell hole where he had lain looking at the cloudy sky, the Bach sonata playing in his head. It happened at times like this, mainly; under stress or strain his mind revolted and he found himself once more looking at those same bloody clouds.

Forcing the unbidden imagery from his mind, Rathbone went to his car, but then he had a thought. What would 'He' do? Well, obviously, Holmes would go to examine the spot from which the photo had been taken. After all, it was clearly taken just two days ago, when he had last met 'her.' Aside from the fact the two hadn't kissed like that before, the girl in the picture was clearly wearing the same dress. More worrying, perhaps, was the man she was kissing so passionately was unmistakably Philip Basil St. John Rathbone. If he'd been wearing his MC for the picture and a deerstalker, it couldn't have been any worse.

He reached the kerb and walked along it, to where a small collection of cigarette ends lay. This was odd in itself – no-one in California threw their butts out of the window, not unless they enjoyed brushfires, but when the tall actor stooped to examine them, he discovered they were foreign, a brand he was unfamiliar with. Quickly, he wrapped one or two of the most intact specimens in his handkerchief and pocketed it, worried his behaviour might attract attention. A quick comparison showed the photograph was almost perfectly aligned now; bending at the knee produced a precise match. Taken from a car, here, by someone prepared to spend some time waiting. He needed a drink. But, then again these days there were few times when he didn't.

Cursing his lack of second sight, Rathbone pulled the Chevrolet up on Bellagio and cut the engine, coasting the last few yards to stop short of the side gate. She was at home – ironically complaining of one of her 'headaches.' Ouida Rathbone often developed these, especially when Basil tried to stand up to her incessant demands. Although not sexual, *never* sexual, these came on a predictable and endless cycle. The only time he could be reasonably safe from these barrages was after she'd thrown a party. $10,000 was a cheap one, and although he was earning anything up to $800,000 a year, Mrs. R's mania for socialising meant by the end of that year they'd be lucky to break even. Plus, the way she insisted on interfering at the studios he worked for meant he was in constant danger of incurring the wrath of the feared studio heads, any one of whom could leave a career in tatters with a sideways glance at a pushy spouse. Damn the woman! Not for the first time, one of the world's most famous men, a decorated veteran of the First War, found himself screwing up the courage to sneak into his own home.

Luckily, it was the German Shepherd, Moritza, who had been waiting to welcome her master and after a brief and playful romp, he was able to dart into the house and retrieve his pocket book from the desk in the library, unseen and unchallenged by anyone but Nellie, the Rathbone's maid. An English girl, Nellie

186

agreed she hadn't seen her employer with a girlish grin and a giggle. Mrs. Rathbone was sleeping – baby Cynthia, a tot of just two, was with the nanny in her playroom. For a moment, the ache to look in on her had been overwhelming, but the risk of another Ouida tantrum (Which would set Cynthia off into a fit of inconsolable sobbing and wailing; more than his heart could stand) outweighed paternal feeling and he'd left the way he'd come.

The car was getting low on gas, so he pulled into a Gilmore and waited while the pretty attendant filled the tank. When she recognised him, she gave him a wide grin and a side profile; everyone wanted to be in pictures, it seemed. She handed him his change from the leather holder around her waist and was still dazzling the air as he tipped her and drove off. Spotting a phone booth, he stopped and after consulting the pocket book, dialled an HO number, bypassing the switchboard at MGM to call Eddie Mannix' private line. The *very* private line. Almost instantly, the gruff voice answered.

'Mannix.'

'Mr. Mannix, it's Basil Rathbone.'

'Then you can call me Eddie, Mr. Rathbone; we're old friends, remember?'

'Yes, but… well, it's complicated.' There was a snort of laughter from the other end.

'If it wasn't, you'd have gone through the switchboard, right? That's why you have this number. Without any details, what's the nature of the trouble?'

Taking a deep breath and closing his eyes to blot out the image of the French sky, the Englishman told him.

'Blackmail. And it's bad this time.'

'Okay; stay calm, I'm sending someone. Where are you?.'

A fleeting moment of panic hit the actor, but he kept his voice calm.

'Someone? Why not you?.'

'Because I'm trying to keep on top of about three different things at once; half of Hollywood's having an abortion and the other half's running jaywalkers down like it's the season. Don't worry – the guy I'm sending is the cream. So, the address please...'

'I'll be at the Cock n' Bull on the Sunset Strip. In twenty minutes.'

'And so will the guy.'

'How will I recognise him?'

'He'll be the guy looking for Sherlock Holmes.'

The Cock n' Bull was the Sunset Strip's attempt at a British pub; all oak beams and leaded glass, the frequent haunt of lonely expatriate actors where Jack Morgan had invented the Moscow Mule, served in his trademark copper mugs. As Rathbone walked into the dark, welcoming interior, his nose was assailed with the unmistakable smell of roast beef and Yorkshire pudding. He wasn't hungry though, going to his customary table in a comparatively quiet corner. As he passed by one table, Errol Flynn slumped noisily to the floor where he promptly fell asleep. Rathbone ignored the drunk and seated himself, watching dispassionately as a bus boy did his best to quietly rouse him, before settling on dragging him out the back, presumably for a face full of water. Checking his watch, he saw twenty minutes had passed, but then looked up as a stocky, middle aged man took the seat opposite, clicking his fingers for service and dumping his hat on an adjacent chair.

This new arrival had the obvious look of ex-cop about him, the rumpled suit and tired, dull brown eyes spoke of long nights sitting watching. Thinning, slicked back black hair with the first signs of grey complemented a boxer's face with a day's stubble. The man looked as if he enjoyed a drink, an impression confirmed when he ordered a large scotch on the rocks for himself before remembering his client's presence. Rathbone nodded for the same. Waiting until the drinks arrived and the waiter had left them alone, the stocky man spoke. 'Eddie said it was blackmail. You gotta note?' Nodding, Rathbone took a pull of his scotch before looking around to make sure no-one was showing any interest. A look of disgust washed over the pug face. 'This isn't a movie. Nobody gives a shit.' One eyebrow raised, Rathbone handed over the envelope, which the man held at length as if he were long sighted. Turning the envelope, the contents spilled out onto the table and he took each into his large fists to examine. He read the letter. (Following page)

Dear Mister Rathbone,

Unless you follow my instructions, this charming photograph shall find it's way into the hands of the Examiner. I am not interested in money, but will contact you soon with instructions and the equipment suitable to carry out your orders.

Do NOT go to the police or the picture goes public.

X

'Yuh. Guy's a nut.' Seeing the actor's face had frozen into a pale mask, the man shrugged and grinned; a lopsided sneer. He pushed the note and picture back across the table, where Rathbone nervously pocketed them.

'You can ignore this crap.' Anxious, Rathbone clenched his

fists in a gesture of impotence.

'But the picture! He clearly states he will go to the papers.'

'Paper. Singular. And I'm gonna go there first; got a pal at the Examiner's copy desk; he'll bury this.'

'But how can I be sure? Can I even trust you? I don't even know your name...' Rising to leave, the burly man swallowed the rest of his drink in one quick motion.

'You can trust me. Eddie sent me. And the name's Barton, Harry to my friends.' With that, he reached across for his hat, planted it lopsidedly on his head, winked and left Rathbone alone with both his thoughts and the bill. He realised he hadn't even shown Barton the cigarette butts.

The next morning, Rathbone woke early, going down-stairs to find the cook and ordered a ham omelette with orange juice for breakfast. For some reason, he had slept an untroubled sleep, the first time in over a month. Of his wife, Ouida, there was no sign. Looking through the picture window of the dining room, he could see Tom, the Japanese houseboy, busily clipping the rose bushes. Nellie appeared with breakfast and both the Los Angeles and London Times and he ate heartily, reading of yesterday's events in California and last week's in London. The papers, when they came at all, tended to come erratically from the besieged island. Not for the first time, he felt a twinge of guilt at not having gone 'home' as Niven had promptly – and patriotically, done. Never mind; of what use was an actor nearing fifty? Besides, his military experience had ended a lifetime ago, or so it seemed. He'd talk it over with Willie when he got the chance.

Casting aside Roosevelt's peace offer to Japan, Rathbone checked his watch. Nearly seven a.m. Time to look in on Cynthia and then head to the studio. The child was already wide awake, playing happily with her favourite, a giant stuffed teddy bear.

Seeing the master of the house, the nurse smiled and stood aside as her father scooped her up in his arms with a joyful whoop. Giggling delightedly, the little girl clung onto her daddy as he whirled her round in a circle. Suddenly, a voice from the door shattered the happy moment. It was Ouida, down uncharacteristically early.

'So, you've remembered our child?' Desperate that the inevitable scene didn't upset little Cynthia, Basil tried to take her out of the room by placing a hand on her arm, but she pulled away with a look of pure hatred.

Shorter than her husband by a wide margin, heavily built and dark of eye and hair, Ouida Rathbone was approaching her fifty fifth birthday. She had been born plain Eunie Branch, but took the name Rathbone when she married in 1926, her fourth marriage and his second. According her official biography, she was born in Madrid; those in the know said Little Rock, Arkansas. Jealous to the point of obsession, manipulative and bitter, this was the woman who had gradually turned life in Hollywood from one of gaiety and joy to misery, at least in private. For all public intents and purposes, they were 'the' Hollywood couple, in love and carefree. The truth was Ouida's reckless spending had more than once driven the couple's finances into the red. Now she faced her husband and with a malicious grin, announced her intention to host another party. Grimly, he stood silent as she added the final barb;

'And Basil? I shall need to visit Valentina for the dress.'

That day, after recording yet another radio show, Rathbone dropped into the production office at MGM; the studio was being asked to loan him out by Universal for another Holmes film and an assistant handed him Universal's contract for perusal. The working title was *Sherlock Holmes saves London*. A contemporary thriller, 'bringing the much-loved character created by Sir. Arthur Conan Doyle into the modern age.' Whatever that meant… still, the money was good; $20,000 and he signed without hesitation. Shooting was scheduled for next year. As his schedule was currently pretty much confined to radio, with only the odd magazine shoot, this was welcome news.

His thoughts darkened as he realised Ouida would almost certainly spend the lot. Why didn't he have the courage to just divorce the damn creature? Angrily, he thought of just walking out; if he didn't earn it, she couldn't spend it!. The thought passed, as always, sentiment taking over. Despite himself, he could never bring himself to hate the woman who so clearly resented his success.

'Mr. Rathbone?' The assistant was looking concerned. Assuming a lightness he didn't feel, the actor smiled self-deprecatingly.

'Sorry, dear boy – just thinking how I could spend it all. You were saying?'

'The contract, sir?' Apologetically, the actor handed the contract over before leaving the office for the second recording session of the day at NBC.

The next morning, dawn spread across the hills of Bel Air and down into the valleys, a late Santa Ana wind blasting its heat down from the hills. Rathbone's Chevrolet turned into the gates of the Limejuicer Club, an exclusive club set up by and for British expats at the time of the Great War. The club took the privacy of its members seriously and Rathbone was held up at the gatehouse while the guard checked his membership.

'Almost due for renewal, sir. Subscriptions have to be in before January, you know.' Rathbone didn't appreciate the reminder. Clearly, Ouida had failed to renew his membership. Again.

'I know, Martin, thank you.' Answering the guard's salute with a casual wave, he drove up the narrow drive as it wound its way half a mile through the lemon trees. It was still not quite twenty to seven as he parked beneath the marquee for a porter to heft the golf clubs from the trunk.

That morning, Rathbone made up a foursome with his friend George Huston and Katharine Hepburn, along with a real Hollywood character, 'Mysterious' Montague. John Montague was a legend in his own right; no one had known the slightest thing about the man, or how he could afford memberships to the most prestigious clubs. He had taken on all comers at golf and beaten them all, often with trick shots. Famously, he once challenged Bing Crosby to a game equipped with a baseball bat, a shovel and a rake; putting off with the slugger, blasting free of a sand trap with the shovel and finishing by using the rake pool cue style to sink the birdie. It was only when Time magazine had run a feature on 'Mysterious' Montague that a New York cop recognised him as one Laverne Moore, a wanted armed robber. Somehow – mainly thanks to his generous friends in 'Tinseltown,' Moore/Montague was acquitted, despite having left his personalised golf clubs at the scene of the crime. Although his game was now past its best, he was still a formidable opponent and his notoriety value had only enhanced his mystique.

The four took to the course, Rathbone's handicap was an eight, so he was paired with Huston while Miss Hepburn played with Montague. Hepburn was a keen golfer and the pair were soon ahead, coming in with an eagle on the first. Despite Rathbone's magnificent shot onto the fairway, his pair finished the hole with a bogey as Huston managed to slice into the rough. And so the game continued, Montague adding gaiety to the affair with a lively selection of stunts and goofing; at one point on the seventh he produced an iron with an India rubber shaft – and still managed to bring the ball down thirty feet from the flag. His playing made an otherwise pleasant round of golf into a joy, as did the flask he produced from the hollow handle of his driver. The proceedings descended into farce somewhat and, by the twelfth hole, Rathbone had all but given up hope of catching the exuberant pair. Hepburn was magnificent, exceeding herself with a birdie after a rare slip from her partner left her in the sand. All in all, an exceptional if comical game which Hepburn and Montague won with a fantastic 66, with Rathbone and Huston limping home at 82.

Thanking the others for a great game, Rathbone went to change. As he did, he noticed a slim, youngish dark-haired girl who seemed to be waiting for someone. Hepburn went up to her and in full view of anyone who cared to watch, gave her a passionate kiss, to which the girl responded with gusto. Hollywood… Rathbone smiled and went on inside.

After the customary drinks, Rathbone found he was starving, but eschewed the club steak for simpler fare; he was ravenous, though and plumped on a little place he knew that offered hamburger steak. He called for his car and lit a cigarette while he waited, tipping the valet and climbing into the Chevy. As he did, he noticed an envelope on the passenger seat, but as the valet was still grinning and saluting, he flipped a jaunty salute back and drove off down the drive, pausing only when out of sight to tear open the envelope. It was from 'X', only this time it wasn't a letter, but a card.

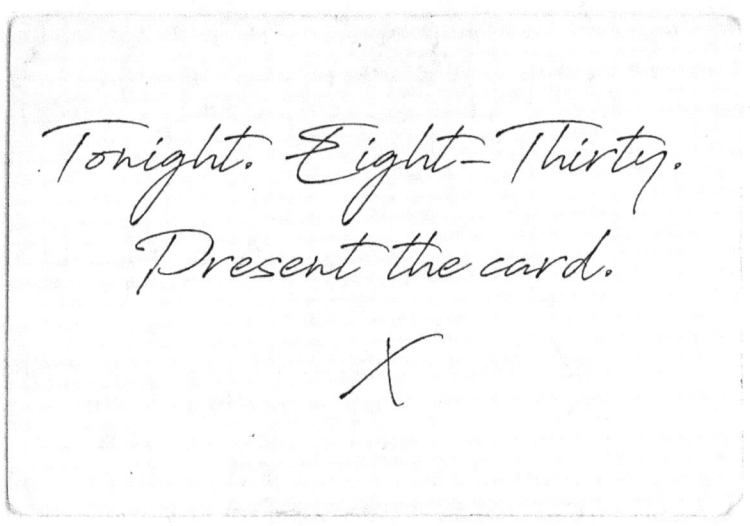

'CORMORANT'
SKIPPER J. HARRIS
SAN PEDRO WHARF
CHARTER HIRE. DAY RATES. FULL SERVICE
TELEPHONE HA-4237
BOOKINGS

And on the back of the card was this note;

Tonight. Eight—Thirty.
Present the card.

X

At eight-twenty precisely, a battered station wagon came to a halt in a dirt parking lot by the wharf in San Pedro. A 1939 Ford Deluxe 'Woody', Rathbone kept the car for its practicality and the powerful V8 under the hood. A good car to make a getaway from kidnappers in. He was convinced that was it; some gangster type was going to hold him for ransom. Under his sport jacket he carried a Colt .38, a studio gun, but the bullets inside the cylinders weren't blanks. A friend in the property department had 'loaned' him the piece with a shoulder holster, no questions asked. If there were any rough stuff, he'd be within his rights to defend himself. It wasn't the first time he'd carried a gun 'for real' – and he was determined this would end now.

After searching for five minutes, he found 'Cormorant' tied up at the third jetty he tried. Pulling the gun from the shoulder holster, he checked the cylinders before replacing it. There was a single light burning in the wheel house and he made his way cautiously up the gangplank. As he stepped on deck, a burly figure became visible in the wheel house, stepping up from below. Rathbone knocked on the glass, startling the man.

'Cheesus Fuckin' H.Christ boy, what the hell d'ya mean sneaking up on a man's boat?' Peering through the window at the dark figure, the grizzled features twisted into a suspicious scowl before his eyebrows rose in apparent recognition. 'Oh. The movie feller. You'd best come below.'

Keenly aware of the weight of the pistol, Rathbone prayed that Harris wouldn't notice the bulge under his jacket. Refusing the offer of a seat in the cramped cabin, he stood and waited while the man examined the card the actor had presented. Satisfied, the captain reached into his pocket for a Zippo lighter, sparking the wheel to burn the card, which he dropped out of an open porthole before it could burn his fingers. Patting the pockets of his denims, he produced a pipe and tobacco. Seeing his visitor was standing tensely, he waved a hand dismissively. 'You can sit down, boy – we got business needs to be discussed. An' Jack Harris don't do no business without first he gets a pipe.'

Deciding he was in no immediate danger, Rathbone seated himself at the bench behind the table, pulling out a pack of Pall Malls and lighting up. When in Rome... Harris was tamping his pipe as his visitor blew a plume up into the damp air between them. The Englishman watched abstractedly as the seaman lit his pipe, puffing speculatively to warm the bowl and dry the tobacco. The smell was fairly off-putting, but the actor's manners precluded him from commenting on the foul mixture. It seemed Harris was not a connoisseur. Finally, the weathered face creased into a belligerent stare and the captain poked the stem of his pipe at Rathbone.

'I'm out. You tell 'em. Jack Harris is out. Running the odd bale of dope up's one thing, and this ain't it. I do this, I'm done. You tell 'em.'

'Tell whom, precisely?'

'This 'Y', that's who.' Harris made the letter in the air with the stem of his pipe. 'Who d'ya think I meant? Henry Ford?' A thought occurred and Rathbone voiced it.

'Am I to perceive that you receive instruction from someone calling himself 'Y'?'

'You purr-seeves what you want, mister. I'm out and that's all there is. You take the bag and do whatever with it. Jack Harris, he's going back to fishin'.'

With that, the fisherman reached down for a small canvas shoulder bag, which he put on the table, pushing it towards the actor with a look that brooked no argument. Without touching the bag, Rathbone leaned closer, eyeing the sailor intently.

'Are you the one who's been blackmailing me?'

'Don't blackmail but no one. Don't know about blackmail. Jack Harris is a...' Rathbone held up a hand impatiently.

'Yes, yes, I know; Jack Harris is a fisherman. I want to know who is blackmailing me. If not you, who is this 'Y' person?'

'Don't know, don't want to neither. I gets a call, nummore than three weeks ago; says something's got to be fetched from a steamer off Catalina.'

'And you didn't know the voice?'

'No I did not.'

The man seemed genuine enough. Rathbone put out his cigarette and decided against another.

'What was the name?' Seeing the lack of comprehension in the older man's eyes, Rathbone rubbed the bridge of his nose with forefinger and thumb. 'The steamer; what was its name?'

'Calliope, sailing out of Panama.'

'And what did this Mr. 'Y' look like?'

'Didn't look no mister to me, Hollywood. It was a woman – not half bad lookin' too. Back out East, New York or Chicago I was thinkin'. Blonde, might be 5'5 and classy enough not to need paint in the afternoon heat. Hard to find them girls, these days, I guess. Not that I was askin'.'

With the bag under his arm, Rathbone left the Cormorant and trudged the gangplank back to where he'd left the Woody. Seconds later, he spun out in a cloud of dust and headed for the dark hills. Had he been more observant, he might have noticed the pickup truck parked behind a chandler's store. The man inside took a few more frames to make sure; you never could tell at night, even with a steady hand, a truck door to brace against and a Leica III with a custom seventy-millimetre lens. Satisfied, he stowed the camera beneath the passenger seat and got out of the truck. Hauling a can of gasoline from the bed, he started walking towards the Cormorant.

Sunday morning broke to find Rathbone alone by his pool, chain smoking and drinking a large scotch. He had barely slept, just enough to make it through the day if he could get something from the doctor. Not a habitual pill taker, the night had left him drained. Doctor Wyman wasn't at work when he'd called, but the receptionist had just arrived and offered a house call. Wyman was nothing but discreet. In his study drawer Rathbone locked the contents of the bag Harris had given him. It was those items, plus the letter of instruction with them, that had caused him so much anguish. All night, he had tossed and turned, agonised by the decision he knew he must make. Going to the police? Well, that was what he should do, of course. That meant a clear conscience... and financial and social ruin. Bad enough the war in Europe was threatening to consume the land he thought of as home, but with America seemingly considering an alliance with Great Britain and Free France, the whole world was at risk of going up in flames.

Twenty minutes later, with a pocket of little white pills in his breast pocket and one in his stomach, Rathbone climbed into the Chevrolet and started the engine, putting it into gear before he noticed the envelope affixed to the windshield beneath a wiper. Hands shaking, he opened it. Dear God, no! There was another photo, again of him, but this time he was walking onto a gangplank, the butt of his borrowed revolver not quite visible in the grainy shot. There could be no doubt about identity however, as the image clearly showed him in three-quarter profile. There was a newspaper cutting, too, an article on an arson at San Pedro. A boat named Cormorant. A body. Murder. That was it. For a moment, time slowed to a standstill and Rathbone simply stared dumbly at the newsprint. Someone had been there, someone took that photo and then waited for him to leave. Suddenly, he let out an anguished cry, clapping a hand to his mouth as if hoping to stifle a sound he had already made. He picked up the photo again, turning it to find a note (following page.)

Such a fetching
photograph – You, about
to murder a man, setting
his boat on fire in an
attempt to conceal your
felonious conduct.

You will go to Sunset
Park, tonight – 31st
Street. look for
Headlights

X

Angrier than at any time in the years since the Great War, Rathbone took the curves hard, slamming the wheel around to negotiate the curves of the Holmby hills, tyres squealing their protest. By the time he'd made town, the brakes stank and the smell of oil and hot metal came at him around the windshield. Only the sight of a police cruiser brought him back to earth, braking hard against the fading drums to bring the car down to a more respectable speed just in time. Opening the dash, he found a pack of cigarettes, shook one loose and lit up. More for the sound of human contact than anything more rational, he flipped on the radio, band music filling the void.

He drove idly, without direction. There was nothing on for the day and although he already felt the guilt at not spending it with Cynthia, he felt he had to escape somehow. She wouldn't be awake until the afternoon and he knew he would have until then at least to himself. For a moment, he considered calling 'her' and asking her to meet him at Cheedie's place on the beach. But that was madness; whoever this 'X' bastard was, he'd be watching. Another photo for his collection, or worse, a film! Suddenly, he noticed he was close to Alpine Drive. Why not?

That Sunday, rather than playing with the Hollywood MCC as was his habit, Nigel Bruce was at home with his beloved 'Bunny', the two girls Jennifer and Pauline charging about the Spanish-style house and causing mayhem. As usual, when Rathbone was admitted 'Willie' was leading the girls in a spirited assault on some fantasy castle or other, the whole time whooping like an Indian chief and using a cricket bat to deflect all sorts of projectiles that were being enthusiastically hurled down the stairs at the siege party. Laughing despite himself, Rathbone joined in, grabbing an India rubber ball and tossing it towards his compatriot.

'The fuse is lit! Send it into the ramparts!' Promptly, Bruce swung at the 'bomb', sending it hurling through a glass panel in the living room door.

The game was over, Violet – Bunny, coming in furious from the kitchen to find her husband red faced, trying to hide the bat behind his portly frame. Bursting into gaiety, she shook a finger and, noticing their guest standing awkwardly, folded her arms.

'Basil! I might have known.' The actor's attempt at apology was waved away and he was presented with a dustpan and brush. Sheepishly, he set to work cleaning away the glass.

'Bad eh?' Bruce looked out over his garden impassively.

'The very worst. Blackmail.'

'Bastards. Hanging's too good for 'em.' His guest nodded in agreement, sipping his Glenfiddich and letting the fire warm his gullet. Although early, Bruce had taken a glass for companionship's sake. Rathbone was, after all was said and done, one of his many close friends out here in the unreality of Tinseltown, as well as the reason his earnings were currently higher than ever. Life was good, more than good with things as they were and the thought of blackmail was a disquieting one indeed.

'What about that studio feller?'

'Eddie Mannix?'

'The same.'

'I've called him in already; sent round the most extraordinary character. He doesn't know the latest and I'm in two minds about letting him in on it. Thought I'd try you out, old man.'

'Holmes and Watson together on the case, what?'

'Well… more someone I can trust. You see, there's been a murder.' At this, Bruce went into a fit of convulsive choking. He'd been taking a hefty sip and the 'M' word was too much to swallow.

'Fucking Hell! What in Christ's name have you gotten into?'

Over the next fifteen minutes, Rathbone told his friend everything; Bruce already knew about the affair, that was old news. The way Ouida treated 'Ratters', as he called him it was only a matter of time, however gallant his fellow Englishman had been during years of abuse and tantrums. The fact someone had photographed his friend and colleague with the girl and was blackmailing him into whatever was being planned here was intolerable and he instantly volunteered to accompany him to Sunset Park that night. Suddenly, Bunny appeared in the garden, her face ashen. Grabbing for his walking cane, Bruce pulled himself to his feet, his old wounds causing him pain as he did.

'Whatever is the matter, darling girl? Have those little hellcats chopped up the maid?'

'You'd better…' The words died in her throat as, clearly distraught, she threw back a hand to indicate the house. Rathbone led the way.

The radio in the lounge was on, a tense voice breaking into the Jello program.

'From the NBC Newsroom in Los Angeles. President Roosevelt said in a statement today, that the Japanese have attacked Pearl Harbor in Hawaii from the air. I'll repeat that – President Roosevelt...' There was stunned silence as a special bulletin advised all personnel of the Sheriff and Police Departments to stand by on a two-platoon basis. All auxiliaries were advised to stand by and the civilian population asked to remain calm. The defiantly jazzy music that followed this only

served to deepen the sense of foreboding in the room. It was Bruce who broke the silence.

'Well old man, it's come here too, hasn't it?' A hand to her face, Bunny ran from the room to her children. Rathbone's jaw tightened, but he said nothing. The world was in flames. And he finally knew what must be done.

That night, the Woody rolled to a halt partway down 31st Street. After a few moments, a pair of headlights blinked once, twice, thrice and the station wagon's lights answered in quick succession. The Woody's V8 purred and the dark shape of a pickup pulled out from the kerb, turned towards the old Clover Field, followed by the wagon. Almost instantly, the glow in the sky beyond the roads of houses was explained as the gigantic bulk of the Douglas Aircraft Corporation complex loomed from the muggy night. Turning to the right, the pickup drawled along the perimeter of the monstrous structure, driving some half-mile to come to a halt by a row of myrtle bushes. Everywhere, there was construction work underway, wherever the eye looked gangs of workers were busy, despite the late hour transforming the already large structures into giants. The old runway had been torn up in favour of a five thousand feet long replacement and the instant the station wagon's motor stopped, the noise was immediate, even from this distance.

The door of the pickup opened and a burly figure emerged, walking back in a leisurely, unhurried gait that suggested the owner knew who was in charge. Bending down to talk through the open window of the station wagon, the voice that emerged from the shadows was harsh, dry.

'Okay. You're here. You bring the stuff we sent you?' The driver nodded, once, holding up the canvas bag. 'Atta boy. We got fifteen minutes, maybe less, so get changed – and don't screw around. Shift change is comin' up.' Suddenly, a dull metallic rod was shoved from the open rear window of the Woody.

'This is a gun. Please do not make the mistake of assuming its report would be heard over all this din... and remain perfectly still.' The shadow seemed unimpressed by Rathbone's ploy.

'Oh. Okay. Whatever you like, bud; but whichever of you is the Limey's still goin' in, so...'

The door creaked open and Rathbone emerged, his face gaunt and angular in the reflected glow from the complex. There were no nearby street lights out here, though the bare traces of what would soon be roads could be dimly made out. Levelling his borrowed revolver at the man's chest, the actor felt his hands shaking. If he opened fire now, perhaps he could still salvage something from this mess, but Willie was in the driving seat and he had no wish to cause his friend any distress. Nonetheless, anger flashed through him at the man's insolent manner.

'Who are you? 'X'? Another lackey like Harris? Answer man, or I'll shoot you in the stomach.'

'I wouldn't do that, mister.'

'And just why not?'

'It's my stomach for beginners, second I'm not 'X' – you shoot me and he'll carry out his threats, you'll wind up sucking gas in San Quentin. All we want is you put on them duds and do like we say and everything's peachy.' Suddenly, the man's manner changed abruptly. 'Say, is that Nigel Bruce? Oh wow! Whadd'ya know? Holmes and Watson in the same place! Holy shit!'

The driver's door was flung open and a furious Bruce struggled out of the wagon to grab the man by a fistful of shirt.

'Now you listen here you, you bugger, just tell this 'X' fellow whatever his plan is, there's no place for Basil in any of it.'

206

Smiling, the man effortlessly pushed Bruce's sixteen stones back against the car as if he were a child, receiving a savage right hook for his efforts. Most men would have hit the ground, but this was clearly not most men. Stepping back, he rubbed his jaw.

'Okay. That's the way you feel, that's the way you feel. But Sherlock here's got about five minutes to change before I drive outta here and the roof comes down on his cosy little life. I'll wait by my truck, so's you don't get no more feelings. You punch pretty good, but I was working the docks when I was fourteen and I took better.' The figure retreated, leaving the two Britishers alone.

'Oh… fuck it.' Bruce watched as his friend threw off his sports jacket and trousers to shrug himself into a pair of denim overalls and threw the canvas bag over his shoulder. With an old slouch hat and a quick application of an oily rag he managed to become the image of an aircraft fitter or mechanic. The brutish figure detached himself from his pickup and loomed out of the darkness, his manner indicating approval.

'You look the part.' Rathbone's face set hard in cold fury.

'Oh, piss off will you? Just tell me what it is you want of me and let's get this farce over with.' The man made an expansive shrug.

'Fine with me. You go inside the nearest personnel entrance to the right. Present your identity card at the booth – don't worry about punching in, it's been taken care of so you show a full shift. You go straight through to Works canteen five and head for the johns. Third stall along, behind the tank. You'll find a package taped to the tank. That goes in the bag; there's a hidden flap at the back. Then you go out another exit and I'll be waiting. That's it.'

(Above)
The false I.D. card given to Rathbone

Bruce made as if to confront the man, but Rathbone put a hand on his shoulder.

'It's the only way, Willie; you'd best wait in the car.' Bruce looked up at his friend.

'But, damn it, it's espionage! What these people are asking, it's monstrous.'

'I know. But I have no choice. I'll be framed for murder if I don't go through with it.' Turning to the thug, he narrowed his eyes. 'But I promise this, I swear – if I ever hear from you, 'X' or any of your abysmal gang again, I'll be happy to spend my remaining days on death row. And I'll shoot the next one of you to show his face.' The man held his hands up.

'I just do what they tell me. But this is all there is.' without another word, Rathbone turned on his heel and left the man to

Bruce's bulldog stare. He only hoped Willie wouldn't try to strangle the man before he could retrieve the package.

Sunday gave way to Monday in a mist of half-remembered dreams and fevered nightmare. Waking earlier than usual, Basil Rathbone went for a shower, washing and shaving himself. With the application of some pomade and some fresh clothes. he felt better than he had in months. As he ate his bacon and eggs, he allowed his thoughts to drift to the previous night. It had all gone smoothly, of course; the package was right there behind the toilet cistern, the blueprints, specifications and operational data for the Douglas Aircraft Company's top-secret bomber, the XB-19. A four engined giant, the XB was the largest plane built for the USAAF and it was unthinkable plans for such a devastating aircraft could find their way into the wrong hands.

Rathbone had taken the thick envelope and, nervously, made his way back out of the huge building. To his intense relief, he hadn't been accosted or even approached at the security booth. The pickup was waiting along the road and, without a word, he tossed the bag through the open window. Starting the engine, the amiable figure inside told him he could keep the outfit and drove off. Willie had been waiting, incandescent with rage. They had driven back to Bel Air with hardly a word spoken. As he drank his coffee, the Englishman reflected that it was better that he had kept Willie out of it. If this went wrong… well, he wanted to be able to say he had acted alone.

That day, there were no more unusual letters; that, at least was something of a relief. How it could conceivably get worse was, however beyond him. Meeting up with 'Willie' Bruce and the other cast members in the lounge, the talk was all of the attack at

Pearl Harbor. Seeking to lighten the mood, the actor in Rathbone came into force as he joked and punned through a last-ditch rehearsal, though it was noticable Bruce was not joining in the merriment. Then, into the studio.

Knox looked over and winked as the music played. 'The Adventures of Sherlock Holmes, starring Basil Rathbone and Nigel Bruce...' A foley man rang an old fashioned pull doorbell and Bruce fidgeted with his moustache awaiting his cue.

'Holmes, was that the bell?'

'I wasn't aware of it, Watson.' The foley man had quickly skipped over to a wooden construction that resembled three stair treads, which he made a show of climbing noisily. The earnest young man playing John Openshaw stepped to the microphone with Mrs. Hudson, who announced that Holmes had a visitor. The show went on from there, the drama of the Five Orange Pips playing out amidst various sound effects, dramatic acting and Rathbone himself mugging throughout, as if he were a naughty child on the last day of a school term. Finally, Bruce announced the demise of the Georgia sloop the Lone Star, sunk with all hands and the end of another mystery. Manning stepped forward smoothly and the closing fanfare played.

'In just a moment Doctor Watson will be back to tell us about next week's story. Ladies and gentlemen, when colds are prevalent, act wisely...'

By the time Rathbone had entered the lounge, Bruce had already left the building. Clearly this 'treachery' would take some forgiving – and a hell of a lot of explaining. Lighting a cigarette, the actor stole smoothly from the lounge and headed towards his Chevrolet. That night, Ouida having one of her 'heads,' Rathbone dined alone at the Brown Derby, the famous restaurant at North

Vine – as opposed to the hat-shaped affair on Wilshire Boulevard. There were a few famous faces in the house, notably Joan Crawford visible in a gallery booth, radiant in a sparkling cocktail dress, dining with a Paramount executive. Interesting… a small party was 'in' downstairs, but Rathbone quickly went upstairs to his regular spot, a relatively secluded booth.

It was a little early for dinner, so he ordered a scotch on the rocks, gazing down across the busier scene downstairs as waiters came and went, satisfying the human needs of the clientele. His thoughts drifted, the sky over France, the mournful notes of the sonata in his ears, long and drawn out, the bow skipping and caressing the strings. Would he ever find peace like that again? His reverie was shattered by a ripple of silver silk at his shoulder. The blonde who stood there was petite, no more than five four, but her smile involved more than her teeth. Eyes that flashed green one moment and blue the next seemed to be gently appraising him. At her throat and ears emeralds shot their fire in mute challenge. For the longest moment Rathbone felt as if he were being bathed in light.

'May I sit?' The words came through the air and seemed to form in it like flickering shimmers from water. Realising he seemed rude, Rathbone leapt to his feet and held out a hand to indicate his assent.

'My name is Cora.'

'Basil.' Her accent, he noted, was somewhere between continents, America, but with a trace of… somewhere European, perhaps.

'But of course; I see so few films these days, yet your face is instantly familiar.' Rathbone smiled, hoping against hope this wasn't a fan who'd paid her way past the normally strict Brown Derby door. An attentive wine waiter hovered discreetly and the

Englishman asked;

'What will you have?'

'Have? Why I haven't the faintest. Perhaps in the spirit of the times, a French 75, or perhaps an Aviation cocktail.' Rathbone looked up despite himself and caught the mischief hanging on her words.

'Why not? Two Aviation cocktails it is, thank you.' The waiter vanished and Rathbone fixed the woman with a fascinated gaze. 'Can I take it you are familiar with the Calliope?'

'My, what a quick study you are. One might almost think it not unexpected, given your current role, naturally.'

Smiling his most dazzling smile, the actor reached for his lighter as she produced a packet of cigarettes and fitted one into an emerald-green holder. Holding out the lighter for her, he reached over with his other hand and took up the packet, one cool brow raising as she watched him examine it.

'Forgive me; but identifying unusual brands has become rather a thing with me lately.' The packet was plain, save a crest and the word 'Brinkmann.' Seeing Rathbone's brow crease in recognition, Cora took them back from him, smiling.

'They're German. I get them from an admirer.'

'I'm no admirer of Germans, I'm afraid.' Exhaling smoke through her pearl-white teeth, the woman shrugged.

'So few people are, these days. And I understand you fought in the last war.'

'I doubt it.' The perfect face remained impassive, save a slightly raised brow. Despite himself, Rathbone took the edge from his next words. 'That you understand, that is. It was a time in my life I have no wish to revisit. As for this... what is this, exactly, if you don't mind enlightening me?'

212

The waiter arrived with the cocktails and Rathbone thanked him, waiting until he had melted away again until looking towards Cora's radiant, milky-white skin. Finishing the cigarette, she raised her glass with a mock air of ceremony, the pale sky-blue colour afforded by the crème de violette deliciously cool-looking.

'To aviators everywhere.' When Rathbone showed no sign of touching his own glass, she shrugged. 'Well, happy landings, anyway. Ooh! That's the ticket!. Now...' She folded her arms, sending a ripple of emerald and diamond into incandescent coruscation. 'What shall we talk about?.' Lighting himself a cigarette, Rathbone inhaled/exhaled before answering.

'I could be hung you know, for what you and your friends compelled me to do.'

'But that *would* be a pity, wouldn't it? – better to just forget it ever happened, go back to your films… but, of course...' She let it hang in the air, unspoken.

Flushed with anger, he made a fist, helpless, impotent.

'Of course what? There's more isn't there? What is it this time, steal a bloody plane? Or will money get you loathsome traitors off of my back?.'

'A traitor, Mr. Rathbone is someone willing to betray their own country. I have no country, none of my own, that is. I do what I do for reasons of my own – plus, it pays better than singing ever did… but that's another life, for another time. No, we were so impressed with what you've done for us we decided to make you an offer. A partnership, if you will.'

'Partnership?'

'Partnership. After all, the war has been raging so horribly for two years now, with only one clear winner. Surely it would be, shall we say prudent to choose the winning side?'

213

Rathbone finally took a sip of his cocktail, the sourness of the gin and the aftertaste of violet enough to divert his thoughts for a moment. Taking another, he sat back. He had decided to play along.

'Very well. I must confess it had been preying on my mind – not that America's not been good to me, you understand, but I've always wanted more.'

'And you shall have it, Basil So much more!.' Cora leaned forward, her eyes intense now.

'There's a man, you know him as 'X' of course, but he's a remarkable man. He's been working here in the States to help bring about victory. You shall meet him, when he calls for you; I shall arrange that meeting, of course. We have to be awfully aware of security.' There was something terrible in her eyes, Rathbone decided, a despair that she'd hidden until now. It was if the girl were caught up in something beyond her and was desperate to unburden herself before whatever it was consumed her. He listened as she outlined the arrangements she would make for the meeting with 'X.'

Although it was clear the offer was there, they hadn't slept together. A shared, surprisingly passionate kiss was as far as it went, but all Rathbone could think of was meeting with this mysterious 'X' at last. Besides, he could never betray his heart. A man might betray many things, he reflected as he drove home through the warm streets. Country, friends, family even... never his heart. And he knew where his heart lay; with the girl that he loved so dearly. The one in the photograph. He'd learned something; the German cigarettes the girl smoked were the same type as the butts he'd found. Somehow he couldn't see Cora taking long-range photographs – it didn't seem to fit her type, plus there hadn't been any lipstick on the butts. Her German admirer, perhaps? Another Santa Ana was blowing, the scorching wind that came down from the mountains and bathed L.A. in dust. He had to work hard to find music on the radio that night. The war, everywhere the war. Finally he made it home and was asleep five minutes after he'd looked in on little Cynthia.

Where do you meet the head of a subversive organisation? A coffee shop? Hardly; a cinema, perhaps? Not if you are someone with access to a major studio. With an eye for the drama of the situation, Rathbone had let it be known the most secure place to meet with 'X' was the backlot at MGM; all Cora had to do was provide her employer with a name; after some debate they settled on 'John Rutherford'. Rathbone would see to it Mr. Rutherford, an out of town investor for the purposes of the exercise, presented himself at the main security gate at seven sharp the next day. Coolly, she had assented and the stage, so to speak, was set for a lesson in betrayal.

An unseasonal rain greeted early birds on that far-off day, with the odd peal of thunder as background in the hills over town, but the real storm was in the Rathbone house; Ouida was awake early. What started with anguished pleadings from her husband not to upset the baby soon descended into bitter recriminations and the throwing of pots and glassware. Celia, the Mexican maid ran from the kitchen screaming as Ouida hurled a pan of water at her retreating husband. Furious, he took the station wagon and screeched out of the drive, nearly hitting an ice truck. He'd called a frantic NBC executive from home, apologising that his voice was failing him; the Santa Ana, no doubt. How long? A day, no more. Yes, he would rest his voice. Yes, he would take something for it. Driving south on Beverly Glen Boulevard, he turned onto Olympic, turning the plan over in his head. There was of course

215

no way he would ever work for these swine; they represented everything he'd fought against in the war, everything England was fighting now. England. How the word resonated. He'd offered his services at the outset, naturally, only to be told 'Stay,' in a terse missive from the War Office. Better to remain in Hollywood, went the thinking. 'Too old' was what they'd meant… well, he'd show them otherwise.

Pulling into the famous MGM gates, he surprised Sam, the security guard, who waved him through with a salute. You didn't need a pass when your face *was* your pass. Parking, he took a brisk walk to the colossal property department, emerging after ten minutes with another pistol, this time a more concealable affair, a little Colt .32 automatic. Sitting flat against his ribs, the Colt felt surprisingly heavy, but sat reassuringly. Idly, he wondered what Sam would have to say had he known he'd shortly be giving a visitor's pass to an enemy agent. There was plenty of time to kill, so Rathbone went to the commissary restaurant for the second breakfast of the day. Hopefully, this one wouldn't be thrown at him.

The town was abandoned, which wouldn't have taken long by the look of the single, forlorn and dusty street. The general store sat empty and neglected, the sheriff's office was deserted. A single figure stood at the top of the street, silhouetted against the harsh sun that beat down on the town. All was not as it seemed, however; open the door of that little cabin, for instance and you'd find yourself staring at the back of a New York City street. Walk around behind the saloon and you'd see it was just a facade. Nothing as it seemed; a perfect reflection of events. A little after ten and a little buggy rolled up, deposited its passenger and then rolled away back in the direction whence it came. The man who stretched his legs was somewhat over six feet, broad of shoulder and of an aristocratic bearing. His eyes looked around through celluloid sunglasses as if he were thinking of buying the place. Finally, he deigned to notice the solitary figure at the far end of the street and began a slow, unhurried walk to meet him.

'X', I presume?'

'Mr. Rathbone. Or should I call you Volksgenosse Rathbone?' The voice was cultured, unmistakably of German origin despite the hint of California creeping in.

'*Volksgenosse?*'

'Forgive me; it means 'Folk Comrade.' Ever since the Führer was dragged into this abysmal and divisive war I have rarely spoken German unless to the members of my group.' He held out a well-manicured hand, which the actor took, keeping the tension he felt out of the handshake.

'So, what do you make of the studio?'

'Decadent. Decadent and wasteful. You should be using it for propaganda, to counter the lies of the Internationalists and Bolsheviks, not making… cowboy films.' He said the word 'cowboy' as if it tasted of bile.

'Oh, but surely there's room for escapism, even in the Third Reich, comrade?. After all, the workers need their diversions.' The man smiled, a thin, taut exercise in re-arrangement of his facial muscles.

'We do not use the term 'Third' to describe the Reich. It stinks of impermanence; after all, Dr. Goebbels has reiterated the Führer's wish that the Reich be referred to as the Großdeutsches Reich, erm, the Greater German Reich, if you will.' *This man must be the life and soul at parties…* no sooner than he had thought it, the Englishman let the image drop.

The two walked along the huge backlot, the most recognisable twenty-nine acres on Earth, discussing the state of things in general and the war in specific. They walked past a life-size railroad terminal, before coming to Castle Finckenstein, an imposing edifice featured in several films. At the moment, a crew was busy rigging lights for a shoot and Rathbone took his guest away towards the brownstone street. All at once, they were in the heart of a city, an eerie and abandoned New York with no signs of life save the two men walking along the sidewalk together.

Pausing, 'X' turned to face Rathbone.

'You have questions of me – I sense this.'

'What do you expect of me? I cannot in all good conscience serve a cause that uses blackmail as motivation – for me to be of any use to you I must have your word the blackmail ends here and as of this minute.'

'Just so. For the purpose of clarity, I should state the methods used to ensure your cooperation did not sit well with me. However, my feelings on this matter are unimportant. We must subvert our own interests for the common cause. You have my word on this; there will be no more photographs, no more threats. But let me say this; if you betray us, fail us in any capacity, we shall be ruthless in our desire to eradicate you.' This time there was no attempt at a smile. The threat delivered, 'X' walked on, leaving his new recruit to digest his words or catch up as he pleased.

The process tank, a gigantic basin filled with water was in use, production was winding up on a Conrad Veidt picture, named, ironically *Nazi Agent*. A model of a ship, some thirty feet long was on the water, about to be sunk. A rigger recognised Rathbone and the actor returned his wave with a broad smile.

'We worked together on *The Hound of the Baskervilles*. Perhaps you've seen it?' Watching the proceedings with a clinical interest, 'X' looked around to check no-one was within earshot before replying.

'No; but Cora tells me you make an excellent Holmes.

Indeed I had thought of asking you to work for UFA, Dr. Goebbel's organisation. They make quite excellent films, by the way.'

'*Sherlock Holmes Versus the Soviet Union,* perhaps?' Seeing Rathbone's cynicism, the German snorted what might have been a laugh.

'Perhaps it was a stupid idea. After all, you are established here – quite the star, I hear. It would be foolish to use you in this fashion. No, here we need eyes within the film industry of Hollywood. Already it has come to my notice that Communism is rife amongst the bourgeoisie that control the studios with their labour teamster unions… we must be ready to subvert and liquidate these when the time comes.'

Walking on, the two men shared what might have almost been a companionable silence until Rathbone asked the question;

'When the time comes you say? Has Germany plans to invade the United States?'

'We won't need any such undertaking. We shall take over using the people; our sources tell us the populace is rife for exploitation. After all, the Great Depression is barely history; workers are crying out for better wages, better and fairer treatment. The Party will provide for their needs and they will provide the basis for a popular movement such as the one sweeping Europe in the nineteen-twenties.' Horrified, Rathbone produced and lit a cigarette to cover his reaction.

So that was it! They planned to foment unrest, to create a Nazi movement such as the one that consigned the Weimar Republic to the dustbin of history. It was unthinkable; an army of otherwise decent Americans blinded by propaganda and driven by basic want. Of course, things in America were far from perfect; he understood that. The thought of poor Americans being gulled by these thugs was too much. For a moment, he considered simply shooting the man there and then – but that wasn't the plan. He had to humour this monster, if only for the time it took to reach the gates. Thankfully, that was less than ten minutes or so.

Rathbone waved his seditious visitor away at the gate, relieved to be out of his stultifying company. Seemingly satisfied with his new recruit, 'X' had told him to expect a summons in the next few days, but when he had asked for more details, the Nazi would only say it would be to help cement his loyalty. By now in despair, Rathbone only hoped the FBI were as good as their word.

The next day, after recording another episode, Basil Rathbone took a chance and drove to Cheedie's beach house. He'd called 'her' from the studio, all the cloak and dagger business overwhelming him. After hearing the atrocious news from Pearl Harbor, he'd called Eddie Mannix at the studio and asked for a confidential meeting with an FBI man he trusted. Naturally, Mannix knew just the man, an Agent Charles. They'd met at a roadside hotdog and burger stall, of all places. The FBI man was dressed like a car salesman rather than a G-Man, but soon impressed the actor with his quick grasp of the situation. He'd even produced a photograph of Cora, taken with some trick camera at a train station or the like. They'd known the Nazis were plotting, of course; but agents in Hollywood? The FBI man had taken some convincing, the blackmail notes being the clincher. They needed time to form an effective plan, so he told the Englishman to string 'X' along while they put a trap into place. Relieved, Rathbone had immediately agreed. Now, as he drove into Cheedie's driveway, he had only one thought on his mind. Ida.

It was just past three in the morning when the Woody

drove out of the beach house and turned for Sunset once more. Arriving home some half hour later, the exhausted actor quietly made for his bedroom and was asleep within five minutes, the afterglow of passionate lovemaking the finest sedative nature could offer.

After lunch with his agent Lew Wasserman of MCA, Rathbone had the rest of the day to himself. Another recording that morning and the series was nearly done. Already, Universal was working full-tilt putting together the next Holmes film and he had a wardrobe call in a day or two. Nigel Bruce was already 'on board' and it looked as if the film would be set in the present day, with Holmes and Watson chasing Nazi spies or some such nonsense. It was a little after two when he found Cora sitting in his Chevrolet listening to Jimmy Dorsey. With a cheery smile and a throwaway gesture she told him it was time. When he made to get behind the wheel, she shook a slender finger and indicated the sleek Packard soft top parked a few spaces from the Chevy.

They drove north, along coastal Highway 101. And kept driving. The eight cylinders purred, and on the straights Cora gave all one hundred and sixty horses their head. Her driving was, Rathbone noted, that of a professional. She took the racing line on corners, didn't take unnecessary risks and her changes were smooth. After an hour or so, she pulled over at a roadside eatery and the two consumed burgers and soda with hardly a word spoken. Despite all of it, Rathbone felt sorry for the girl; he had the strongest feeling she was being coerced in some way, blackmailed even. When they did speak, they spoke of nothing and everything; the hot weather, the almost empty road and the feeling that the war wasn't somehow real, at least not on the West Coast. They got back into the Packard and continued their journey northwards.

A little after five, Cora pulled off the highway onto a side road leading off towards a low range of hills that were sitting hazy and expectant in the medium distance. After ten miles it seemed they were no closer, but all of a sudden the big car was climbing the curves and in a few miles they turned in to a driveway. Two men stood guarding an apparently ramshackle gate, the sort of thing ranches used to have in the days before automobiles. There was even a bell, a dull brass affair that looked as if it hadn't been rung since McKinley took office. It was only when the gates swung shut behind them that Rathbone looked in the mirror to see the armour plating covering the reverse of the gates. Someone had gone to a lot of trouble to make this place seem rundown. It didn't bode well. He'd been told the FBI would be keeping tabs on his movements, but couldn't see how they'd manage it out here; a squirrel moving out on these hills would stand out like a Chinaman in Parliament.

The house was a two-storey affair that contrived to look like a bungalow, an adobe affair with the look of Old Spain. That is, if Old Spain had men with high-powered rifles patrolling the roof and grounds. Of all things, there were Nazi banners hung either side of the main entrance, the swastika somehow more obscene in this incongruous setting. Two braziers to either side of the flags sat unlit, but two guards, these in full tropical uniform, snapped to attention, the machine-pistols across their chests looking like they'd just been unwrapped from the factory for the occasion. As he climbed from the Packard to unwind his legs, Rathbone noted the silver 'SS' insignia at their necks and the hard, scarred bodies. These weren't tin soldiers, he decided; they reminded him of the hardened, battle-scarred men he had faced in France. The heavy hardwood doors were swung open by some unseen mechanism and 'X' strutted out to greet his guest.

The bowl had been a quirk of nature originally, but human hands had excavated and shaped and now the amphitheatre waited expectantly. Around three sides of the cavernous space, braziers burned, lighting the pole banners held proudly by the standard bearers below. The scene resembled nothing so much as a pagan sacrifice from a De Mille picture, and for a moment Rathbone had to stifle the giggles as he was led ceremoniously to the dais set centre stage. Behind the lectern, a severe older man stood, in full ceremonial SS uniform. His left sleeve, empty, was pinned to his tunic, a vivid mensur scar on his left cheek doubtless a memento of a student duel. He waited, eyes like coals, for 'X' to bring Rathbone before him. The silver oak leaves on his collar and the cross at his throat vied with a chestful of medal ribbons; First War, Rathbone decided.

Finally, the man spoke, his voice gravel.
'Good evening. I am Standartenfuhrer Schramm, of the Brandenberg Division, currently on detached duty with the Abwehr. Does this mean anything to you, Mr. Rathbone?' Schramm's English was clinical, but he pronounced 'Rathbone' as 'Wrath-bonn.' Finding himself standing at attention, the Englishman admitted it did not. Without blinking once, Schramm continued. 'That is to be expected. The Abwehr is perhaps the counterpart of your English Military Intelligence Department Six, the much vaunted Secret Service. I should explain that my rank has the equivalent of Colonel. You are here to confirm your loyalty and for this a small ceremony is in order. Has he been prepared?' This last to 'X', who shook his head curtly before responding.
'There has not been sufficient opportunity. Security considerations have made it impracticable, Standartenfuhrer.' Despite Schramm's rank, it seemed 'X' was very much the superior; there was no hint of deference despite the dazzling array

of decorations on the older man's chest.

'So. You have, I think already proved your bravery; the Military Cross, I think?' The actor shrugged modestly.

The next few minutes were among the most difficult of Rathbone's life. As the colonel spoke the words of the SS loyalty oath, he repeated them. Rather childishly, he had attempted to cross the toes of his right foot as he spoke the hated words.

'I vow to you, Adolf Hitler, as Führer and chancellor of the German Reich, loyalty and bravery. I vow to you and to the leaders that you set for me, absolute allegiance until death. So help me God.' The words left a bitter taste, but he worked hard not to betray any sign of distaste, thinking instead of these men squirming in the gas chamber or before a firing squad. Finally, Schramm moved from behind the lectern and surprised the Englishman by both the sword he turned out to be wearing and then by handing over a small and rather plain paper envelope. Risking a glance down, Rathbone saw it contained the Iron Cross.

'It is my honour to inform you that the Führer, Adolf Hitler himself has awarded you the *Eisernes Kreuz*, in the second class, for your actions in securing the blueprints of the American bomber.' Rathbone was damned if he was going to take this lying down.

'Well, one usually doesn't travel second-class, but thanks all the same.' For a moment, it seemed as if the colonel was struggling with the urge to draw his sword and eviscerate the Britisher, the scar on his face raw and flushed.

Coughing discretely, 'X' took Rathbone by the arm and led him back to the house, where a small group of men waited, all blindfolded. These were labourers and artisans, judging by their garb and Rathbone saw one was holding a cab driver's hat between stubby fingers. Without turning, he addressed his host.

'New recruits?'

'Just so. The masks are so they cannot discern the identity of our most prestigious new operative – at least, until the time has come for action.'

'You seem to have thought of everything.'

'The German fondness of exactness and efficiency is much admired, I think. It should be so; we have, indeed, thought of everything. You will realise this in a moment.' A thrill of subdued fear jolted Rathbone's spine, but he continued walking. He only hoped he hadn't been uncovered as an infiltrator; he was in no position to try anything, least of all escape.

The library was straight out of a film set in Bavaria; oak panelling and bookshelves, a heavy mahogany desk with a Nazi eagle and the obligatory bust of Hitler on a marble plinth. Over the fireplace hung a portrait of *Der Führer*, gazing out over a sweeping landscape. 'X' went to a wall hanging, a faded and tattered fragment of tapestry. Sweeping the ancient cloth aside, he revealed a wall safe, setting about the dials and careful to shield the combination with his body. To instil trust, Rathbone made a point of casually examining Hitler's bust until the German had closed the safe once more, turning to see him spreading a sheaf of papers and plans across the baize of the desk.

'Please, come closer so you may see the next phase of our action here.' Leaning over the desk, Rathbone saw a sight that made his blood run ice cold. The sheet was a blueprint for a four-engined bomber, the letters printed below it proclaimed it to be the *'Amerika Bomber'*, the implication was clear even before 'X' confirmed it. This was to be a long-range bomber for use against American military installations and factories.

Wordlessly, the Nazi removed the blueprint to show a map of the Los Angeles area. Several areas were marked in red; among them, Rathbone saw was the Douglas Aircraft Factory.

'There are seven Japanese submarines off the West Coast as we speak. They have the capacity to launch both aircraft and artillery strikes against shore and inland targets, plus a small landing force specially trained to conduct blitzkrieg-style raids where needed. Along with our own U-Boats in the Atlantic, this should prove sufficient to cause fear and panic among the civilian populace – and force the decadent gangsters of Washington to sue for peace.'

'I see. Do you think it will be enough?; I mean, the Amerika Bomber, how many are there?' Chuckling as if to a private joke, 'X' wagged a finger.

'You understand I have shown you too much already. The bombers will come; in point of fact, Japan has been developing what they call 'Project Z', a six engine machine with extraordinary capacity. It can reach the American Midwest from Japan.' Nodding thoughtfully, the actor tried to remember as much as he could; if the FBI didn't get their hands on these plans it would be down to him to give them as much as he could.

It was past midnight when the Packard threw up dust from the driveway. Once on the road South, Rathbone lit two cigarettes, handing one wordlessly to Cora. After ten miles or so, she pulled over and cut the engine.

'If it's all the same, old girl I'd rather just get home...' Without answering, she leant over and kissed him on the mouth. Despite himself, despite the atrocious circumstances, he found himself responding. Pulling away, she opened her door and, lifting her dress, showed him that she was naked beneath. Her body was perfect, her legs long and shapely, the soft golden triangle between inviting and her hard-nippled breasts beautifully pert in the light from the dashboard, but the gentleman in him had been ingrained from childhood.

'Cora... we can't. I have a wife...'

'And a mistress. I've seen her, remember? Pretty little starlet, batting those British doe eyes at you. I can give you so much more…'

'And what do you expect in return?' Seeing her frown, Rathbone had suddenly had enough. 'Oh for God's sake! This isn't a bloody game! These people are deadly serious.' Leaning over as she dropped the hem of her dress, he pointed two fingers at her, cigarette between them.

'Ever since we met I've had the damndest feeling your heart's not in this – any of it.'

'And you? Where does your heart lie, Mister Basil Rathbone?.'

With Rathbone now at the wheel, the big Packard roared towards Los Angeles, visible now as a yellow/orange glow against the sky. Cora sat next to him, mostly silent save what might have almost been an occasional sobbing. Finally, with a few miles until Malibu, he pulled over onto a dirt track leading down to the sea. Puzzled, the girl sat as he went around to the passenger door and wrenched it open, his jaw set. She saw the Colt in his hand and her head dropped onto her chest. Taking her roughly by an arm, he yanked her from the seat and marched her roughly down to the shoreline. It went against the grain, but his heart, though heavy, was like stone. He saw the lights of the fishing fleet that twinkled offshore and it struck him there would have to be a blackout; already rumours of aircraft carriers and submarines were spreading like wildfire. Resolute, he cocked the weapon and held it by his side. Frozen in place, she looked out over the sea.

'I shall give you one chance, Cora – and one chance alone. Are you loyal to the Nazis? Their cause?' She turned, her hair silver in the night air. She was crying, a shudder running through her as she looked into the mouth of the automatic. Into the mouth of death itself. A single word escaped her – more a moan than coherent speech. The word was 'No.'

They sat there, the two of them on a blanket he'd found in the trunk of the car. There was a pint of rye too. For emergencies, she'd said. Over a pull of the whiskey, it all came out. Her name was Cora; Cora Bradley, born in a one-car nowhere town in Missouri to an alcoholic father and a sick mother, who died when she was three. After one beating too many, she'd packed her few things and stole away to the big city; first St. Louis, then Chicago. The Windy City was not an easy place to make a living in the 'thirties, but she had looks and a voice and found work as a torcher in the clubs that flourished after Prohibition had ended the year before. There had been men, naturally; her first time had been with a sax player, a hophead negro with a winning smile and easy charm. Others followed, as they will and soon there was no trace of the wide-eyed small town girl from the sticks. On a whim she'd bought a ticket on a Greyhound all the way to El Paso, where she crossed the border headed for... wherever she could get to. Which turned out to be Cuba, after a series of adventures through Mexico – one of which ended with three men shot and her escaping out of a bordel window just ahead of the federales.

It was getting cold, so Rathbone draped his jacket around her shoulders, the gun laying forgotten on the blanket. They were out of cigarettes, so they shared the last.

'And what did you find in Cuba?' Handing him the cigarette, she brushed her hair from her face and considered her answer.

'I found Tim.'

'Tim?'

'Tim. Timothy Maxwell-Haymer; rather a playboy, with a paper job in his father's hotel chain. Poor Tim, he never understood work – or women, come to that. But, he had a yacht and we sailed the Caribbean for a summer… that wonderful summer. Oh, it couldn't last; he wasn't the type for a girl like me, so I jumped ship in Panama and headed to Peru.'

'Peru is hardly the Caribbean, I'd say.' Rathbone's voice chided gently, a smile on his lips. She slapped his arm playfully.

'Pedant. We'd sailed through the canal; Tim was headed north to San Francisco – the business of course. We parted friends, as well as you can be friends when one of you cleans the other out for $5,000.' She let out a wry laugh, shrugging her slim shoulders. 'You can guess the rest.' Suddenly, she got to her feet, handing the actor his jacket back.

'Oh, but surely there's more to Cora's story than that?'

'Another time. Another beach. Anyway, it involves Germans and I've seen enough to last me a lifetime. I'll take you home.'

Nothing happened the next day, apart from more recording sessions and an early script for the new film. In it, Sherlock Holmes would be pitted against Nazi spies attempting the overthrow of England. It seemed laughable, but the money was good and after all, it mirrored what Rathbone had been caught up in in the real world. It was the following day that it all started to unwind. First Cora had showed up again at NBC, with further instructions for the coming attack. There was a script, a sheet of typed paper which she handed to him. On the appointed hour, just as the first wave of sub-launched planes went over, he was to go to one of the announcer's booths near the master control room, where two of the X-Network stooges would be ready to take over the station's output. In painfully stilted English, the script called for him to identify himself to the listening public, then call for them to stay in their homes as the combined forces of the Reich and Imperial Japan swept over Los Angeles. The audacity and conceit of it was galling; even with a thousand planes they couldn't hope to make a dent in a city the size of LA! All the same, he took the paper and folded it away into his jacket pocket.

On his way home (Ouida was planning a party for the weekend and the maid had called to warn him of the tantrum she was throwing) Rathbone stopped at Musso Franks on Hollywood Boulevard for a stiffener. Or two. He took a booth towards the rear as even at that early hour, the place was teeming. He ordered a scotch on the rocks and waited with a cigarette. The man in the next booth got up, reaching for his hat, which he dropped on the seat across from the Englishman. About to berate the man, Rathbone groaned inwardly as the pug face of Harry Barton folded itself into what might have passed for a smile on a bull mastiff.

'Hey, what are the odds? Hi old pally.' The waiter arrived with the scotch and Barton held up a finger for another, waiting a long while until it arrived before speaking another word.

'Well, here we are.' Rathbone stubbed out his cigarette and smiled, ruefully.

'Aren't we just?' With a wink and a widening of the grin, the big man winked at the Englishman.

'Here's mud in your eye, chum.' Raising his glass as if for a toast, he emptied half of it in one slobbering gulp, causing Rathbone to wince. Bad manners he could forgive, but abusing good scotch was beyond the pale!

'So...' Barton reached into his pockets and pulled out a decrepit looking pipe which was held together with tape, then patted himself down to find some tobacco. Rathbone watched, idly fascinated as thick fingers filled and tamped the pipe, then produced a match to be sparked along a dirty thumbnail. Clouds of a surprisingly pleasant aroma began filling the booth. Despite himself, Rathbone found himself warming to the man. 'So, Mr.

Barton...'

'Harry, please.'

'Harry then. To what do I owe the pleasure?.'

'An old pal of mine, guy named Tom Fealey, works for the FBI on the West Coast up in 'Cisco. Works the Counter-Espionage desk, at least one of them; since Pearl they've been buying more office furniture than Sears can ship, if you get me.'

'I do. Business booming, as you might say.'

'Literally; but you would know where the booming's going to happen, right?' Rathbone leaned back as a young couple walked past to a booth, then leaned forward conspiratorially.

'I can't discuss it, Harry; your friend may not know, but I've already made contact with his, em, organisation. They are fully informed as to the execrable mess I've been sucked into and the effort I'm making to extricate myself from it.' Barton snapped a finger and held up two fingers to the waiter, who affected not to notice the rough manner.

Drinks refreshed, the ex-cop resumed the confabulation.

'Eddie's worried. Gotta tell ya, Eddie's worried. As a matter of fact, his words to me today were; 'Tell that goddam Limey he's over his head with these punks and get him the fuck outa there while he's got a face to sell.' So, I tell you; don't expect you and that military cross of yours to pay much mind, but I tell you; Eddie's pulling chunks a'hair out and eating the carpet over there.' Rathbone's face assumed a mock sympathy.

'Poor Eddie; perhaps I should buy him a new rug. And one for the floor, come to think of it.' The belly laugh that erupted from the pug faced Barton sent the whole place into a shocked silence for a moment, a meaty hand slapping the table for emphasis.

'Atta boy! I knew you weren't one o' them Brit pansies!. And I got a reply for you all my own, pal.'

'Which is?'

The creased face moved closer, the dull brown eyes now fiery coals, the expression now one of cold menace. The voice was low, steady and sent a shock of unease through the outwardly unruffled actor.

'You're not only over your head, you're fukkin' drowning. Eddie don't like that a million dollar picture star drowns; bad for the studio, bad for business. So, Mister Military Fukkin' Cross, you got yourself a babysitter – don't think of sayin' no neither, or I'll be babysitting you outside your room in the General while you eat baby food through toobs.'

Parking the Chevrolet in his garage, Rathbone paused to compose himself and walked into the storm. Broken glass and crockery greeted him, as did the plaintive wail from the nursery. Coldly, he ignored the dishevelled, manic form of what had once been his wife and walked through to his daughter. The only love remaining in that house.

A few hours later, the phone rang and the Mexican cook, Eupesnia called out to the garden where the master of the house was playing happily with little Cynthia and the dogs. Bunty was catching her favourite ball and Moritza was involved in a friendly tussle with little Leo, all to the delight of the child. For a while, Rathbone had never been happier, especially as Ouida had stormed off to town with the stated intention of bankrupting him, using his infidelity as a lever to his wallet. Instead of rising to her bait, the Englishman had simply walked into his study, taken a cheque book from the desk and handed it to her with an icy smile and the instructions to spend the bloody lot. The small act of rebellion had felt like the victory after a long and bitter war – which, in a way it had been. He determined there and then to live his life as he saw fit; so long as Cynthia was protected from the woman who had never shown her the slightest attention, unless that is, outsiders were present. A show-mother for a showbusiness family.

Answering the phone with a nod and smile to Eupesnia, he waited until the cook had retreated before answering. The voice at the other end was Cora's, breathless and agitated. She was calling from the ranch, she said and had little time before she was missed. The plans had been brought forward as Colonel Schramm had insisted on after the ceremony, he hadn't trusted the English actor and apparently he carried more weight than it seemed; Germany had agreed to his demand. The attacks started that very night at ten. Before Rathbone could question her further, there was a muffled voice as if someone had entered the room. The line went dead.

Instantly, he called the number the FBI man had given him. It was answered before the second ring.

'Hello.'

'Good evening; I'm calling for Agent Charles.'

'Hold the line, caller.' There was some electronic clickery before a second, unfamiliar voice came on.

'Agent Charles speaking.' His brow furrowed, Rathbone stood impatiently.

'This isn't the Agent Charles I met the other day. Put me onto him at once. This is Basil Rathbone.'

'Sherlock Holmes, eh? How did you get this number?.'

'How do you think? Agent Charles gave me his card!.' Agitated, Rathbone slapped a palm against his leg, before holding the hand flat against his waist, pressing hard as if to stem a bleeding wound.

'Well, there's no record of a meeting here, assuming you *are* Mr. Rathbone – but we're very busy here at the moment; why not pay a visit to the Los Angeles Field Office?. It's at...'

'Damn it all! I'm not some crank! This is of vital importance! I have information of an imminent attack on American soil!.'

'Okey. Please hold; I'll transfer the call to our Intelligence desk.' Angrily, Rathbone slammed the phone down. Opening the locked drawer at the bottom of his desk, he took out the Colt automatic, hefting it for a moment before slipping on a sport coat from the stand, slipping the pistol into the inside pocket. He'd do this alone if he had to.

Barton was leaning against the fender of his car, a 1939 Hudson, when the Chevrolet pulled out of the gates. Tossing the matchstick he'd been chewing, he screwed his burly frame into the coupé and fired the starter. In his rear-view mirror, Rathbone saw he was being tailed. So be it. If Barton wanted to come along, he wasn't going to stop him.

It wasn't much of a plan – in fact it wasn't a plan at all. All that Rathbone could think of was somehow sneaking into a heavily armed compound to rescue the girl. With a pistol. The more he thought it through, the worse it got, until noticing he needed gas, he pulled over at a Conoco and went inside, asking the pump attendant to fill the Chevy and check the oil and water. Just in case… inside, he bought two packs of Chesterfields and a bar of chocolate. Just in case. Remembering he carried a flashlight in the trunk, he added two batteries for good measure. It felt good to be *doing* something, whatever that something was.

Outside, as the attendant finished filling and checking the car, he found Barton standing there, a sly grin on his face. 'Come on, what you gonna do? offer them some candy?'

Defiantly, the actor threw his purchases onto the passenger seat and tipped the attendant.

'I have not the slightest idea. All I know is, there's a girl and she's in trouble.' The pug face was not unkind.

'When ain't there? Look… I know enough to know you ain't got a hope, but mebbe we can do something about the odds – unless you think you really are Sherlock Holmes. I'm offering a hand, is all.' Looking at the dull brown eyes, Rathbone felt as if the ground were falling away beneath his feet. The man was right; he didn't stand a chance. Alone, that is. He needed someone he could trust.

'So that's it, Willie. The whole sordid thing laid bare.' Awkwardly, Rathbone waited for his friend to respond to the news that one of the most famous actors on Earth was infiltrating a Nazi sabotage network. In his sitting room, Nigel Bruce stood as solidly as any statue, the very picture of British resolve. Without a single word, he left the room, leaving his visitors to exchange baffled looks. After a long while, however, Bruce re-emerged with a large box under one arm and a leather bag filled with cartridges. Setting it down on a table, he unlatched it to reveal two venerable-looking shotguns.

'Christ! I didn't know you had a gun room, old boy.' Bruce favoured his friend with an unblinking glance.

'Hardly; these were in the attic; family heirlooms, what?' Leaning forward, Barton inspected the label inside the lid. *Samuel Nock, Gun Maker to his Majesty A.D. 1790.*

'You sure these things are safe to fire Mister Bruce?'

'My lad, these were fired every season for one hundred and twenty years; you can rest assured they will fire again if need be.'

'Well, okay; we can use 'em to scare the natives plenty, I guess… best give them a pull through and get moving. Now… the plan…' Pulling a Shell road map from a pocket, the ex-cop laid down his ideas on how they were going to save both California from enemy invasion and a wayward girl from death.

Lieutenant Commander Ichirō Anabuki of the Imperial Japanese Navy Submarine 1-X gripped the handles of the long-range periscope as he examined the coastline of Santa Monica intently. The control room was silent, save for the clicking of the hydroplane controls, the young ensign working hard to maintain a precise depth. More than a foot or two of periscope visible here in these enemy waters would spell disaster for the submarine and her complement of ninety four men and the twelve special-purpose troops, the *Teishin Shudan* raiders who had been crammed on top of the already crowded crew for the long trip from Japan. Stopping off at the secret Japanese sub base at Magdalena Bay in Baja, the raiders had practised beach landings while the sub was refuelled and provisioned for the trip northwards. Now the culmination of all the hard work was about to bear fruit; the time was a little after nine p.m. At nine-forty precisely, the sub would surface to enable the commando troops to embark in their rubber boats and the scout-bomber plane to be assembled on deck and launched. Suppressing a grin, Anabuki thought of the reception that would await him on his return home.

The lights of Venice Amusement Pier still burned their defiance, though for how long was anyone's guess. Strict black-out regulations were coming into force and the merry makers that rode the Dippsy-Doodle were shrieking and screaming with delight. Who knew what tomorrow would bring? Who knew that, even now they were being watched by keen eyes from beneath the calm waters of the Pacific?

The shrill tones of the phone sounded just as the trio was

preparing to leave, Rathbone snatching the receiver from the cradle to hear Agent Charles' voice.

'Yes? How did you find me here?'

'Good to talk to you too. I just got word from one of our surveillance teams. The compound is empty; they cleared out some time before eight. Any idea why?' Irritably, Rathbone clutched the receiver tightly, his knuckles white against the bakelite.

'I received a call from Cora – the girl. She said they hadn't trusted me and the attack was being brought forward. to tonight.'

'Well; they're gone, at any rate. I called to warn you not to try anything stupid. Stay out of the way, let us deal with them.' With that, the line went dead. Resolute, the actor turned to his companions. Bruce's expression would have done a prize bulldog credit.

'What news, then?'

'They've left the ranch. They must be attempting escape before the attack goes in. We have to move… and quickly!'

At nine-thirty, the Woody drove onto the packed sand track leading beneath the boardwalk of the Venice pier, coming to a halt beside a dimly lit shack. Inside an office of sorts, two men sat in dilapidated leather chairs smoking and listening to a news broadcast warning of enemy shipping raiders and possible air raids. Barton knocked twice rapidly, opening the door before the second had faded from earshot. One of the men, older than his companion and shorter by a head, threw down his pipe and pulled his fat little body from the upholstery with an effort.

'We're all paid up, copper – blow.'

'I'm not the police any more, Lenny; so sit your fat ass down and listen to what's coming, or I'll tear the kid's arm off and beat you silly with the wet end.' The younger man flushed at this, but something in the big man's manner told him to let it slide.

A few minutes later and Barton emerged from the shack alone, giving the two Englishmen in the car the nod. All set.

'Lenny O'Connell's an old sparring partner of mine – in both senses of the word, back in the day I was strike busting, and Len's boys were doing some busting back. He runs the Longshoreman's local here.' Rathbone was anxious.

'Is he reliable?' The ham face looked grim.

'Put it this way; he don't like nobody gets to blow up his boys' livelihood none.' As they got out of the car, Bruce was startled to see the vague shapes of perhaps a dozen men detaching themselves from the shadows. One had a leather change bag round his waist, another carried a vicious-looking boat hook.

'Where's the fire, Mister?' Asked a gruff voice. He was answered from the open doorway of the office, the fat man's face puce with anger as he pointed out to sea.

'Out there. And it's Japa-nees.'

Warrant Flying Officer Hideshi Kimoto clambered into the cockpit of the Yokosuka scout/bomber, giving the thumbs-up to the deck crew as he fired the starter. Behind him, in the observer/gunner's seat, Petty Officer Eisuke Morishita waited for the thump of the steam catapult that would launch the seaplane into the air. Already, the Teishin Shudan had embarked in their three rubber boats, laden with weapons and explosives. They would make as much noise as possible, blow up the pier and kill all the Americans they could... but their mission was only the diversion that would enable the Nazi team to enter the Douglas plant unchecked and challenged. Once there, Kimoto knew, the plan called for the Germans to set off flares marking the vital installations and buildings, which he and the five other bomber pilots would then devastate with the incendiary bombs each carried. By the time the American authorities realised the true target was not some vacuous pleasure beach, it would be too late. A crewman held up a dim red torch and Kimoto held his breath.

A second later, the torch whipped downwards and the awesome thump of the catapult threw the plane forwards as if a giant hand had swatted a fly. At maximum revs, the heavily-laden aircraft lurched forwards and clawed its way into the darkness. The attack was under way.

The lead boat bumped gently against the pilings beneath the pier, and instantly nimble hands were at work to tie the boat to the oil-scummed structure. Their faces blacked out, the raiders set to work, passing explosives from hand to hand to the men climbing the slippery wooden poles, their progress made easier by the iron spikes they wore on their boots. As the demolition team set to work, the remaining two boats moved closer to the shore, the men in them armed with sub-machine guns and light machine guns of the latest type, along with grenade launchers and mortars. Once ashore, they were to form a firing line with the heavier weapons as the remaining quartet went forward armed with grenades and satchel explosives. None of these men were married, as none was expected to survive. The chosen foursome had all been issued with short swords for the ritual of seppuku. Before the boats had quite reached the damp sand, the roar of aero engines came from the dark sea behind them and the Yokosuka flew past in perfect formation, six shadows of death passing overhead.

The first man onto the beach had gone no more than a few steps when he halted, his nose assailed by a harsh odour. Before he could identify the source, an equally harsh voice called out;
'Light the bastards up!' In the sudden silence the subdued *whumph* of a gas-soaked rag being lit sounded clearly – and then all hell was unleashed on the beach. A burst of machine gun fire ripped the darkness apart, the crump of a grenade exploding and the *boomph-boomph* of shotguns being discharged all mixed with the screams of terrified men. From their viewpoint beneath the

pier Rathbone's group watched as the battle unfolded, the longshoremen fighting a savage hand to hand with the nearest raiders and Bruce furiously firing each of his shotguns in turn as the younger man from the shack reloaded. Revolver in hand, Barton stood to one side, watching keenly and raising the pistol to fire the odd shot. The sea itself was now on fire, burning forms rolling furiously on the damp sand in frantic attempts to extinguish the flames. A human torch suddenly reared from the melee and Rathbone fired into the writhing form at point-blank range, watching in silent horror as the bubbling, hissing figure sank back into the flames that consumed it.

By now, the patrons above the pier had realised something terrible was unfolding and a stampede began towards the landward end of the massive structure. The burp-burp of a machine gun sounded, splinters exploding from the safety rail above. A young woman screamed, pitching forward onto the decking to lie still. Outraged, Bruce swung his shotgun and gave the gunner both barrels. He was rewarded with a high pitched shriek and then a brief silence that was gone as fast as it came, the ping of a grenade launcher sounding, followed by a shockingly loud **krak** and more screams from above. It was clear the target was the fleeing merrymakers and, his blood up, Rathbone charged forwards into the hail of hot metal slashing through the humid air. He had seen the muzzle flash of the small mortar and ran through the loosely packed sand as fast as his feet would carry him, cursing his decision not to wear boots. A smouldering Japanese raider appeared, raising his pistol, but as suddenly as he had appeared he disappeared in a dark spray of what must have been his blood, the report from Bruce's shotgun setting his fellow countryman's ears ringing. Looking back briefly, Rathbone saw Bruce striding stiff-legged along the beach like he was on a parade ground, reloading his own weapon now to send another volley into the enemy. The grenade launcher fired once more, but the tall

Englishman looming from the darkness was the last thing the mortarman saw, his chest torn apart by both Rathbone's Colt and Barton's revolver, the big man seeming to appear and disappear at will out of the murky scene.

Suddenly a burst of swearing and cursing came from Bruce. Dashing back to his friend, Rathbone could see he had taken a wound to the shoulder. Shrapnel, possibly; it was impossible to tell. Despite the injury, Bruce handed his friend the shotgun and held out a handful of shells.

'You want me to have some sport, eh, Willie?' Forcing levity into the words, Rathbone broke the shotgun and fed two cartridges in. Bruce spluttered in furious indignation at the presumption.

'Sport my arse, you bloody fool – hand me that fucking gun!' No sooner had he regained his weapon than Bruce fired again, discharging both barrels at the rubber boat a fleeing pair of raiders were desperately trying to refloat. The boat exploded into shreds and the two soldiers sat comically on the remnants for a moment, then turned to find themselves surrounded by fiery carnage, the flames from the beach making grim silhouettes of the longshoremen who advanced slowly on the pair. Before they could reach them, however, they had drawn their ritual swords and committed seppuku, disembowelling themselves as they knelt on the sand. The last raiders died in dignified agony on the very beach they had travelled so far to attack.

The sabotage team had laid their explosives and were halfway back to the 1-X when their leader realised something had gone wrong. The battle from the beach had been spectacular, but it was clear it had failed. More worrying, from his point of view was that his watch now showed past the time due for the explosives to detonate. A problem with the Bakafun explosive, perhaps? The answer was provided by the sudden glare of a searchlight from the end of the pier. The Americans had found the explosives! The ghastly knowledge of failure in his throat, the team leader drew his pistol, knowing he would never see his homeland again.

'Looks worse than it is; I've got the metal out, just need some powder and a few sutures. How did you say this happened?.' Flapping a hand up dismissively, Bruce replied;   'Fishing accident.' The Doctor eyed his late night patient with a suspicion evident from the way his bushy brows beetled, but kept his thoughts to himself. He'd been at Belleau in 1918 as an orderly; he knew shrapnel wounds when he saw them. The twisted shard of steel was discarded in a kidney dish. Mostly to make conversation, he addressed the oddly familiar Briton.
'Big air raid tonight.' Bruce tried to keep his composure, feigning disinterest.
'Oh, really?'
'Yep. The Douglas factory got it, but good. My sister works in the canteen, gave me a call in case I was worried. Said not to; worry, that is. Funny, really...'
'Oh? funny how?.'
'Well, there was the darnedest racket from the beach down Santa Monica way a while back. Air raid drill, the radio said. Well… that's you patched up.' Eyeing the piece of shell casing wryly, the physician smiled at his patient. Thanking the Doctor for his prompt attention at such an unsociable hour, Bruce paid him in cash and left.

The first light of the false dawn was beginning to colour the sky as Bruce rejoined his friend in the Woody, which he'd parked in a side street in a belated attempt at discretion. Without speaking, Rathbone handed his friend a lit cigarette.

'Thanks, old man.'

'Have you heard – about the aircraft factory I mean?'

'Doctor said they'd been hit and quite badly… we both saw those bombers. Seems we failed, Ratters.'

'Yes. Yes I'm afraid we did.'

'Still, we haven't found the girl, Cora, whatever her name is.' Inhaling, Bruce broke into a spluttering cough, wiping his mouth. 'Damn things, made of horse shit and old bus tickets, what?' Despite the gravity of the situation, Rathbone smiled at the old joke.

'Yes they are rather rough on the throat. You know I was thinking...'

'About what? Invading Japan?' The voice of Agent Charles broke into the actor's reverie, though neither man in the car had had the slightest idea he was there.

The Woody coasted to a halt onto a vacant lot. There waiting for them was Harry Barton, standing by an unfamiliar Buick, around which several FBI men were stood examining a map by flashlight. A large area behind the lot was smouldering, a large group of fire engines at the site of what had clearly been a massive conflagration, what looked like a row of aircraft frames burning merrily. A covered military truck pulled out, throwing dust over everything, two Military Police on motorcycles roaring out to pass the truck and lead it down the road. Jerking a meaty thumb over his shoulder, Barton leered at the new arrivals.

'There goes the Douglas plant.' Weary, Rathbone was in no mood for games.

'We must be two miles from the Douglas plant. What's the meaning of all this?'

'Oh, no meaning; just that some film studio guys built a phoney plant; complete with dummy planes outta ply and canvas and some other guys, seems *they* went around changing road signs so some Germanic types got confused. The same Germanic types in that truck, as it happens.'

Pointing in the direction the army truck had departed to, Barton explained;
'They were picked up by the Feds after setting off some flares and just before the Imperial Japanese Navy bombed the bajeezus out of nothing.' So… it was all over. Anxious, Rathbone asked about the girl, but Barton knew nothing and the FBI was saying the same. Suddenly tired beyond his years, the actor turned away and walked back to the station wagon.

After dropping Bruce off at North Alpine Drive, Rathbone was taking Sunset West towards home when a Police K-Car pulled him over. The plainclothes cop that approached him waved away his proffered license and leaned in close.
'You're Rathbone, right?' Ignoring the look of confusion, the cop continued; 'We gotta call from headquarters; hope it makes sense to you, 'cos it don't none to us. Anyway; *Tell Rathbone bad guys left truck – meet mooring station USN Resolve immediate. Charles.* That mean anything to you?'
'It certainly does, officer, but I'm very much afraid I'm going to have to break some traffic laws now.' The cop's face creased at this.
'Anything to do with that ruckus down at Venice tonight?'
'I cannot answer that, officer. It is, however a matter of security.' Jabbing his thumb at his own chest, the cop smiled, a wolfish grin.
'I was ten years in the Marines, and you got a police escort.' Tapping the door jamb, the cop trotted back to his car and got onto the radio.

Sirens wailing and lights flashing, two prowl cars

screamed down to the beach north of the Venice pier, itself still smouldering from the attempt to destroy it. The FBI had cordoned the pier off whilst some of the braver and more agile stevedores and longshoremen passed up an alarming amount of undetonated explosives. Behind the police cars came the Woody and behind that the K-Car. Just short of Castle Rock, the cars cut the lights and sirens and pulled off by a gate, the path beyond leading onto scrub and the beach itself. There, hanging in the half light was a gigantic gray cigar, ghostly yet familiar. As the group approached, a shape resolved itself into the features of Agent Charles.

'My, don't you like to get around?' Before Rathbone could formulate any meaningful reply, a voice called out from the direction of the imposing form suspended over the beach.
'Wind's rising. We don't launch now we don't launch at all.' Clapping the Englishman on the shoulder, Charles grinned.
'Up for one last trip?'

The U.S. Navy blimp Resolve rose gracefully into a turn, its twin Warner radials and their combined 330 horses powering the craft effortlessly into the lightening sky over the beach. Two pilots sat up front, behind a bewildering array of dials and switches. Within minutes, they were at a dizzying height and cruising at just under forty knots. From the gondola, Rathbone could see the coastline falling away in both directions, the view superb despite the crowded cabin. As well as the Navy pilots and himself, Agent Charles and a chief petty officer were aboard. This last, an otherwise avuncular fellow by the name of Macnaughten would only say he was a 'specialist' when questioned. He wore a webbing belt from which a large and unpleasant looking knife hung in its sheath and a 1911 model .45 in case the other leg felt left out. The large canvas bags he'd brought with him he used as a seat, making it clear by his body language no-one else was to touch them. The Resolve continued on its flight along the coast, heading Northwest, parallel to Topanga and Malibu.

At six-thirty, the sun had risen and the scene was set for another perfect day in California. From his lofty vantage point, Basil Rathbone could see the tiny dots of people on the beach and the wakes of the pleasure boats. What he couldn't see was the purpose of this flight, but Agent Charles just smiled and winked when he asked. It all became suddenly clear a few minutes later; the unmistakable shape of a massive submarine lurking beneath the surface of the dark water perhaps five miles off Malibu pier sent a thrill of recognition through the occupants of the airship. CPO Macnaughten ripped open his bags and Rathbone was alarmed to see a number of dull green and yellow objects – clearly some kind of explosive devices.

Grinning, the chief grabbed a bag and stepped forward to open the door as, far below, a speedboat detached itself from its moorings at the pier and knifed through the water towards the sub.

'There they go, right on time.' The voice belonged to Agent Charles and Rathbone realised there was information to which he had not been privy. He'd noticed a pair of binoculars hanging from a strut and took them, focusing them on the smaller craft. There were five of them aboard, but there was no mistaking the dazzling blonde hair of one passenger sat in back of the speeding boat.

Yelling to the pilots, Chief Macnaughten told them to hold a position over the sub.

'Bombs away!' Pulling a pin, the chief cheerfully dropped the small tube he'd selected down towards the sub, smoke trailing from the falling device. Shouting back into the cabin to make himself heard, he pointed a finger below. 'Depth Charge Marker;

shows me wind drift, helps me aim.' Rathbone was tempted to ask 'Aim what?' But he watched silently as Macnaughten held up two ominous and bulky yellow cylinders.

'Hey Sherlock; you can do the honors!' Realising the chief's intentions, Rathbone stepped forward and grasped the two rings on the charges, pulling them clear with firm yanks. These dropped some forty feet before a puff of smoke came from each, trailing all the way down to the water. Both fell a few feet wide of the submarine. For a second or two, it seemed as if they had been duds, but then two roiling gouts of water erupted from the surface and visible ripples of shock waves could be seen buffeting the submerged vessel.

Two more yellow depth charges were dropped before the submarine broke the surface, one seeming to hit the sub squarely on the deck aft of the conning tower. By now it was clear the sub was damaged, a stream of black smoke issuing from the tower. Through the binoculars, Rathbone could see the sailors scrambling onto the surface and down onto the deck, which was still streaming seawater. A fire and repairs party no doubt. Without any apparent motion, the Resolve was still over the sub as it began to turn for the open sea. Another two yellow bombs did their work and, appalled, the actor saw one sweep the majority of the repair party away in a blinding flash and an instant cloud of smoke. Chief Macnaughten shouted down, as if the doomed men could somehow hear him.
'That's for Pearl, ya slanty bastards!' Switching focus to the speedboat, the Englishman could see it was almost upon the sub, but a tussle of some kind seemed to be taking place; two of the men trying to get at the wheel. Helpless to intervene, he watched as the boat suddenly turned straight for the retreating submarine and then careened off of the casing. There was only one thought in his head as he shouted to the pilots to take the

airship down.

The control room fire was out, but there was still the inferno in the engine-room compartment to deal with; the 1-X still had power from her batteries, but desperately needed the diesels re-started if she was to have any hope of surviving the aerial onslaught. Lieutenant Commander Anabuki was directing the fire control party below himself, despite the heavy casualties they were suffering. He himself had sustained terrible burns from the super-heated steam that was hissing from numerous pipes, scalding flesh from bone. He could, of course, seal off the compartment and dive, but with battery reserves uncertain, it would have been the height of foolhardiness. Curse the Americans and their flying toy!

At that moment, the 'flying toy' was descending over the stricken sub, Rathbone hanging out of the doorway with a borrowed Colt .45 and a spare clip, plus an unusual grenade-type device that Chief Macnaughten had quickly schooled him on correct usage. Top Secret, the Chief had said, adding he'd rather the actor blew his 'idiot self' to pieces than let it fall intact into enemy hands. Agent Charles had made a determined effort to dissuade the Englishman from his suicidal foray, but to no avail. Cora was down there – as was 'X.' America wasn't safe while the Nazi drew breath, and Cora... well, Cora was just a girl in a man's world; she didn't belong.

The port pilot yelled out that they were at forty feet and, taking a breath, Rathbone executed a rather amateurish swan dive down into the Pacific. He splashed through oil, going down to what seemed to be the very depths of the ocean, finally emerging with a splutter and gasps for breath alongside the sub just afore the speedboat. The craft had been lashed to the hull to enable the transfer of the passengers, who were already being led up a ladder to the conning tower, Cora being last. Grabbing at the boat, he was shocked to discover the speed it was being pulled through the water; far too fast to give him any chance of securing a grip. And then he realised with a sudden terror that he was being pulled, inexorably towards the submarine's propeller as it churned and thrashed water a few feet below the surface. He was a dead man.

The body that dropped from nowhere splashed into the water besides the doomed Rathbone, a whipcord arm wrapped itself around his waist and, inexplicably at first, the two men surged forwards through the water. The battered actor realised it was Chief Macnaughten, tied to a rope trailed from the Resolve. The airship was towing them at the same speed as the sub, which made breathing next to impossible. Half drowned, the actor and the chief crashed into the stern of the speedboat and with an inhuman effort, the Navy specialist hauled first his charge and them himself over the transom to lie, gasping on the deck. Next, he checked Rathbone was all right, before crawling forward, his profile low as a cat, to the mooring rope. Checking he still had the big Colt and the grenade, the Englishman followed Machaughten as the Navy man shimmied monkey style below the rope to the casing. Luckily, the outer hull was perforated with slits; something technical, Rathbone assumed. These apertures made climbing comparatively simple and the Chief was laying prone on the wooden decking besides a dangerous looking deck gun as the actor reached him. There were two crewmen atop the conning tower and the Chief trained his own .45 on them.

The danger, however, came not from in front, but behind; unseen by either of the covert boarders, the aft hatch had been opened at a signal from the canny crew on the conning tower, two crewmen emerging, one armed with a curious looking machine pistol with a long and curved magazine, the other a rifle. Watchful eyes had seen the danger from above, however and grenades began raining down onto the deck around the hatch, the second killing or injuring the pair as Macnaughten whipped round to open fire, receiving a slug in the shoulder for his pains. Groaning, he slumped forward, spat and lifted his head with what seemed a superhuman effort. More crewmen were emerging, hampered by the body of one of the wounded men and the shots that Rathbone sent whining and crashing off the open hatch coaming. Adding his own fire, the chief roared the words;

'Go, damnit!' Rathbone got to his feet to run to the ladder where Cora was being helped over into the conning tower.

The sound of her name came to her over the noise of battle and the roar of the fire below and, frightened, Cora looked back to see the crazy Englishman starting on the ladder below. Just then, the submarine gave a mighty shudder, then another, before starting to slip beneath the waves. The 1-X was doomed. Hesitating, Cora let out a shriek as an oil-slick hand grabbed her shoulder. It was 'X', and he carried one of the odd machine pistols. The smoke from below became noticeably more intense as an overpowering hissing sound came from seemingly all around the conning tower. The sea had found a way in somewhere and the sub's descent seemed to slow perceptibly. The shouts of desperate men came from below and behind, frantic shouts from the blocked hatch that the chief was still raining fire on.

Looking up, Rathbone saw he had perhaps five feet yet to climb – and the gaping mouth of a machine pistol trained on his head, 'X's features contorted with rage and fury.

'Du dreckiges Schwein! Verräter!*' The pistol fired a long burst, the rounds sparking off the ladder and sending metal flying… but only one round hit its intended target, an agony of white heat searing through Rathbone's left bicep. Drawing his borrowed Colt, he saw it would not be needed; 'X's body falling slowly back away from the rim of the tower. With a sickly grin, Cora popped up waving a tiny and shiny automatic.

'Dad always told me to look after myself; only good advice he ever gave a girl.' Despite the pain he was in, Rathbone couldn't resist laughing.

'For God's sake!; I'm supposed to be rescuing you!'

*'You dirty swine! Traitor!'

EPILOGUE

Of course, no such events ever took place. Officially, the incident at the Venice Amusement Pier was a fire that got out of control briefly, before the Santa Monica Fire Department managed to get it under control. The Navy Blimp Resolve conducted a 'training exercise' with a U.S. Navy Submarine that long-forgotten day; and the Douglas Aircraft Company installed a clever camouflage scheme against aerial attack, with help from MGM's props men; an entire neighborhood was erected atop the plant, complete with houses, roads and shrubbery – all built on netting stretched between a vast network of poles. As for the Hollywood Nazi spy ring?; pure fabrication, a myth, a rumor. True, local rumor had it that a ranch outside Paso Robles had been raided by the FBI; some old timers even today will tell you they took away truck loads of radio transmitters, weapons, explosives and even a bust of Hitler. What do they know?. Certainly, the Japanese submarine 1-X was reported missing following a routine patrol of the Pacific, doubtless lost forever; another of the multitude of mysteries thrown up by the long and savage War of '39 to '45, along with several other Japanese subs that never returned home.

And what of the people I mention in this wild and fanciful tale? Well, as many know, Basil Rathbone enjoyed ever greater success and fame playing the character that endeared him to so many; along with Nigel Bruce, he made a total of fourteen Sherlock Holmes movies and some two hundred and twenty episodes on radio, before quitting Hollywood for the New York stage, winning a Tony award in the process. He died aged seventy-five on the twenty-first of July, 1967. Nigel Bruce remained in Hollywood, never forgiving his friend for abandoning the series that had made them into superstars. He died at fifty-eight on

October the eighth, 1953 in Santa Monica.

Of course, no Agent Charles ever existed, although by curious coincidence a Zachary Charles went on to serve with distinction in the Wartime OSS, before being assigned to the FBI's Washington Bureau, where he rose to head a secretive section devoted to uncovering communist sympathisers. He retired in 1974, to Maryland with his wife and four children. He died in 1990, at home in his sleep. Likewise, the U.S. Navy has no records for a Chief Petty Officer Macnaughten – at least none who could have been present aboard any blimp at the time the story is set. The service of one Chief Petty Officer Harold 'Lumps' Macnaughten, however, is not in doubt. As one of the U.S. Navy's elite Underwater Demolition Teams, his career stretched across the globe, most notably in the Pacific where he led a team clearing underwater mines and obstacles at Iwo Jima and Okinawa. He retired to run a cab business in Chicago, living until the ripe old age of ninety-two. His first-born son, William served with the Navy SEALS in Vietnam. He was killed in 1970, saving the lives of his team when an ambush against a Viet Cong tax collector turned into a major firefight with a North Vietnamese unit.

And so to Cora. By now, the news Cora Bradley appears in no official birth certificate ever issued in Missouri will surprise no one. Cora Bryant, on the other hand is a patient at an exclusive nursing home at the outskirts of Reno, Nevada. Nothing is known of her earlier years, but in 1945 she married a GI and they went into the nightclub business; her as both singer and joint owner. No-one knew how she came by the stake she needed to build the 'Starlite Rooms', but for a while it was rumored a wealthy British friend had helped set her up in what soon became one of the most popular joints in town. Don't bother looking; I've changed the name of the place at her request. Although her husband passed in

1980, she has happy memories – and three children; Basil, Nigel and Charles, and a host of grand and great grandchildren to keep her busy.

I don't know the why of anything, even when I pretend most diligently I do. The truth is the last time I had any idea why or what I was supposed to do I was lying in a shell hole, looking up at the sky. My mind was filled with a Bach keyboard sonata, which was one of the last I'd learned, I forget which one now. I absolutely knew I was about to die and I was completely happy and at peace, in a way I never was before or since, not even with you, in our best moments...

- Philip St.John Basil Rathbone – 1892-1967.

THE END

Also by Mark Sohn

It is the year 1888. A madman stalks the East End of London and only Sherlock Holmes and his trusted colleague and scribe, Dr. John Watson, stand between him and the women he preys upon. However, the world's first consulting detective is plunged into a web of intrigue and deceit. Is Jack the Ripper acting alone?. Is there a conspiracy to murder fallen women in Whitechapel?. How far must Holmes go to stop it?. Add a plot to steal the most famous jewels in existence and a sinister figure known only as,The Professor' and you have more than one mystery to be solved.

www.ingramcontent.com/pod-product-compliance
Lightning Source LLC
Chambersburg PA
CBHW071137260626
47162CB00003B/818